STOLEN CHILD

To Marlene! You matter! Psalm 62:8 [illegible]

What Readers Are Saying About Stolen Child:

I found that her second book, Stolen Child surpassed the first....It was certainly worth the wait. I couldn't put it down! I love predicting storylines and this book kept me guessing during most of the main dramatic parts. Now to wait for the 3rd book, which I am sure will not disappoint! *Rachael*

Again, it was a book I could barely put down. Each chapter drew you further into the story and the excitement....I of course, loved the ever deepening love story of Asha and Mark. I don't want to spoil any of it, but boy is it exciting and romantic! *Laura*

Stayed up all night tonight to finish the book; it was truly inspiring and well written. I'm so glad I read it, by far one of the best books. *Megan*

This is a must follow-up for the first book in the Stolen Series by this author. In fact, I'd have this book on hand to read before finishing the first. It continues the story of the adopted Indian American girl who goes back to India to follow her roots and find her birth parents. As with the first novel, this one includes intrigue and a view of Indian culture seldom seen in the west. The story is exciting with a bit of romance. It's a fast read with a great ending. I hope to read more books by this author. *Lillian*

I could not put these books down once I started reading them. *Michele*

The bad thing about finding a favorite "new" writer is when you finish reading the 2 books she has out, there is nothing to go back and read lol! Can't wait for your next book and the future ones after that! *Mary*

I loved the first book in the series so much and couldn't wait to read the sequel. It did not disappoint! I didn't want the book to end so I tried to stretch it out as much as possible. However, that didn't work too well because I couldn't wait to see what happened. Even though the topic is on the "dark side of life", it was written in an uplifting yet realistic way that didn't drag me down. It was a very compelling book that I would highly recommend.
Sue

...couldn't put it down. *Janice*

Wow! What a story of hope!...you will be on the edge of your seat waiting to find out what happens next. This one moved me to tears ….I love that both of these book end positively, offering hope. *Kimberly*

Actually, this story turned out differently than what I thought it was going to be. I had a hard time putting it down and just had to keep reading to find out how it ended! *Linda*

This sequel is even better than the first book of this 3 book series. I have to admit that I am a very picky reader. I tend to figure out books quite easily and if I am not into a book by the 2nd chapter, I normally don't finish it. The first book was very good, but I have to say that this one blew the first book out of the water. *Rachael*

Definitely a series I want!!! ….I couldn't put it down. Can't wait for the next one, but will be sad its the last one. *Michelle*

I ordered this book the day it came out. I had been waiting for it since I finished reading the first book in the series, Stolen Woman. Kimberly takes you on a great adventure as you read what Asha is going through. You feel as if you're on the journey with her. I found myself praying for Asha's safety as I was reading and holding my breath as she and her birth mother were in the storm. This is a must read. It opened my eyes to things about Human Trafficking that I never thought of before. I am not normally a reader and I read this book twice. This is another great book by Kimberly Rae. *Karen*

I loved the first novel in this series and was waiting with baited breath for the second one. I can't say enough good about this book. I have given it to my mother and grandmother who both loved it! My mother said she loved it because the chapters are short and she could fit it into her busy schedule by reading a chapter when she had a moment. I loved it because once I got started I couldn't put it down. What a lovely continuation of the story. I think Kimberly's writing has grown and matured with this book and everyone I know who has read it agrees. None of us can decide which one we like better...Stolen Woman or Stolen Child. *JD*

Loved it….made you want to keep reading to see what was going to happen. *Jackie*

Loved the books ! What a powerful message they send! I could not put them down. *Lois*

Great for teens and for any with cold feet about being exposed to the dark reality of human trafficking. I was hesitant, too, until I found myself immersed in the careful writing abilities of Kimberly Rae. Her passion for the hurting rubs off in this compelling story of true, Biblical love and victory over evil. *Bethany*

Great series on Human Trafficking! Plus this author is amazing! *Mary Beth*

I stumbled on this series and felt I HAD to buy it. I am now hooked. This is a life changing book if you let it!! *Melanie*

STOLEN CHILD

www.stolenwoman.org

First Edition, September 2011
Second Edition, May 2012
Third Edition, December 2012

Printed in South Carolina, the United States of America

ISBN-13: 978-1466325302
ISBN-10: 1466325305

The characters and events in this book are fictional. The author takes full responsibility and apologizes for any mistakes in cultural understanding or expression.

STOLEN SERIES, BOOK 2

STOLEN CHILD

KIMBERLY RAE

For the children
still longing to be loved.

Character Pronunciation Guide:

Rashid—pronounced Rah-sheed

Ahmad—pronounced Ah-mahd

Asha—pronounced Ah-shah

Milo—pronounced Mee-low

Didi—pronounced Dee-dee, means "Big Sister"

Dada—pronounced Dah-dah, means "Big Brother"

Neena—pronounced Nee-nah

Sumi—pronounced Shoo-mee

Dokhan—pronounced Doe-kahn, a small side-of-the-road shop

Hatigram—pronounced Hah-tee-grahm, a fictional area in Bangladesh meaning "village of elephants."

Cultural Note from the Author: I have recently been informed that Bangladesh has changed drastically over the past years. Most people have cell phones, knowledge of the outside world, and there are new laws to combat child trafficking, including a law forbidding foreign adoption of Bangladeshi children. The Bangladesh in this story is the country I remember from my time there over a decade ago.

PROLOGUE

She had been screaming for hours.

Ahmad crouched just outside the hut, his back to the rickety bamboo. Sweat beaded across the patch of skin above his upper lip. *Why didn't she stop*?

Finally, a climatic, ragged cry of pain ripped through the air. It was followed by a smaller, but no less violent, cry of a newborn.

"A son!" The words of a woman inside were jubilant. "A son." Relieved.

Ahmad let out a breath, then sucked in another. A boy. A small, thin smile curved up one corner of his mouth.

He cast a quick look in all directions to make certain no one saw him, then slipped off into the night.

"Are you certain?" The young man Rashid was hesitant.

"Do you question me?" Ahmad's voice was hard. Gritty. "I saw the child myself."

"And it's a boy?"

"A son." The man's smile was not warm. "A sweet little boy some barren couple will pay dearly for."

Rashid broke out in a cold sweat. "I'm not sure I can do this."

There was a harsh laugh, and Ahmad's words were cold. "You want to be a man, don't you, Little Brother?"

Rashid gritted his teeth. He did not see how stealing and selling a baby made him a man. He offered one last, feeble argument. "But he said we could take the baby if it was a girl."

Ahmad snorted in disdain. "As if we care what that weak, pathetic cigarette-seller says. We'll tell him Sumi and Alia were mistaken. That it was really a girl." An evil grin spread across his face, one that ran shudders down Rashid's back. The knowledge that Ahmad was actually enjoying this double betrayal filled him with terror. What else was he capable of?

"Besides," Ahmad continued, "what can he do about it? Once the baby is sold, if he talks, the greatest shame is on him."

Ahmad clapped his hands together. The sound echoed in the darkness, scaring several roosting birds into flight above them. "He is trapped." Ahmad smiled with glee. "It's perfect."

Rashid felt his limbs quiver. He was just feeling certain he would be sick when Ahmad returned his attention to him. "Now, you go and get the baby. Make sure no one sees you." Rashid watched him smile coldly. "We wouldn't want you to get arrested for child trafficking, now would we, Little Brother?"

At that moment, it became clear. Ahmad would steal the baby regardless, but if Rashid crossed him, Ahmad would find some way to make him regret it for life.

Rashid's shoulders dropped. There was no way out, for him or the baby.

He nodded, then with slow steps left to do his brother's bidding.

Sumi's voice was strained. She looked across the hut to her sister. "What do we do? The pains keep coming. It's as if the baby has not come yet."

Alia, standing to the left, finished cleaning the new baby. She glanced at their young niece, Shazari, who thrashed on the woven mat.

"I'm dying," Shazari moaned. "I must be dying."

Suddenly, Alia set the baby into his prepared basket and hastened toward the young woman.

"What is it?" Sumi asked. "What?"

Alia's face was pale. Her voice was a mere whisper. "There is another."

Sumi gasped. "Two babies? Twins?"

The young woman's cries increased until the second child entered the world. A beautiful baby girl.

"What will we tell the husband?" Sumi moved the firstborn in his basket to the back of the room, next to the young mother's exhausted form. "He will not be happy to hear there are two—"

"—more mouths to feed." Alia finished, heaving a weary sigh. She wrapped the newborn in an extra blanket found near the door.

"Don't forget the mark," Sumi reminded.

Alia took care as she dipped her hand into the waning fire's ashes and rubbed a round black circle onto the baby's forehead. "Don't want the Evil Eye to get you," she murmured.

When the young mother revived and cried out for help, both aunts rushed to her side.

As they worked to calm her, handing her the firstborn baby boy to nurse, the tiny baby girl wriggled in her tightly-wrapped blanket. One small fist escaped to wave victoriously through the air.

And at that moment, as loved ones comforted Shazari with news of both a baby boy and girl, hands reached just inside the door, quietly picked up the second-born baby, and fled with her into the night.

Part One

Father to the fatherless, defender of widows

— this is God, whose dwelling is holy.

God places the lonely in families.

Psalms 68:5-6

CHAPTER ONE

The body can be taken. Used. Bartered over like a trinket. Sold again and again until its value is gone completely.

The will can be crushed. Chained until subdued. Painted over. Even shadowed by outward submission.

But the soul, hidden behind the paint, beneath an outer crust of cynicism or bitterness or even demonstrative meekness, cannot be taken. Cannot be sold.

The soul is the place where hope endures. And it can only be given as, bit by tiny bit, it is brought into the light, palm open, made vulnerable to a man or a dream or one more chance to live. Not just survive but really live. And if, as each part is brought into the open, it is shattered, the soul can be destroyed.

Is it any wonder so many of us are afraid?

Asha looked at the words she had just written. Her parents would worry if they read them. Mark would frown in concern. Mark's father would probably tease her about being melodramatic.

Only Rani would really understand. And Ruth.

But Ruth was dead now.

And Rani was not here.

With a quick impulsive movement, Asha scribbled the words out, her pen scratching back and forth with a fierceness that broke through the page like an open wound.

Snapping the notebook closed, she set it aside, and turned her attention to the beauty around her.

She had hiked her favorite pinnacle in the Blue Ridge Mountains—Mount Pisgah—as an escape. Escape from the stress of studying for finals. Escape from her parents' quiet, questioning glances.

But the thing she wanted to escape most could not be left at the bottom of the mountain trail. The faces of the stolen girls forced to work the red-light districts in Kolkata, India, continued to haunt her even after a year back in America. The helplessness she felt in the face of their need followed her, taunted her, attacked her with guilt.

"You need to let it go. Get back to your life," her mother said soon after her return.

Asha had sighed. "Thanks for bringing me here, Mom." She looked over the selection of specialty coffees, something she used to enjoy. "You go ahead and get one. I . . . I'm just not thirsty today."

"It's not that much money," Maryanne Rogers whispered.

"Not to you, I know that." How could she explain? "Mom, my favorite drink here costs nearly four dollars. How can I buy one knowing there are girls out there forced to sell themselves for less than that?"

"Asha, you enjoying something nice does not make their situation any worse."

"I know. It's just that—that—I can't figure out how to enjoy myself when so many others are suffering."

Her mother frowned. "You've been carrying the weight of the world on your shoulders since you got back."

Asha stared down at the cup of ice water she had chosen. "Not at first," she said softly. "I couldn't wait to come back and show everyone my pictures and tell them about Milo and the orphans, and the possibility of rescuing more girls."

"But . . . ?"

"But after they looked and said a few nice things, everyone went back to their normal lives. It's like they were just pictures, not real people."

The frown deepened. "Honey, you can't expect them to care the same way you do. They haven't been there."

Asha wondered if her mother was speaking for others, or more for herself. "I know. Life here hasn't changed."

"But you have."

"Yes." She touched her mother's hand. "But I'll try not to burden you with it anymore, Mom."

Maryanne Rogers finally smiled. "I want you to be happy, honey. Here." She pushed her latte in Asha's direction. "Taste this. It's divine."

That afternoon Asha had put her photos away. She tucked the memories and the stories and the overwhelming burden someplace deep inside where only she could see them.

And now it seemed she had carried them up the mountain with her.

With a sigh, she grabbed a bottle of water from her backpack and took several long drinks. Lifting her face, she poured the remainder over her warm cocoa-colored skin, closing her eyes as the liquid ran in rivulets down her face and neck.

As the water evaporated under the hot June sun, Asha's thoughts drifted to the night before when her father had joined her outside on the porch swing.

"So how many days does it take to pack?" he teased. "I'm glad to see you're finally done."

"Not quite," Asha admitted with a smile. "I just can't decide about the little things. Like soap. It seems smart to take shampoo and body wash for my trip to the village, but what if the bottles burst in my luggage all over my clothes?"

Her dad had chuckled. "Well, I wouldn't be able to help with decisions like that. In the military they told us exactly what we were bringing."

"You don't talk much about those days."

"Your mother doesn't like to hear my war stories." He gave a small shrug. "And that's what I came out here to talk to you about."

"Your war stories?"

He smiled. "No, your mother."

Asha looked up at him in surprise.

"Your mother wants to believe the world is basically good," he said, looking up into the night sky as the swing beneath them creaked under their weight. "She doesn't like hearing about the hard stuff—especially things she can't do anything about. She likes to do good here and there and that's her way of making a difference in the world."

He turned to her in a rare moment of openness. "While you were in India last summer, she told me adopting you was the most important thing she had ever done, and the idea of you throwing yourself into some evil place . . . well, she was scared you'd get sucked in by the evil and never be able to get out."

The middle-aged man chuckled again—it sounded rather forced to Asha's ears—and awkwardly patted her hand. "She thinks if you ignore things, they'll go away." Another chuckle. Another creak of the swing. His final words were little above a whisper. "You refuse to ignore the evil in the world, Asha. That's good, because you're going to do something about it. But be careful you don't let it take over. There is good in the world, too. Don't forget that, okay?"

With that, he stood and retreated to the house, leaving Asha dumbfounded and silent on the porch.

Today, trying in some way to apply his advice, she had run away to her favorite place.

Looking around now, soaking in the panorama of beauty in every direction, Asha tried to set aside for a moment the excitement and fear that battled for precedence within her regarding her upcoming trip back to India.

Trees, lush with summertime foliage, covered the scenery in a green carpet, as if God had taken a huge rug, dropped it upon the earth, and decided not to smooth out the lumps and ridges to add character and depth to the landscape. Below, a hazy fog smoked around Mount Pisgah. It almost hid her car from view where it sat parked at the bottom of the trail, facing outward as if it too were enjoying the view.

Sitting atop the mountain with no person or building or telephone pole as far as the eye could see was refreshing in the best kind of way. It was like music for the eyes—a song thousands of years old that never changed, but somehow always felt brand new.

Refreshed, Asha reached for her notebook once again. She thumbed past her scribbles and scratches until she found a blank page.

She would write to Mark. Just the thought put a smile on her face. "I can't wait to talk to you in person," she whispered.

Somewhere along the way, as the e-mails had flown from India to America and back again, Asha had slowly realized Mark had become her best friend. He was so good for her. So stable and solid. So balanced. He never gave in to extremes of emotion. He never seemed to get stressed.

Asha needed that, especially today, and she could think of nothing more enjoyable at that moment than writing to her best friend from atop one of the most beautiful places in the world.

She would write to him about how she felt about the coming trip. About how she was looking forward to seeing India again. And the orphanage kids and Milo. And him. Perhaps she would even mention a little about her feelings about the planned trip to Bangladesh to find her birth family. About how her insides seemed all knotted up when she imagined finding her birth parents and talking with them for the first time.

Mark would understand how she was feeling. Mark always understood.

Picking up her pen, Asha once again poured out her heart on paper, but this time she did it with a smile.

CHAPTER TWO

Mark stood in the hallway just outside the room. He willed himself not to pace as his father was doing. When Dr. Andersen opened the door, he turned expectantly.

"I can tell you don't have anything good to say."

The statement had come from John Stephens, Mark's father. Mark remained quiet, waiting.

"You're right," Elijah Andersen said, "and I'm sorry for it."

"He's not going to recover this time, is he?"

"No, I'm afraid not. His body is just too weak."

Mark felt an ache in his chest. Though expected, the news still brought pain. His grandfather, Lloyd Stephens, patriarch of the mission there in Kolkata, India, was dying.

While his father followed the doctor toward the front door, asking more questions, Mark tried to reroute his mind, to focus on something else, something to muffle the sadness.

Would now be a good time to ask his dad about finally moving off the compound and living among the Indian people as he believed God wanted him to? Not that he would go anytime soon. He would want to be near his grandmother for a few weeks and help any way he could. And of course he would want to be close when Asha returned.

An elderly, heart-shaped face peeked around the corner through the open door. Mark turned to fold his grandmother in his arms, feeling how small she suddenly seemed, how frail. "I'm so sorry, Grams."

Glistening eyes accompanied her smile as Eleanor Stephens looked up at her grandson. "He's been struggling for so long. I am happy he will finally be free from the pain of this sickness. You know how much he's hated the limitations his body has put on him these past few years." She sighed, then patted Mark's back reassuringly and led him into the room. "He wants to speak with you."

Hollow, sunken eyes barely lifted as Mark pulled a chair close to his grandfather's bedside. Lloyd Stephens spoke first. "Your girl . . . Asha. She is coming back." A weakened hand reached up. Mark took it in his own. "She is coming back, right?"

"Yes, she is coming back."

Mark allowed his thoughts to drift toward the woman he was almost certain he wanted to spend the rest of his life with. They had never talked of love in their e-mails back and forth over the past year. He had not told her his feelings for her had only grown stronger over their time apart.

"I remember when she came last summer." A rattling chuckle came from the bed. "That girl had you tied in knots right from the beginning. She'll be good for you. Keep you guessing."

Mark's mouth tipped into a half-grin. That was true enough.

He still found Asha fascinatingly—and frustratingly—mysterious. There was still so much he did not understand about her. He loved her passion for those in need, but was baffled at how she could fly into a project or problem without really thinking through all the variables beforehand. He loved her strong emotion, but fought frustration when the results of her emotion did not follow reason.

Somehow, however, despite the fact that she seemed like one of those trick algebraic word problems that had no real solution, he still found himself inexorably drawn to her. It was not reasonable for him to look forward to her e-mails all day long, yet he still did. It did not make sense to enjoy her personality as it was so completely divergent from his own. Yet he did.

And it was very out of character for him to adore her quirks and overreactions to things, but he could not seem to keep that embarrassingly cheesy grin off his face whenever he remembered them.

She was the brightest part of his day, an escape from the shroud of tension hanging over the compound that predicted coming upheaval like dark clouds predict a storm.

His grandfather coughed and Mark quickly reached for the glass of water on his bedside table. After taking a small sip, Lloyd Stephens said, "How is the house coming along?"

Mark mentally pictured the house he had begun for himself, but would now finish for her. "It's almost done. It's been nice being able to work on it these past couple of weeks."

His grandfather nodded, understanding what Mark had left unsaid. That physical labor to do in the evenings helped after sitting close to the aged man through the afternoons, watching helplessly as he slipped away.

Mark saw the understanding and cringed. "It's helped keep me from being nervous about Asha coming back," he said, trying to divert both their thoughts. "She's only got one week here before her trip to Bangladesh."

"To find her real parents."

Mark nodded. He did not like the time frame. A week was too much time to not say anything, but not enough time to know if he was ready to say what he thought he wanted to say.

"When will she return?"

"That's the thing." Mark exhaled, shifting in the worn wicker chair. "She won't tell me."

He looked out the window at the high wall surrounding the compound, the wall he had come to think of as intended to keep him in. "It's like she's planned everything up to getting there and hopefully finding her parents, and then nothing after that. I can't figure her out. I ask if she's thinking a week, a month? She just keeps saying she doesn't know."

Lloyd Stephens' smile was gentle. "Perhaps that is the truth."

Mark let out a frustrated breath. "Yeah, I know. I'm starting to get nervous that this is the way my whole life is going to be from now on—not having a clue what's happening and not being able to do anything about it."

Another chuckle from the bed. "As time goes by, you both will learn to love each other better."

"Well, I'm not sure love is part of the equation yet, Gramps. I'm—"

A soft hand touched his shoulder. "He needs to rest now, dear." Eleanor Stephens had returned to the room. She smiled. "You can come back in a few hours, okay?"

"Okay." Mark squeezed his grandfather's hand. He should have noticed he was tired. "I'll see you later this afternoon."

He rose and quietly left the room, stopping just outside in the hallway to lean back against the wall. His neck ached. He reached a hand back to knead the tight muscles.

His father returned from outside, his normally jovial face flat and solemn.

"Son, I'm sure you realize what this means."

Mark was still pondering the house, and Asha. "What?"

His father's forehead was lined, his eyebrows pulled close together. "I have to take over responsibility of this compound now. I am stepping into those shoes because there's no one else to do it. And you," he pointed a finger, "have to step up and take responsibility to continue the rest of your grandfather's ministries."

This caught Mark's attention. "Dad, please don't joke at a time like this. It's not funny."

"I'm not joking, Son."

Mark looked into his father's face and felt a sudden nausea. "You can't mean that." Mark remembered their location and lowered his voice to a whisper. "I've spent years preparing to begin my own work. I've been waiting for the chance to get started. I—"

"Are you going to let fifty years of service just die out because you want to run off and do something else?"

Mark motioned for his father to join him as he walked from the house into the sunshine outside. Once far enough away to not be overheard, Mark spoke again. "Grandpa did do a great work." Self-control kept his arms at his sides and his face calm. "But does a good work have to be continued just because it is a good work? Grandpa did what God called him to do. What about what God has called *me* to do? Am I required to give that up to continue someone else's calling?"

His father's jaw clenched. "I don't understand you at all." He turned away. "This whole compound is on the verge of collapse and all you can think about is your personal goals for the future."

Mark felt a jolt at his words. Was that really what was happening? Was the ministry as a whole really in such a precarious position?

If it was, what was he supposed to do about it? Did his father really think that by trying to keep everything exactly the same as his grandfather did it, it would keep all the problems away?

When John Stephens ended the conversation by walking away, Mark tried to think. Tried to pray.

"God, I don't get it. I've prayed for a year that You'd get them to let me off the compound, not tied down even more in it. What am I supposed to do?"

Mark started pacing, but that felt useless. What he needed was a project. Something hands-on, that did not require delving into his emotions or trying to figure anyone out.

Turning on his heel, Mark headed with sudden purpose across the compound. He would build a swing to hang from the tree behind Asha's house. Last summer, she had liked doing her devotions outdoors.

Yes, a swing would be nice. He would get some wood out of the shed, grab his tool chest, and pound some nails until, hopefully, the boil of his emotions settled into a simmer.

CHAPTER THREE

"I'm never coming with you on any trail ever again. Do you hear me, Asha?"

Asha's best friend, Amy, heaved deep breaths and leaned over her generously padded thighs. "You know I have no desire for anything that even resembles exercise," she panted, pointing an accusing finger toward her college friend. "You said it wasn't a long trek to the waterfall. What is this, like, three miles or something?"

Asha suppressed a smile. For the past four years, she had been "dragging" her friend on one physical activity after another, and each time Amy vowed never to go with her again. Asha felt sure Amy enjoyed complaining about the effort as much as Asha enjoyed her boisterous friend's company.

"I think it's a little less than one mile altogether."

"Right. And it's only a few short steps to the top of the Empire State Building, too."

Asha laughed. "It's not much farther to the waterfall. It'll be worth it. Trust me."

"Yeah, sure," Amy huffed, dragging her legs dramatically. "Says the girl who runs all over the world by herself and calls getting nearly killed in Kolkata an adventure. I don't trust your idea of fun for one minute!"

Asha grinned and changed the subject. "It feels so good to get outside for awhile," she said, pulling away a large branch that had fallen across the trail. "Now that the semester is finally over, I wanted to get as far away from technology as possible. No laptop, no e-mails, no Facebook and especially no grade postings. I even left my phone back in the car at the edge of the trail."

"You know your mom would have a conniption if she heard that. The closer you get to going back to India, the more protective she's gotten." Amy stopped and leaned against an obliging tree.

"No kidding," Asha agreed. "But the last thing I wanted today was to get to a beautiful waterfall and start enjoying the first moment of peace we've had in two weeks, and have my phone start screeching at me. It's been incessant lately!"

"You know you're exaggerating."

"I know. It's just that these past weeks of finals and goodbyes are really getting to me. Taking those extra classes on cultural anthropology and language acquisition will really help in the future, but all those added hours were just too much."

Her friend smiled indulgently. "Yeah, you being all driven and enthusiastic is great, but just because you decide to become superwoman doesn't mean you get any more hours in your day than the rest of us normal people."

Amy did not see the wry smile cross Asha's face. She was busy removing a pesky ant from her sleeve.

"So you're saying maybe I pushed too hard?"

A loud "Hummph" was Amy's initial answer. "The real question is, when do you ever not? When are you going to learn to stop overextending yourself?"

Asha shrugged. "Not in the next three weeks, that's for sure. With packing, updating my shots, getting all my papers finalized and getting together with everybody I need to say goodbye to, I think I'm going to be wiped out before I even get on the plane. That's why I wanted to come here today so badly. I think it will be my last chance to visit the mountains before all the craziness starts."

"Starts?" Amy had stopped walking again and was sitting on a fallen tree. "What do you call this entire last semester?"

Asha was about to respond when the welcome sound of rushing water teased the edge of her senses. "Hey, I hear the falls! Come on!"

Leaving Amy to her slow drudging pace, Asha rushed ahead and around one last turn in the trail. There, twenty feet in the air, water jumped and danced and threw itself off the edge of a jagged series of rocks, falling with abandon toward the small pool below, like a hundred happy children diving into a lake on the first day of summer vacation.

Asha drank in the scene, breathed in its peace and joy, delighted in the moment of solitary beauty that was all her own.

She heard Amy approach from behind. "Wow." Her voice bounced off the falling water. "Cool."

They sat quietly for several minutes, soaking weary feet in the cool water.

Asha could have remained soaking in both the water and the quietness all day long, but Amy had enjoyed her fill—of the silence at least.

"So what do your parents really think about you going back to Bangladesh to find your birth family?"

Asha winced. Of all the subjects, her friend could not have picked any that would unsettle this peaceful scene more. Like a Picasso painting, the beauty and symmetry of the waterfall setting seemed to jangle and jar before her eyes. Now instead, she saw her mother's slim hands clenching and unclenching where they rested on the table. Her father's confused face as he asked her why she felt she needed to find her birth family. Their strong reaction to her request that she be allowed to search.

"They don't seem to understand that I need to know what happened." Asha sighed, heavy with guilt over a lifetime of feelings that had never been accepted. "My parents have no desire to know the circumstances about my birth and why I was given up for adoption. They apparently didn't want to know anything back then, and they don't want to know now. It's like they think I won't love them as much if I find out or something."

"But they did give you enough to get started, right?"

Asha splashed her feet back and forth in the water, nodding with gratefulness. "In information and money. I couldn't believe it when they told me about the money they had set aside for when I graduated from college. I feel bad about using it—I know they wanted it to be for me starting a small business or getting further education." Asha bit her lip. "But when they said it was to be used for whatever I wanted most to do with my life, the thing that kept coming into my heart was finding my birth family."

For a few moments the only sounds around them were peaceful. Birds calling and water splashing into the pool. Then, braving a small moment of vulnerability, Asha revealed in a whisper, "I just feel like I can't begin any kind of life until I find out."

Amy turned to view her friend. "Find out what?"

Asha lifted her face—the face of a woman, though the voice revealed the heart of a lost and frightened child. "Why they gave me up. What was wrong with me that they didn't want me."

The soft words trailed away.

With a shake of the head, Asha forced her thoughts back to the present. "Anyway." She bounced up and offered a hand to Amy. "I was shocked when my parents told me I could use the money to go find my biological family in Bangladesh. All my life they resisted every time I asked them if I could search for them, as if there was some great secret behind the whole thing. Now I've got total freedom to go find them. It's kind of scary."

"Do you still think there's a big secret?" Amy asked curiously as they started back down the trail.

"I don't know. They told me the name of the Australian nurse who arranged for me to be adopted. She works at a free clinic in Bangladesh—someplace called Hatigram. My mom said when the nurse first told them about me, she offered to tell them all about my situation, but they didn't want to know. Can you imagine? How could they not want to know?"

Amy thought for a moment. "Well, maybe they were afraid if they heard too much about your real parents, they wouldn't be able to feel like you were really theirs."

Asha had never considered that before. Her parents being afraid? They always seemed so in control, especially of their feelings. Suddenly a new thought so completely overtook her, she forgot to focus on the trail and lost her footing. What if . . . what if they were as good at shutting away their true feelings as she had become?

Amy grabbed Asha's arm to keep her from falling. "Watch it there. So last time I talked to you, you'd e-mailed the nurse. Have you heard back from her?"

Nodding, Asha brushed a strand of hair back from her face. It fell again. "Twice. She's willing to meet with me, so I got my tickets to go." Just the thought brought butterflies back into her stomach. "I'll have to fly to a city and then ride a bus to the clinic. I guess it's way out in the middle of nowhere. She said she'd rather just tell me all about it over e-mail, but I told her I wanted to ask my birth parents myself. If we can find them, that is. She said she knows where they used to live, but isn't sure if they are still there."

Back in the car, Amy drank down half a bottle of water. Wiping her mouth, she asked, "What about India?" She grinned. "And Mark?"

Asha pulled onto the road. She smiled but did not look at her friend, the winding roads down the mountain commanding her attention. "I'll spend a week in India first then go to Bangladesh. Kolkata is so close, it hardly cost anything more to stop there. Then after Bangladesh I'll go back to India, and after that . . . I'm not sure. So much is just unknown."

Amy's grin spread even wider. "Like whether or not you're going to marry a certain American missionary dude—who by the way I have yet to meet? How can you marry somebody I haven't even met and approved of?"

As Asha tried to frame a vague response, Amy continued. "Then again, considering he's already, like, saved your life and all that, I guess he's got a firm check-mark in the prince charming category, so what more do you need?"

What more did she need? So much, Asha wanted to say. She forgot her friend's presence as her mind concentrated on the road and her heart concentrated on Mark. "The truth is," she whispered, imagining his face before her, not realizing she was speaking aloud. "I'm not totally sure how I really feel about him. I'm afraid the guy I fell in love with is more what my imagination has created than the real thing. What if I get there and he isn't all I remember him to be? What if I'm making it up?"

They had reached the bottom of the mountain road. Turning, taking in one last look at the peaceful expanse in every direction, she sighed. "And what if, sometime this past year, he changed his mind about how he feels about me?"

"Well," Amy's voice pulled Asha from her thoughts. "I guess you'll know the answer to a whole lot of your questions pretty soon."

Asha's hands clenched the wheel. The thought should be comforting.

But it wasn't.

CHAPTER FOUR

Eight thousand miles away, a woman pulled the face veil of her *burkah* down to shade her skin from the relentless tropical sun. As quickly as her aged bones would go, she rushed to Shazari's hut.

"It happened again," she said the moment her eyes encountered her niece. "Another baby has been taken."

Shazari stood and turned away. "I don't want to hear about it."

"It was your neighbor's daughter-in-law's baby," the woman continued undeterred. "The child was only a few weeks old."

"You talk too much."

"They said they had even offered sacrifices to keep the curse away." The woman shivered and rubbed her arms. "But during the night last night, while they all slept—"

"Stop. Just stop it!" Shazari shrieked. "I said I didn't want to hear about it!"

She pushed past Alia and left the hut, but not before the woman could see tears running down her niece's weathered cheeks.

CHAPTER FIVE

"Ladies and gentlemen, welcome—"

Asha looked out the window as the plane taxied down the runway, wishing security had not been so tight and her parents could have seen her off at the actual gate instead of out in the airport lobby. Goodbyes were lousy in general, and having to say them in the middle of a hundred bustling travelers made it worse.

Her mother had hugged her fiercely and told her with tears that they loved her and wanted her to be happy, whatever that took. Asha had looked from her mother's eyes to her father's, and saw in them the acceptance of her trip and the purpose for it. She felt as if one of her heaviest pieces of luggage had been taken away.

"I don't know how to thank you." She reached up to hug them both. "Not just for this. For—for everything. For taking me in. For—for loving me. For—"

"Stop, stop," Asha's mother pleaded. "I'm already crying." She waved her beautifully manicured nails in front of her eyes and attempted a smile. "Do you want me to melt?"

Her father had already handed his wife a handkerchief before Asha could reply. He looked at his watch. "You should probably get going."

"I know." Asha patted her father's arm. "It's your fatherly duty to make sure I'm always on time."

"Well, an international plane flight is definitely a circumstance when one does not wish to be late."

Asha smiled and hugged them both again. She turned to go through security before anyone had a chance to say anything else that would feel too emotional.

Now, with America falling behind, the plane moved up and away, forward, toward her future. Whatever it would be.

The trip was long. Longer than she remembered. She tried to sleep, watched several uninteresting movies, tried to read but could not focus.

Eventually the lights dimmed, announcing the night. Passengers covered themselves in airline blankets and tried to find comfortable positions in uncomfortable seats. Asha nodded off several times, but always woke sooner than desired. She tried to quell her feelings. The excitement over going back was overshadowed by another, stronger emotion. It filled her with its questions.

What will it be like to see my birth parents for the first time? Will they welcome me with open arms? Or will they turn away, rejecting me for the second time?

Fear. The feeling was fear.

Once Asha finally acknowledged the problem for what it was, she knew what to do about it. "God has not given me the spirit of fear," she whispered, reaching into her carry-on for her small travel Bible. Opening it to the concordance at the back, she looked up every verse listed under fear. God's promises poured into her anxious heart, washing out the anxieties and replacing them with peace.

And then, finally, after several flights and layovers, India appeared below her. Down through the clouds the plane descended and Asha looked with glistening eyes on the place she had learned to love one summer ago. Lush green fields in fertile patches of farmland gave way to the browns and blacks of the tightly cramped city buildings.

Somehow, more than ever in her life, as the plane touched down on Indian soil, Asha felt like she was coming home.

Her plane had landed surprisingly early. Certain Mark would not be there yet, Asha stepped outside the airport to be part of it all again.

The sights, the sounds that greeted her filled her senses with delight. She had missed the loud cries from the vendors. The multitudes of street children traveling in small herds from one white tourist to another. The blaze of colors flowing from scores of saris as women passed by in every direction. The emotional chatter and wide gestures and bells ringing from a line of eagerly awaiting rickshaw drivers.

Above her, telephone poles and phone lines seemed to go in every direction, intersecting and twining like a woman's tangled hair. Across the street, blue plastic chairs and small tables with even smaller outdoor umbrellas welcomed visitors to stop for a cup of *chai* and a spicy snack.

Even just standing there, with India swirling all around her, she felt swept up in its life.

Yes, that was it. The people of India lived life in capital letters. Everything about them was out loud, passionate.

A group of teenage girls passed by, giggling and gesturing. One looked at her, then after a word to her friends, they all looked her over. Asha looked down. Were they giggling about her clothes? She had changed into a salwar kameez before landing so she would not stand out as a foreigner.

After feeling the hot wash of embarrassment flood her, Asha started to retreat back into the airport. Then she remembered her Indian friend Ruth's wise words. "When you get the feeling you are doing something out of place, or people are looking at you and you're feeling you stand out for the wrong reasons, just stop and take a close look at the details. You might find it is something as simple as the fact that you forgot to remove your shoes before entering the church, or you are using the wrong hand, or giving the wrong greeting. Don't crouch away when you start feeling embarrassed. Stop, think, discover the reason and then you can make the adjustment."

Dear Ruth. How Asha missed her.

So Asha looked. She noticed their hair, long and straight. Hers was also, having grown several inches over the past year. She noticed their earrings and nose rings. She had no nose ring, but neither did several of the girls in the group, so that could not be it.

Their salwar kameez outfits were of various colors and materials . . .

Then she saw it. Their kameez tops. Every one of their tops were straight-cut, had slits on the sides up to the hips, and they only came down to several inches above the knees.

Asha looked down again at her own kameez top, flowing long and loose over her balloon "underwear" pants. Her top was at least six inches longer, cut in an A-shape, with slits that only came up to where the new tops started.

The style must have changed while she was gone. Or perhaps it had been that way last year, too? Perhaps the wardrobe full of clothes for short-termers at the guest house only had old-fashioned ones.

Could she have been that unobservant?

It was possible. With a whole new world to absorb, it was plausible she could have been walking around totally out of style and never noticed it.

But not today. Today, her first day back, Asha had felt the embarrassment of standing out and not only did she resist it, but she would conquer it.

She looked at her watch. There was still half an hour before the plane had been scheduled to land. With a grin, and a burst of renewed energy, Asha grabbed her suitcases, threw her carry-on over her shoulder, and marched to the nearest rickety trolley.

"Can you tell me where I could buy a salwar kameez?"

The driver pointed toward the Departure gate of the airport.

"No, I don't want to leave," she tried again. Had her Bengali gotten that bad over the past year? "I want to buy an outfit."

He gave the little head-jiggle Asha remembered and explained that there were clothes for sale in the Departure section of the airport.

"Oh!" He had understood her after all. "Thank you!"

It was time to start living life in capital letters. And she would begin by buying the most Indian-looking outfit she could find.

Twenty-five minutes later Asha emerged, head high, slim body clad in a stylish, fiery orange and red salwar kameez, the *orna* draped over both shoulders and trailing flamboyantly behind her as she re-crossed the airport to the Arrival gate.

Back inside, Asha dodged the flow of new arrivals and edged through the waiting crowd. Finding a spot nearly all her own, she dropped her carry-on from her shoulder to rest on one of her suitcases and turned full circle to survey the scene all around her.

The airport was cluttered with people, noises, baggage, and even one traumatized goat that had wandered in from the street and could not find its way back out.

She smiled. Then she laughed. Oh, it felt good to be back.

"Asha."

She turned and suddenly, he was there. He was there, and he was looking at her.

For a moment, the feelings were too much, and time had to stand still to catch them all.

Asha forgot to breathe. She could not think of one single thing to say. But her eyes spoke, and finally her mouth followed.

"Hello," she said softly.

He watched her lips move and smiled.

"Hi."

His smile brought back a hundred memories, and Asha remembered to breathe again.

He was here. They were together after a long, long time.

Now what?

CHAPTER SIX

She was standing just a few yards away, all bright colors and beauty. Mark felt his throat clamp up, as if he had just swallowed a large *rupee* coin.

Her hair was longer, he noticed. Her eyes sparkled and her lips shimmered with some kind of gloss or something. And where did she get that great outfit? It set off the color of her dark skin just right.

He saw her lips move. "Hello." Such a simple greeting. After a year of shared opinions and thoughts over e-mails, now in real life what was there big enough to say?

Hello was as good a place as any to start. He smiled. "Hi." When her lips curved and bloomed into a smile in return, Mark caught his breath. She was as beautiful as he remembered.

He was walking toward her before he even consciously decided to move. Her bright orange outfit was a flame, and he was drawn to her like a moth.

Stopping halfway, Mark recognized with a grin that his analogy meant he was headed for trouble. Was this how Samson gave up his secret to Delilah, even though any sane man could see she was bad news? Was this how Solomon, wisest man in the world, became foolish and drifted from God because of his wives?

Fortunately for me, Mark thought, *the woman generating that invisible, powerful pull in my case is one who loves God and belongs to Him first.*

Maybe he was not a doomed moth after all.

As Mark slowly approached, a wide, secret smile on his face, Asha noted the differences between the reality of his presence and her memories from the summer before.

He was thinner, the contours of the bones on his face stood out. Had he been sick? His sleeves were rolled up to the elbows, something she remembered he liked to do when he was working all day on the compound. He must have forgotten to unroll them.

Her eyes traveled upward again, past buttons, to his face. Now he was standing a mere foot away. He was taller than she remembered. Her head had to tilt upward to look him in the eye.

And his eyes. Oh, his eyes.

Feelings flooded her, from the rush of anticipation, fear, excitement and uncertainty in her heart, to the blush rising from the same region to flash up her neck and face. *Say something*, she thought frantically. *Anything*.

Feigning a lightness she was not even close to feeling, Asha spoke. "You're looking at me as though you haven't seen me for a year."

If it was possible, his smile widened even more. "And I'm very happy to see you," he stated simply. Genuinely.

His hand lifted, as if to touch her cheek, then suddenly he stopped and dropped his arm. "Almost forgot," he chuckled, the timber of his voice warming her from the inside out. She watched him stuff both hands deep into his pockets.

A group of men walked by, their arms around one another in friendship. Asha watched, feeling jealous of their freedom. She fought back the temptation to throw her arms around Mark's broad shoulders, not caring who was watching or how inappropriate it might appear in that culture.

She was still thinking about how wonderful it would feel to hug him when Mark's voice reached out to her. He had shouldered her carry-on and was grabbing the larger of her two suitcases. "I spent the whole time on the way over here trying to think of something memorable to say, like they do in the movies." He grinned, then his face softened tenderly. "But all I could think of to tell you was how much I missed you." He looked at the crowds of people flowing around them, then back at her. "So . . . I really missed you," he stated.

Asha bit her lip to keep it from trembling. She hid her face, bending to lift her other suitcase onto its wheels. "I—I missed you too."

They tried to walk side by side, but with the jostling, pushing crowd Asha finally gave up and settled for just being able to keep Mark in her sights. He looked back regularly, checking to make sure she was still with him. Once they reached the Land Rover, dodging groups of beggars and vendors, Mark heaved her luggage into the back then climbed onto the seat.

"We made it." He looked her way. "Ready?"

She nodded and they were off, inching their way amid the throng of vehicles, people, and two rail-thin cows being goaded by a young shirtless boy using a reed for a prod.

Asha commented on the cows, Mark responded, then they fell into silence again. Asha felt her toes curling inside her shoes, as they always did when she was feeling more emotions than she could handle. She grasped her left hand with her right and began twisting the fingers of her left hand, but then stopped herself. She did not want Mark to see how nervous she was.

Mark made a left turn, sliding slowly through an intersection. Traffic lights hung in all the right places, but the electricity was out, leaving them as blank and useless as museum pieces representing some other, more time-conscious society. Cars, rickshaws and auto taxis were all merging in and out of the intersection from every direction. It took fifteen minutes for them to break free of the tangle.

Mark chuckled. "On days like today, walking is the fastest way to get around. Even the rickshaws have a quicker time of it when the traffic is like this."

Asha was about to smile when she realized Mark was driving on the left side of the road. A car was headed straight toward them. "Mark, that car's going to hit us!"

He glanced at her. *Don't look at me!* she wanted to scream. *Get on the right side of the road!*

When the oncoming car swerved back into the other lane, so close Asha was certain it would clip the side of their vehicle, she flinched.

"We drive on the left side here, remember?" He glanced at her again. Asha could tell he was trying not to look amused. "The car was just passing that rickshaw over there."

"Oh." How could she have forgotten that? Asha slumped down in the chair. Here she was, making a fool of herself, and she hadn't even been in India for two hours yet.

"You've been gone awhile. You'll get the hang of things again in a day or so." Mark smiled but did not look her way, focusing on the road. "It always takes me awhile to get readjusted whenever I've been away, too."

An uncomfortable silence filled the space around them. Asha fidgeted. She bit her lip. She could not think of one interesting thing to say.

Was this the way it was going to be her whole week here?

Was it as she had feared, and the feeling between them was not reality, but merely her imagination?

CHAPTER SEVEN

After the silence reigned for several minutes, Mark finally looked over at Asha with a wry grin. "This is . . . weird, isn't it?"

She let out a small laugh in relief. He had felt it too. "Yes," she admitted. "I'm used to talking to you over e-mail, but not at all in real life anymore."

He sent a grin her way, the wide, full grin she had missed so much. In it, Asha saw her best friend. Whatever they might become, best friend was enough for now. She could be comfortable with that.

"So tell me about your trip," he offered. Asha considered what she would tell him were she e-mailing him, and was able to relax and share several funny stories from her travels. They joked and talked and were almost comfortable by the time the vehicle reached the compound gate.

It was opened by a reed-thin Bengali man wearing the typical wrap-around *lungi* and a long *Punjabi* shirt. He bowed and touched folded hands to his forehead in the traditional greeting. When he stood upright again, a welcoming smile on his face, Asha spoke with pleasure. "It's Milo's father!"

She returned the greeting as Mark drove the Land Rover through the gate and under the nearby awning. "Does he live here on the compound now? Is Milo here, too? He said he would come live with his father and stop living on the streets that day you offered his dad the job. Remember?"

Before Mark had a chance to answer, Asha's door was opened by a boy with only one foot, a crutch, and a huge smile on his face.

"*Didi* Asha!" the boy said, using the term for big sister affectionately. He wagged a finger at her like he had seen the Americans do. "*Didi*, you take too long to come back. Look, I am taller now! Almost a man!"

Asha laughed. She had missed him, this boy who had been part of most of her mishaps and adventures the previous summer. She had hated the thought of him living on the streets again, begging for his food, but now with his father getting a job on the compound, it looked like he had settled down with him.

"So you live here, now?" she asked, marveling at how much he had grown over the past year. He really was almost a man.

Milo grinned and nodded. He used his crutch to point toward the small guard shack near the gate. "I am living here with my father. And my mother and baby sister also came from the village now that we have a house. There is enough money to buy food. And sometimes *Dada* Mark is giving me the jobs to help him fix up the small house for you. He pays me some money. I no more need to be begging. I even take my mother to get an ice cream, and I pay the money myself!"

Feeling tears glaze her eyes, Asha blinked quickly. "God has taken good care of you, my friend."

"Yes!" Milo agreed enthusiastically. "It is true what the big book is saying, that the God knows what we need before we even ask it. Now my family is together and we have good life here. I stay here and work for *Dada* Mark, even though the small house for you is finished." He leaned in to whisper conspiratorially, "And maybe you stay in India, too, *Didi* Asha? Maybe the small house be for you and the man who built it for you?"

Asha blushed. "I don't know," she answered honestly, hoping Mark could not hear their conversation.

"Hmmm." Milo pursed his lips together. Then he grinned again. "Maybe you are not seeing what is—what you say in English?—what is plain like nose on face, but Milo sees." Milo looked back to where Mark was pulling Asha's luggage from the back. Mark caught his look, waved, then glanced at Asha.

"All set," he said. "Ready to go see your new place?"

Milo looked from one to the other. He nodded, pleased with his superior knowledge. "Yes," he confirmed. "Milo sees."

With that, he pivoted deftly with his crutch and began making his way back home, promising to see *Didi* when she came to Bible time at the orphanage tomorrow.

"What was that all about?" Mark handed Asha her carry-on and pulled the two suitcases himself.

Asha shouldered the bag. "Um, about something as plain as the nose on my face, apparently."

Mark raised his eyebrows, but Asha offered no more information.

"So what's this about you and Milo working on a small house?" Asha asked, changing the subject. "I know you've been working on your house here and there this past year, but Milo seems to be confused. He seems to think it's for me."

Mark had led them to the small building, now finished, that had once been intended for himself. "I'm going to be staying with Grandma for awhile. She could use some extra help sometimes, and I know she's feeling lonely these days so I thought it would be good to be around, especially while my dad's out of town for awhile."

Asha looked at the house she knew he had put countless hours into building. She glanced back at him, questions in her eyes.

"It's for you," was all he said, enjoying watching her eyes widen in disbelief.

"Me?" she squeaked out, putting a hand to her heart. All those hours. All that effort. For her?

She looked at the house. It welcomed her with its cheerfully-painted shutters and screened-in porch area. She touched the screen—it was the only building on the compound with a screened in outdoor area. She could be outside in the evening without having to deal with the dreaded mosquitoes.

His thoughtfulness touched something deep inside her. "Mark," she said softly, not daring to look at him. "I don't know what to say."

"Well, don't say anything yet," he said with a laugh. "For all you know, the inside might have crooked walls and beat-up baseboards."

She smiled. "Not if I know you," she countered. Mark was a man of precision and detail. Everything he did, he did thoroughly and well.

And he had done this for her.

She opened the porch screen door and walked the few feet to the front door of the house. It was painted yellow, like sunshine, to match the shutters.

Mark deposited her luggage on the porch, then retreated to stand just outside.

"Um . . ." he stalled, and Asha looked at him questioningly.

"I can't wait to look around and see all you've done," she encouraged. "This was just a wood frame when I left, you know."

He nodded. "I remember." His eyes told her he remembered everything from her time there last summer. She wondered if he was thinking of the day she left, when he had kissed her. Her face flamed.

She was surprised when he took a step backward instead of forward. "I'd really love to show you around and tell you about all the stuff I did on the house." He shuffled his feet a little. "But if you look around . . ." She did. "You'll notice a lot of Bengalis work on the compound . . ." She noticed several in various places within sight. "So . . ." He stalled again and Asha tilted her head, confused. He nodded his head toward several Bengali men working on the compound's other vehicle. Or at least they had been working. From the moment Asha arrived, they had stopped their tasks and watched the newcomer with interest.

"So to protect your reputation," Mark said finally, "not to mention my own, I'm going to head over to Grandma's place and let you get settled in by yourself. You can come over for supper after you've rested a bit. If you want to, that is."

She wanted to. She wanted to ask him to wait outside while she unpacked. She wanted to skip the nap her body needed and continue talking with him. Anything to keep him from walking away.

He took several more steps back, seemingly as reluctant as she to separate. When he did turn and cross the compound to his Grandmother's home, Asha watched until she remembered the men who likely were still watching her. She glanced over toward the garage. Yes, the entire group of men remained standing stock still, staring openly.

Asha quickly lowered her eyes, turned to grab a suitcase, and headed inside the small structure that was to be her home during her stay.

Mark managed to get inside Eleanor Stephens' house without turning around to see if Asha was still there. He willed himself not to go to the window and look for one more glimpse of her face.

Instead, he sat on the living room couch and imagined her walking through his house—now her house. He pictured her noticing the table and chairs he had built, the decorations his grandmother had lovingly contributed, the kitchen cabinets placed low enough for someone of her height to easily access. He knew she would notice every detail, every window frame and piece of wall trim, knowing he had done every piece out of love for her. She would see that, he was certain.

When Eleanor Stephens arrived home, she found her grandson sitting frozen on the edge of the couch as if waiting for an important interview. A soft, gentle smile creased the face that had watched Mark grow from a boy into a man. "She is here, isn't she?"

The voice was full of loving affection. Mark looked up. Seeing the knowing look in her eyes, he grinned. "Using your super-grandma-vision on me again?"

Eleanor Stephens did indeed see into her grandson's heart, and tears touched her eyes. How she wished her husband could have lived long enough to see his grandson love and marry and have children.

Mark stood and approached her. "You're feeling tired, aren't you, Grams? Why don't you go rest for awhile?"

The elderly woman reached up a weary hand to pat her grandson's cheek. "I am a bit tuckered. But there is an important young man in my home who looks like he needs someone to talk with." Her eyes traveled back in time. "Your grandfather was the same way. Whenever he was nervous about something, he either had to talk about it with me, or he would just get stir-crazy." She giggled. "And now that you don't have the house to work on anymore, Mark dear, I'm afraid you'd get so stir-crazy you'd decide to cook dinner, or some other idea that would end in equal disaster."

Mark chuckled, helping lower her into the rocking chair her husband had built before the birth of their first child nearly fifty years ago. "Now Grandma, you know that was just a one-time mistake. That meatloaf wasn't too bad, once you ate past the burnt outer section."

A frail hand covered Eleanor's mouth as she giggled again. "I thought your grandpa's teeth might just fall out, he was trying so hard!" Then she sighed. "Oh, I have had such a blessed life. I have loved and been loved. I have served the Lord, and watched following generations serve Him, too."

She looked from the past over to the man sitting next to her. "And now it is your turn," she spoke lovingly. Then, as if waking herself from her nostalgia, she said pertly, "Now tell me everything. Are you going to propose to that woman or not?"

Two hours later, when Asha knocked on the door, Eleanor Stephens was waiting to greet her.

Asha hugged her warmly, "I'm so happy to see you." She noticed the hints of dark circles under the dear lady's eyes. "I was so sorry to hear about Mr. Stephens," Asha added. "Your husband was a great man."

Not knowing what else to say, Asha was thankful when Mrs. Stephens spoke. "Thank you, my dear. After fifty-two years together, I hardly know how to be by myself anymore. But, truly, I'm not alone. I always have the Lord with me. And for awhile, my grandson, too."

With that she called Mark from the kitchen. "He's helping," Mrs. Stephens explained, then added with a wink, "but don't worry, I'm not letting him actually cook anything."

"I heard that!" came a voice from the kitchen. Asha bit the smile from her lip as Mark came into the room carrying a steaming casserole dish. When he looked at her, the smile burst free.

"Hi," he said.

She thought of their first moments at the airport. "Hello."

Eleanor looked from Mark to Asha. Her sweet sigh inspired them both into action. Suddenly Mark was setting the table and Asha headed to the kitchen to fix drinks.

"I'll never feel far from North Carolina as long as you have this sweet tea," Asha called out from the kitchen, putting ice in each glass. When Mark returned to get the salad from the refrigerator, his arm brushed lightly against her as he passed. Asha momentarily froze. The kitchen was narrow, and he had to brush against her again on his way back out.

Asha chided herself for holding her breath until he had exited the kitchen. Surely it was ridiculous to be so affected by such a small connection. She balanced the three glasses and carefully carried them out to the table, hoping she would make it through dinner without embarrassing herself by melting every time he looked her way.

Dinner was a success. Eleanor Stephens, ever the gracious hostess, kept the conversation going. Asha enjoyed her stories from Mark's childhood, and the easy camaraderie that flowed between them. Mark treated his grandmother with respect and affection, pulling Asha's heart even more toward him.

Once the dishes were cleared away, Mrs. Stephens faked a yawn. "Oh dear, it's been a long day for me," she said, fluttering a hand toward Mark and Asha. "Forgive me for deserting you two children, but I missed my nap today." She winked at Mark. "I'll be just down the hall if you need me."

At the room's end she turned. "Don't you stay up too late, now," she warned with a smile. Then she was gone.

The silence filled the room. Slowly, Asha turned to find Mark watching her. She felt her heart quicken. Her toes curled.

The air between them was electric. He took a step toward her. Then another.

Asha felt rooted to her spot, until he whispered, "Welcome back," and held out his arms. Suddenly, a year's worth of feeling propelled her forward.

She was in his arms. Finally.

A quietness wrapped around them. No words were needed.

Asha sighed. She was in India. She was with Mark.

She was home.

CHAPTER EIGHT

"I wanted to take you out to the banyan tree today," Mark said, looking toward Asha almost shyly as he stepped up onto a heavily ornamented rickshaw. "But that will have to wait until tomorrow or the next day."

Asha climbed in after him, enjoying the feeling of closeness the small rickshaw provided.

"Gopal is a good friend and I just couldn't miss his wedding. I'm glad you didn't mind coming with me."

"Are you kidding? I'm excited about it!" Asha adjusted her *orna*, tucking the long, embroidered edge beneath her to keep it safely away from the rickshaw wheel. "I've missed Indian culture so much, and this is the perfect way to jump back in."

"Well, then." Mark ran his hand out in a sweeping gesture as the rickshaw pulled into the heavy, noisy traffic. "Allow me to give you a little welcome-back cultural tour. We'll take the scenic route."

"Wonderful!" Asha bounced in her seat, eagerly trying to look in every direction at once.

The city was more colorful, more chaotic than she had even remembered. Their rickshaw darted in and out of traffic, the driver's flip-flop clad feet peddling them past a street-side barber. Asha thought he was giving his customer a haircut, until her eyes told her he was actually cleaning out the man's ears with a tiny ladle.

At her little screech, Mark smiled. "You know, sometimes things look primitive here, but India has a rich history that puts other lands to shame," he said. "There are records from over two thousand years ago of an Indian doctor doing brain surgery using herbs as anesthetics." Mark instructed the rickshaw driver to turn left, then continued. "And how about the fact that quadratic equations were being used in India way back in the eleventh century?"

Asha hid a smile. "Well, I'd be more impressed if I knew what a quadratic equation was," she admitted.

"Hmm." Mark frowned. "Okay, I guess that's the kind of stuff that would impress me. Now if I were trying to impress you . . ." He smiled down on her. "Which of course I am . . ." He thought for a moment. "I'd tell you about Mother Teresa's home for the dying, and all her orphanages in Calcutta, now known as Kolkata of course."

He thought for another minute. "What else? I'd tell you about how Indian women use henna dye to put red tints in their hair, and to paint designs on their hands and feet when they get married. You'll probably notice it on the bride as soon as we get to the wedding today. I always thought it was kind of strange how they go to so much trouble to make her look pretty, but then she's supposed to look sad. I remember one wedding where the bride was wearing a red sari—red's the color of joy—but she cried the whole time."

"Why?"

"I can't really blame her—I'd be feeling pretty lousy too if someone had arranged my marriage to somebody I'd never met. I think traditionally they're supposed to look sad because they're leaving their family for good, which is a big deal."

"Wow!" Asha wilted a little in her seat.

Mark noticed. "But don't worry, the wedding today is a joyful one. People are calling it a 'love match' because Gopal and Siti have talked to each other on three separate occasions."

"Are you serious?" Asha said, openmouthed in astonishment. "That's all it takes to make it a love match?"

Mark's gaze caught hers. "Well, sometimes I imagine it only takes once or twice."

She thought of her first meeting with Mark, how they'd argued, and her eyebrows rose in disbelief. It appeared he was suddenly remembering the same thing, for he chuckled. "Of course, with some people, it takes a lot longer before they figure out what a great catch they've got," he teased.

Asha was trying to think of an appropriately tart response when Mark indicated their arrival. Music played from inside a building. People were arriving from every direction to flood the courtyard.

Mark led Asha down the driveway and to the front door, outside of which at least a hundred pairs of shoes waited like spectators refused an entrance. He looked inside the building and muttered, "Guess we should have come earlier. The place is packed."

Turning from the doorway, he led Asha around the outside of the building to a three-foot wide hole in the wall that served as a window. "We can watch the wedding from here."

"Is that allowed?"

"Sure. Look around."

Asha saw that the other windows around the building also framed last-minute arrivals. She put her hands on the open windowsill and smiled. "This window is just the right size. I don't know if I'll ever get used to being in a place where nearly everyone is my height!"

At that moment a hush fell inside the building. Asha watched the groom enter from a side door to sit on a chair in the front. Then along with the crowd inside, she turned her head to the back of the building as the bride entered, her face painted white, a large gold pendant hanging to rest on her forehead, her red sari gleaming with gold accents. Her hands and feet were, indeed, covered with tiny, intricate paisleys and dots.

She was beautiful. Asha felt like a child watching Cinderella. She could not help but imagine herself in that sari, with painted hands and feet, walking toward the man she loved.

She glanced up at Mark. Was it her imagination, or did he just look down at her and wink?

The pastor began speaking and Asha turned her attention to the ceremony. She could understand most of what was being said, thankful she had not lost much of her Bengali despite being in America for a year. Mark filled in the parts she could not understand.

Love match or not, it was clear both bride and groom were incredibly nervous. *Who wouldn't be?* Asha thought. *What would it be like to marry someone you did not even know, or just barely knew?*

"Why do they keep their eyes on the ground the whole time?" Asha whispered, then added quickly, "Never mind. The I-pronounce-you-man-and-wife part is coming. I don't want to miss it."

To Asha's surprise, at the spot where an American couple would have kissed, the pastor took a hand from both bride and groom and placed them together. If it was possible, the two looked even more uncomfortable than before. *How strange it must feel to touch across genders for the first time, and in front of all these people!*

With that, the wedding was over. A young girl walked backwards down the aisle, throwing flower petals at the bride as she exited. The child was doing her job with enthusiasm, flinging the flowers as energetically as she could. Asha bit her lip, trying not to smile as she imagined some of the petals sticking to the bride's coated face.

The congregation sang a song, then the pastor dismissed them all. From there, Mark and Asha joined the other missionaries for the supper of spicy curry and rice.

Asha watched the different missionaries as they mingled and joked with their Bengali friends, marveling at how they had made this place their own world. Though their skin stood out as foreign, it was easy to see their hearts were Indian.

She smiled wryly to herself, knowing her skin fit in perfectly, but her actions showed she was more foreign than any of them. So far she had managed to fail multiple times at getting the curry and rice into her mouth using the fingers of her right hand, leaving curry stains on the thankfully plastic tablecloth as witness to her botched attempts. Her fingers were covered in sticky rice. She had no napkin, and the spices were so strong she was fighting tears, but could not take a drink until she had cleaned her hand. She almost reached her left hand up to wipe her right when she remembered such an action would be completely inappropriate.

Quickly assessing the situation, Mark's grin was teasing—affectionate, she tried to tell herself. He had told her in his family teasing was a sign of affection. She had yet to believe it.

"Forgot how to eat with your fingers, didn't you?" he joked.

He led her to a nearby washing area with faucets. Yellow from the turmeric spice had already stained her fingers, and turned what used to be her mauve nail polish into a strange variation of orange.

"All done?" Mark asked. "It's time to send the couple off."

Asha again followed Mark, this time around the gated driveway to where a car waited for the bride and groom. A car covered in flowers.

She put a hand to her heart. "How beautiful!" Turning to look at Mark, who had shifted to stand behind her, she asked, "Your friend has a car already?"

Mark smiled down at her. "No way. He'll never be able to afford a car his entire life. This one is borrowed from a rich relative who is back on a visit from America. See all those?" He used his chin to point toward the roses all over the hood, trunk and top of the car. "They put them on with scotch tape."

Asha saw his face and laughed, knowing he was imagining what the tape would do to the car's paint job. "Aren't all those flowers expensive?"

"Not here. Well, I mean, considering the average wage, they probably are comparable. A rose like that would cost about . . . probably less than fifteen cents. I don't really know; I haven't ever bought any."

"Oh." Asha felt another of those Cinderella moments. She could not imagine anything more romantic than getting married in a red sari in India, with painted hands, and a car covered in roses.

She had never had these feelings at weddings in America. Did that mean something?

Mark was looking at the departing car as he commented, "Maybe if you stay, someday you'll be driving off in a car like that."

His voice was casual, but Asha saw his throat move as he swallowed.

She tried to lighten the moment. "I doubt I'd be driving. Most men in India have a thing about the guy being in charge, you know."

His smile came back. "Well, hopefully you'll have a love match, and you can sweet-talk the guy into letting you have a turn at the wheel now and then."

"I don't know," she teased. "He might be too uptight, worrying about what the scotch tape is doing to his paint job."

He grinned, looking down at her as if she were the sunshine breaking through after a month of monsoon rains. "Asha," he started. His tone turned husky and she gazed at him, wide-eyed. "I want—"

A voice came over a loudspeaker from a nearby mosque, drowning out any conversation as the call to prayer wailed out in Arabic above them. It blared so loud Asha fought the temptation to reach up like a child and plug her ears.

Mark cocked his head toward the road, and Asha followed gladly as he found a rickshaw and they climbed aboard. She waved back at the other missionaries as they rode away, then settled back to dream of rose-covered cars, and to wonder what it was Mark had almost said.

CHAPTER NINE

Mark's mind felt like a game of ping-pong. Should he ask her today? Should he wait?

They had ridden a rickshaw together through the city early that morning, stopping for breakfast at a side-of-the-road shop, then traveling on to the banyan tree that had been their own special place the previous summer.

All throughout the past year, he had checked and re-checked his feelings and desires. Was he ready to say he loved her? Was he ready to ask her to be his?

A line of sweat ran down Mark's back beneath his shirt as he lowered himself to sit against the tree's sturdy trunk. He loved Asha, of that he was certain. But was he ready to say forever?

Or should he wait? Wait to see if she felt called by God to stay and serve in India on her own, regardless of him?

But then again, how could he keep going without knowing something of how she felt?

Mark was so deep in thought, he barely noticed when Asha sat by his side and began speaking.

She twisted her fingers as she talked about her upcoming trip to Bangladesh.

"I have to go to a city called Chittagong first. One of my friends from college is working at an orphanage there for a year, so I'm going to stay with her overnight before I go on to Hatigram." Asha was rambling, a sure sign she was feeling nervous. "Well, actually, she became my friend after I found out she was going to Bangladesh and I hounded her for information till I'm sure I drove her crazy." She smiled. "I'm looking forward to seeing her, but I don't know how I'll endure being so close and not just rushing straight for Hatigram to meet with Cindy Stewart and have her take me to my family."

Mark smiled absently, still engrossed in his quandary over Asha and their future together.

"I keep imagining what it will be like to actually meet them in person," Asha was saying. "I've dreamed about this my whole life, but there's this big hole in my thoughts once we've been introduced. I can't seem to envision anything after that."

She sighed then. "I'm so afraid they are going to ask why I bothered to come find them. Why would they want to see me now, when they gave me up back when I was born?"

Silence reigned for so long, Mark stopped his pondering and looked down at Asha's face.

She was gazing up at him, biting her lip. Her eyes asked questions he could never hope to answer. Then she spoke. "And Mark, how will I bear it if they reject me again?"

He should have been paying attention. He knew he should have. That was why everything went wrong. But he had been so focused on trying to decipher his own heart that he had only half-listened as Asha had bared hers.

"I really don't think you need to go at all," he offered. Not noticing her jolt in response to his words, he continued. "I don't understand what it is you need to prove." Couldn't she just skip the Bangladesh trip and stay there with him? He looked down at Asha's suddenly pale face. He thought of how fragile her heart was, and how he wanted to protect her from anything or anyone who would hurt her.

"What if they do reject you again?" He hated saying it, hated the way her eyes filled with tears. "Why is it so important to you to find out why they gave you up for adoption over twenty years ago?"

By then Asha was standing, her hands clasped. She turned away, but he heard the tears in her voice. "I thought you understood," she choked out. "I thought you were the one person who understood."

He rose to his feet but stayed behind her. This was not turning out the way he had hoped. "I'm sorry, Asha. I just don't want you to set your heart on something that might end in disappointment. You seem to think what happened to you back then somehow defines who you are now, and that doesn't make any sense to me."

She whirled to face him. "It *is* who I am now. Don't you see? I was given away—*given away*. Like an unwanted toy or the runt of a litter. My own family *did not want me*. Can you even begin to imagine how that feels?"

"Asha, what happened to you as a baby has nothing to do with you now—with who you are." Mark reached for her, but she pulled away.

"It does. It does!" she cried out. She sunk to the ground, covering her face with her hands. "What was wrong with me? What did I do wrong that they didn't want me?"

His heart hurt for her pain, though his mind could not grasp her words. Why would she even think these things?

"Asha, please," he pleaded, kneeling beside her. "You've got to let this go. You can't live your whole life letting what happened to you in the past control you like this."

He had gathered her into his arms as he spoke, and at first she softened against him. However, by the time his words penetrated, Asha had stiffened completely. She pushed away from him and stood. "You aren't even trying to understand."

He sighed. "I'm not trying to be uncaring, Asha." He stood and faced her. "I'm just trying to help you be reasonable about this and think through—"

"Reasonable?" her voice was high-pitched with strain. "*Reasonable*?" She spun away from him. "I don't want to be reasonable!"

Mark was mentally agreeing with her statement when a coldness swept over him as her voice hardened. "Is that what you want? A woman who is reasonable?" Her face turned away. "If that's what you want, then you've found the wrong girl."

She looked at him then and he was stunned by the coldness in her eyes. "You don't want me to be reasonable," she said with sudden fury. "You want me to be you. To think like you and act like you, and not have strong feelings about anything you don't personally think is important enough."

He was following her as she stomped from the banyan tree toward the road. "Asha—" he called after her.

She climbed into a rickshaw, and only spoke once he had joined her and the driver began pedaling them back toward the compound. "My past is important to me. My family, and why they gave me up, is important to me. I am going to find out the truth because it matters, whether you think it does or not."

He started to speak but she cut him off, her voice toneless. "I guess it's good I'm leaving in a few days. It seems like we both need some time apart to figure out what really matters—what we really want."

Mark felt numb, his emotions overloaded and his mind clogged. He tried to mentally replay what had happened, to sort through and decipher what had gone wrong, but the only thing that remained clear was that Asha was angry, hurt, and suddenly glad she was leaving him behind.

They sat in silence the rest of the way back, Mark completely baffled, Asha in tears, present hopes and future dreams crumbling all around them.

CHAPTER TEN

Chickens flapped and squawked and ran for their lives. Alia laughed as she watched. "You have become fat and cannot run fast enough," she teased her friend.

"Fat, ha!" responded the village woman. "Who can become fat when there is not enough rice, and the chickens run away?"

She lunged toward the largest of the animals. "Get over here!"

The chicken bolted, but not soon enough. "Ah-hah, got you!"

The middle-aged woman swung her trophy by the foot in triumph but soon reached to grab the living poultry by the neck to stop its attempts to peck her hands and arms.

Soon, a swift swing with a large machete had sliced off the chicken's head. The woman picked up the deceased animal, her eyes following a younger village woman, one of several hauling water together from the riverbed to their homes.

Her chin pointed. "There is not enough food, and yet she becomes fat."

Bangles on Alia's arm jangled as she gestured toward the girl. "You know what it means."

"She was married two summers ago. It has been more than enough time."

Alia shook her head. "I would not want to be her, not in this village."

"The curse?"

"Bah!" Alia spit to the ground. "It is no curse."

"What do you think it is, then?"

Alia backed into her friend's hut before speaking. She whispered, "I think it is the Evil Eye."

The friend dropped her chicken and rushed to shut the door. "The Evil Eye? Do not speak of it in my home. You will bring its wrath on me!"

"On you? How can it affect you? You have passed the time to carry any more children." Ignoring her friend's furtive gestures of warning, Alia continued, her voice thick with suspense. "The Evil Eye swoops into the village and takes them, one by one."

"Do not say anymore!" The woman's fear propelled her to physically shove Alia from her hut. "I will not have you causing our chickens to die, or our food to poison!"

"Mark my words," Alia whispered toward the house, knowing her friend could hear her behind the slammed door. "The Evil Eye takes them. I know, for it appeared once when I myself was present. One minute the baby was there. The next . . ."

Alia felt herself shudder as her friend inside whimpered in fear.

"The next minute, the baby was gone."

The trip was strained. Neither the hours traveling to the Scarlet Cord, nor even the time there with Rahab and her husband could erase the strain of tension that had followed both Mark and Asha since their visit to the banyan tree two days earlier.

Asha looked out the window as the passing landscape transformed back from green and fertile fields to the bustle and chaos of the city. Her spirit had not responded to the beauty of the fields outside the city. She could not even garner an excitement in response to Rahab's reports of women being rescued from sexual slavery and given hope again, stories which a few days before would have given her heart wings.

She had wanted to be excited. After a year of looking forward to revisiting the Scarlet Cord, she wanted to set aside the whole situation with Mark and focus her heart on the ministry that had filled her thoughts since the previous summer.

But how could she even hope about a future rescuing trafficked women if she and Mark were at such an impasse? How could they have any future at all if he did not understand the core of who she was? Her greatest fears? Her deepest needs?

Did he not know her at all?

The evening following did not prove any better than the trip had been. Asha packed without enthusiasm, slept fitfully through the night, then skipped her morning devotions to avoid the pain of seeing the swing Mark had made just for her.

Mark drove Asha to the airport, his face grim. Even his physical muscles were contracting from the tension filling the vehicle. He could not decide which was worse: trying to talk and possibly ending up in an argument again, or not talking and having to endure things as they were until she returned.

He could not leave things as they were, so he spoke. He explained his viewpoint again. She reiterated hers. They were not getting anywhere, except perhaps farther away from each other.

"I just want you to understand," she pleaded. "Even if you don't agree, I just want you to understand that this is something I have to do."

He did not understand, and could not tell her he did.

I love you.

He almost said it out loud. He almost told her.

But would she believe he loved her if he did not understand her? To Asha, love and understanding seemed one and the same. Could one not be valid without the other?

They stood at the airport gate.

"I guess I'll be in touch sometime," was her muted goodbye.

She turned, but he called her back. His arms reached out involuntarily. "I can't tell you I understand." He saw her stiffen. "But I care about you, and about what happens to you."

He saw tears spring to her eyes, spreading the ache in his chest.

She nodded. "Thanks," she whispered.

He heard her sniff, saw her wipe a finger quickly across her cheek to catch a falling tear. She started to speak, but could not seem to find any words to say.

Finally, she shrugged softly, almost helplessly, and murmured, "Bye, Mark."

Then she was gone.

CHAPTER ELEVEN

How many disappointments could she take? Her argument with Mark was bad enough. How was she going to disguise her disappointment over this?

After her flight to the capital of Bangladesh, another flight to Chittagong, a night's stay with her college friend, then long hours traveling north on a rocking, swerving bus, she had finally arrived at GCC—Grace Christian Clinic—in Hatigram only to hear that Cindy Stewart would be in surgery all afternoon.

Asha's hopes of finding her family that day fell all around her feet, like discarded luggage. She wandered the clinic area aimlessly, following a narrow paved path from the clinic back to a collection of concrete houses, then past them to an incredible view that stretched out over miles of endless rice fields.

Each square patch seemed to have its own shade of green, more shades than even Crayola© could imagine. Asha wondered why. Bordering each side of the crop squares stood small, snake-like mounds of piled dirt and mud, creating tiny fortified walls for the crops—keeping some flooded in several inches of water, keeping others dry. Asha wished someone was nearby who could tell her what the differences meant.

She put a hand up to shade the sun from her eyes. In the distance a small child walked toward a tiny thatch hut, balancing on a sun-hardened mud border like a gymnast on a balance beam. To her left, a person—Asha could not tell if it was a man or woman—bent over harvesting rice, a Chinese-style pointed hat shading the person's head and shoulders, legs calf-deep in muddy water.

Here and there, small huts arose from the landscape, like mushrooms growing out of a freshly-mowed lawn. Far in the distance, as Asha squinted into the sun, she could make out what looked to be a building made of concrete, the only non-natural creation for miles.

Must be a cyclone shelter. She had seen a few in her research about Bangladesh. Asha frowned, thinking the sight of the building likely offered little comfort to the locals. What good was a cyclone shelter if people had to sludge through miles of muddy fields to reach it? Were a real cyclone to hit the area, only those in the closest surrounding areas would make it to its thick, protective walls in time.

A whoop caught Asha's attention. The child who had been balancing on the built-up mud border lost his balance. She watched the mud give way beneath his bare feet, and he lurched, then fell into the rice paddy with a splash.

She smiled and then waved as the boy looked around to see if anyone had noticed his undignified descent. Breaking out in a huge grin, the boy waved back, then scrambled back onto the mud ridge and toward his home.

When one of Cindy's co-workers called Asha in for supper, she waved toward the tiny hut in case the boy might be watching from inside, then left the sanctuary she had found, determined to return if she had the chance.

"You'll have to excuse us, Asha," Danielle was saying while the rest of the nurses laughed at Asha's facial expression. "We all work in a third-world clinic, and this is just life for us."

Asha had been listening, wide-eyed as a child, as the nurses talked about the day's events, including one man who had come in with maggots eating away at a wound he had left untreated for weeks, and a stomach surgery that set loose two handfuls of worms, which, as they were still alive, all started squirming away toward freedom once they fell to the floor below the operating table.

Appetite completely gone, Asha tried not to even look at the spaghetti on her plate. Her mind was conjuring up imagines of it coming to life and wriggling off the table.

"Is it like this all the time?" she asked, her nose unconsciously wrinkling at the idea.

"Well . . ." Danielle started.

"Pretty much," Jane, another nurse, put in with a sigh. "Some days it's worse! For example, we get in a lot of bus accident victims. I'm sure you've noticed how men pile up on top of the buses."

Asha nodded her head.

"Well, you can imagine how awful a bus accident is for the men sitting on top."

Again, Asha nodded.

"So one day an accident victim was brought in. Three men had been impaled by a metal pole right through their middles. People trying to help had pulled the pole out of the first two men, and they died. But the third begged them to leave the pole in and bring him here. He made it. Miraculously the pole had missed all his internal organs." She half-smiled. "But we did have quite the difficult time getting him and his six-foot protruding pole through the emergency room door."

Asha felt like her eyes were bugging out of her head. What a reality TV show this place would make!

"Some things here are devastating," Danielle offered, "but God is so good to us. He is the great Healer and has touched so many lives through this clinic." She smiled. "And when things seem too difficult or discouraging, God sends us reasons to laugh, often when we need them most. Like that lady who had the ear infection, remember her?"

Jane nodded and everyone at the table laughed, except Asha. "What happened?"

"She came in complaining of an ear infection, so we gave her antibiotics and sent her on her way. Well, about a week later, the woman came back saying the medicine didn't work. I was checking her that day, so I asked if she had sold the medicine—we have a big problem with that—but she said she hadn't sold it. I asked her several more questions, and then, finally, I asked her if she had swallowed the pills like she should."

Jane grinned. "Well, she looked at me like I was crazy and said, 'Swallowed them? Of course not! I put them in my ear!'"

Asha laughed. She looked around the table, suddenly glad she had not been able to leave for the village right away. Her respect for these women was high. They faced difficult circumstances on a daily basis, but still found reasons to laugh and enjoy the lives they had chosen.

With a smile, she dug her fork into her spaghetti and tried to eat it without thinking about worms.

CHAPTER TWELVE

Cindy Stewart had returned. The other nurses retired to their separate rooms, and Asha found herself alone in the building's version of a parlor, waiting impatiently for Cindy to shower and change from scrubs worn through a long, hot day.

Asha had so many questions. How far away was her family's village? How long would it take to get there? When could they leave? She felt the impatience like a mosquito bite—a constant itch she could not scratch.

The Muslim call to prayer sounded out from a mosque somewhere in the distance. A fraction of a second later, another one began from another mosque. Then a third chimed in. Like surround sound, the voices came to her from all directions, as if competing against each other.

Cindy Stewart's voice came to Asha from behind. "After hearing that five times a day for twenty years, you'd think I'd be used to it by now," she said, smiling. "I am able to sleep through the first early morning one, but the rest of the day, it still always catches my attention. Reminds me there are over one hundred million people in this country calling out to God in Arabic—a language they do not even understand."

She sighed. "These weary bones are getting tired of such long days." With a smile she added, "I know you've been here for hours already, but welcome to Hatigram."

"Thank you." Asha sat on a worn couch positioned near the window to catch any passing breeze. "I'm curious about the name Hatigram. Doesn't that translate to mean 'village of elephants'?"

"Sure does." Cindy settled onto a chair facing the couch. "Hatigram got its name because elephants come down from the hills during the winter months looking for food. It's not unusual for us to see a few around Christmastime."

"Wow." Asha ached to ask when she could see her family, but did not want to be rude. "So how old were you when you came out here?"

The nurse smiled. "I came fresh out of college, full of idealism and energy. Along the way I've been bedridden for months with malaria, typhoid, and an unknown strain of Hepatitis. I've learned to set aside some of my ideals and accept reality, hard as it is sometimes. And most of all, I've seen God at work in big and small ways, and learned to love who He really is—even the times I do not understand His ways."

Crossing the room to the kitchen, she filled two glasses with boiled, filtered water, then returned to hand one to Asha. "But you didn't come all this way to ask me about my philosophies on life in a third-world country."

Asha felt herself unconsciously sit up straighter. She gripped her glass, already slippery from condensation. Though darkness had fallen before six in the evening, the night air brought no coolness with it, only a damp heat that left her feeling as sweaty as the glass in her hand.

"I need to tell you about your birth family," Cindy said, "and the circumstances that brought you into my neighborhood, literally."

Asha stiffened. "Thank you," she inserted quickly, "but I really want to ask my family about it in person."

Cindy shook her head. "I know you are Bengali by birth, but you do not understand the Asian way. First of all, it would be completely inappropriate for you to barge into their home and ask such direct questions, especially when you first meet them."

Asha felt herself bristling. She had no intention of "barging" into anyone's home. Especially not her own family's. Then again, if that is how they would perceive it, it would not matter whether she intended to do so or not. Maybe she should listen to Cindy's advice.

Taking a deep breath, Asha forced herself to settle back onto the couch and say, "All right. Can you please tell me why?"

Cindy nodded with an understanding smile. "For one, elders are to be highly respected. A child does not question parents. And in this particular situation, it would be very uncomfortable to them for you to even bring up the subject for a very long time. For you to show up and broach the subject immediately would be deeply hurtful and disrespectful."

What does respect have to do with it? Asha wondered impatiently. *I came all this way to find out the truth. I need to know!*

"Westerners value independence, forthrightness, and information—all things that give us a bad reputation in Asian countries. Here, relationships are more important than tasks. Direct communication is considered aggressive. Harmony is desired above all things, often even above truth."

Asha sighed. Cindy was right; she did not understand the Asian way at all.

Setting aside her now-empty glass, Cindy leaned back in her chair and crossed one leg over the other comfortably. "When you go tomorrow—"

Tomorrow! The word rang like joy in Asha's ears.

"—I will not be joining you. They are going to see you as an American and a foreigner, and my presence would only make it more difficult for them to remember you are one of them. I want to make things as easy as possible for you, so I am sending you with a Bangladeshi nurse who knows your village."

Curiosity ignited, Asha edged forward on the couch. Cindy continued.

"It will be important for you to treat your parents with great respect. Not as equals. As higher than you. Bangladesh has a beautiful, but complex, culture. Don't assume that things are happening or not happening for the reasons that immediately come to mind, and try not to react emotionally before finding out what's really going on."

"I have no idea how to do that," Asha admitted. She felt more queasy than the first time she had gotten behind the wheel in driver's ed class.

Nodding, Cindy pulled out a small book titled *Bangladesh at a Glance*. She handed it to Asha. "Take this, and study it before you go."

Asha murmured her thanks as she took it. She was about to begin leafing through its pages when Cindy's words stopped her hand in mid-air.

"And now I will tell you your story."

Asha stood, dropping the book onto the couch. "Can't I go and get to know them, and then ask them about it?" Cindy was a very nice person, but Asha had not come all this way to hear about her past from a stranger. Not that she would not be a stranger to her family as well, but it just did not feel right talking about such a deeply personal experience with anyone but her own parents.

"No, Asha. There are things you have to know before you meet your parents. It's important."

Asha began pacing, circling behind the couch. This was not how she had planned things. How she had imagined her life-long questions being answered.

"Asha, please sit down."

Asha could not. But she did stop pacing. She stood behind the couch, leaning over to brace her arms on it, holding herself still.

"All right." Asha's voice was tight. She gripped the back of the couch. "Whatever the big secret is, please just tell me and get it over with." She felt ashamed at how brash her voice sounded and tried to soften it. "I'm sorry. What is this big thing I have to know before I meet my parents?"

Cindy studied Asha's face for several moments. She closed her eyes and Asha wondered if she was praying.

Then her words came and Asha's world exploded. "Your parents did not give you up," Cindy said, her voice giving facts but betraying no feeling. "Asha, you were a victim of child trafficking. You were stolen from your family, and offered for sale. To me."

Asha's face blanched. Her stomach reeled.

It could not be true. It could not be.

She felt herself taking in huge gulps of air, as if she were suffocating. Of all the things she had imagined, of all the scenarios she had constructed of what might have happened at her birth, this had never even been a thought.

Stolen. And sold.

Her mind could not hold in such a possibility. Even her body fought to reject the news.

Asha fled out the door, ran behind the house, and threw up.

CHAPTER THIRTEEN

She was heaving. Dry, racking heaves that hurt. Asha held one hand pressed to the outer wall of the house, keeping her upright. The other hand clutched at her stomach as it churned and contracted.

Finally, her body settled. Without thought, Asha used her *orna* to wipe her mouth, then used another part of it to wipe the dampness from her face and neck.

She let the *orna* drop to the ground and fell back against the wall of the house, letting her body slide down until she was sitting on the ground.

A great confusion overtook her. She wanted to sob, to cry out, to curl up into a ball and reject the news she had just heard.

She had been sold? She had been stolen? Why?

Why would anyone steal a baby?

Asha pictured a baby being wrenched from a mother's arms, imagined the pain, the fear, the terrible anguish a mother would face losing a child to a thief. Waiting for word. Hoping against hope the baby would be returned.

She heard the sound of sobbing and only then realized she was crying. Pulling her knees to her chest, Asha wrapped her arms around her legs and gave in to the tears. She cried for herself, for her mother, for all the years of feeling unwanted when the truth was she had not been abandoned by her family, but taken away.

Why hadn't Cindy Stewart taken her back to her family? She said she knew them. Why had she sent her away to be adopted by Americans?

A hundred questions clouded Asha's soul, tormenting her with whys and what ifs that only Cindy Stewart could answer. It took a full ten minutes before Asha had gained enough control of herself to even consider returning to face the woman who had decided her fate so many years ago. How could she have chosen to send her away instead of returning her to her family? How could she buy a baby in the first place?

Asha had been bought, with money. The thought was so degrading. Nausea returned to her empty belly. Asha breathed deeply to contain it, holding her midsection tightly. She felt herself rocking back and forth, like a lost child.

Suddenly she froze. That is what she was. A lost child.

Still, even now, she felt lost. Helpless. Afraid. Wanting her mother but not knowing how to find her way home.

Tears came again, this time for all that was lost. All that was taken away.

God, how could You let this happen?

There was no answer. Only silence, broken by the soft sounds of crickets and night birds.

Asha lowered her head in despair. At that moment, she felt completely and totally alone.

Half an hour later the door opened and Asha entered, walking on legs grown numb from crouching on the ground outside. *As numb as my heart feels.*

She lowered herself onto the couch across from the chair where Cindy Stewart still sat. Cindy looked on Asha with compassion.

"I'm sorry to have to be the one to tell you all of this." Asha heard her, but vaguely, as if she were underwater and someone shouted at her from a distance. Her eyes focused on Cindy's aged shoes, and she could not seem to pry them away to look into her face as she spoke. Images of children being stolen, then sold, like kittens in a box on the side of the road, held her mind captive.

"Asha," Cindy called out. "Asha," she said again, rising to cross the distance between them. She sat close to Asha and firmly took her arm. When Asha did not respond, Cindy gave her arm a quick swat.

Asha blinked, as if waking up from a deep sleep. She looked up. Cindy was sitting next to her. "I'm sorry, what did you say?" she asked politely.

"Asha, look at me," Cindy ordered.

Asha obeyed. Her eyes pointed toward Cindy's, but her gaze was distant. Cindy shook her head and grasped Asha's chin with her hand. "No, really look at me. Focus."

With effort, Asha did as she was told. Cindy spoke clearly and distinctly, and Asha concentrated on the movements of her mouth as she talked.

"I want to tell you everything about what happened when you were brought here. But I'm not sure you can handle it right now. Do you want to wait until tomorrow?"

The words were clear and concise, and brought an immediate response. Asha balked. Wait until tomorrow? For answers to questions her heart had been asking all her life?

"No!" Asha sat upright, pulling her arm free and shaking her head with passion. The action brought her mind back into focus. "No. I want to know. Please."

Her life was on hold until she had these answers. She would beg and plead and get on her knees if she must. She had to know. Tonight. Her voice barely contained the desperation she felt. "Please tell me."

Cindy's eyes studied Asha's. As if assured of something important, she nodded. Asha waited, twisting her fingers, as Cindy stood and returned to her chair several feet away.

"Get comfortable," she said, and Asha wanted to ask if she was joking. Comfortable? How could she possibly even think of comfort at a time like this?

"Get comfortable," Cindy repeated. "It's going to be a long story."

CHAPTER FOURTEEN

"Mark, the phone's for you."

Mark was surprised his father had even answered his cell phone. John Stephens had returned to the compound that morning, and he and Mark were discussing the future of the mission, and the difficult choices Mr. Stephens, now in charge, was having to make. The more Mark listened, the more he understood the pressure his dad had been under, and the reason for his dad's insistence that Mark remain on the compound until the crisis was over.

For once they were really, genuinely communicating.

They had been brainstorming for two hours when the phone rang. "I'll just let it go to voicemail," Mark's father had said. Then Mark saw him glance over at the number, pick it up to look at it again, then quickly answer it.

Must be someone important, Mark thought, returning to the spreadsheet they were creating on an oversized sheet of paper. When he heard his father say, "Yes, yes, he's here. He's right here," and hold the phone out to him, Mark's eyebrows rose in question. Who would be calling him on his dad's cell phone?

"It's Asha."

Mark's hand shot out immediately to reach for the phone. Asha had not left his mind since her departure. He had begun several e-mails to her, but deleted them all, wanting to give her the space she needed. He never imagined she would actually call.

"I can't believe a phone call actually came through," John Stephens said as he handed the phone over. "It's practically a miracle—the phone lines are hardly ever open in both areas at the same time."

Mark nodded and pressed the phone to his ear. He watched in surprise as his father quietly left the room to give him privacy. It flashed across his mind that normally he would have expected his father to come sit even closer, curious, eager to be part of the conversation. *These last weeks of responsibility have changed him.*

But there would be time to analyze that later.

"Asha?" was all he said, still finding it hard to believe she had actually called. Mark thought of all the things he had wanted to tell her before she left. He plunged in. "Asha, I wanted to tell you—"

She had not even heard him. "Mark, you're never going to believe what I just found out. Cindy let me borrow her phone, and the only number I knew there was your dad's. I hope he didn't mind. I just had to call and tell someone, and I can't call my parents because I'm totally freaking out, not to mention it's twelve hours time difference from here to there so it's like nine in the morning for them and they're at work already, and—"

He heard her suck in a deep breath. Her voice sounded different. Mark wondered if she had been crying. Before he had a chance to decide what to say, she had started up again.

"I know I'm rambling," she said quickly. "I'm sorry. I'm just so—I don't even know what to think or how to feel. I—Mark, I wasn't given up for adoption from my birth parents. I mean, I was, but I wasn't."

Mark had gone from concern that maybe she'd been in some kind of accident, to confusion at trying to decipher meaning from the barrage of words coming his way. "Asha," he stuck in before she had a chance to continue. "Asha, I'm here, and I'm listening, but you'll have to slow down. What has happened? First of all, are you all right?"

"I don't know," came the baffling answer. "I don't know if I'm all right. I don't think so."

Maybe she had been in an accident after all. "Are you hurt?" he asked, hating the limitations of being so far away and only having her voice to give him information. He could not see her, not see for himself if she was okay.

"No," she answered quickly, putting him a little more at ease. "No, I'm not hurt. Not physically. I'm just—I'm so overwhelmed. I feel like I'm drowning."

His heart constricted. She must have met her family, and they rejected her again. Mark felt a pain at just the thought. He wished he was there, with her, even though being beside her he would feel as helpless as he was feeling at the moment. But at least he could . . . well, he could do something.

"They didn't give me up, Mark." She was speaking again, rapidly, as if her mind was suddenly tipped over and all the information had to come spilling out. "I was stolen. Stolen, just like those women I care so much about rescuing. I'm one of them. Except I was a baby. I was just a baby, Mark, and they stole me away from my family and tried to sell me. And not for even a decent amount of money either!"

He wanted to smile at her indignation over her price until the meaning of her words fully sunk in. "What?" he asked, dazed. "You were what?"

"They tried to sell me to Cindy Stewart. When she first came out here, before she knew better than to walk alone at night, she was walking home after an emergency c-section when these two guys came up to the fence and called out to her. Can you imagine having somebody come up to you with a baby in their hands, and they say if you don't buy her they're going to sell her into the sex trade? A baby! How could anyone—"

"Wait," Mark interrupted. His head was reeling. "Asha please, I can't keep up. Start at the beginning, okay?" He sat down, gripping the chair next to him with one hand, gripping the phone with the other.

"Okay." He heard her breathe in, as if to collect herself. He focused every muscle he had on listening to her words.

"The night I was born, I was stolen away by these two men—Cindy knows it was the night I was born because later my mother told her—no, wait, I'm getting ahead of myself again. Sorry. These two guys brought me to Cindy. They said they would sell me to her. Cindy didn't know what to do, but she didn't trust the guys. She said the one holding me had a nasty scar running across his jaw, like he'd been in a knife fight. The other one looked scared, and once called the guy holding me "older brother." Cindy said that could mean he really was his brother, or just a family term because of their ages, but—"

She had cut herself off. Mark was processing as quickly as possible when she started speaking again. "I was rambling again. Why do I do that so much when I'm freaked out? The bad guy, the guy with the scar, saw that Cindy was backing away from the fence where they were, so he said if she didn't buy me he was going to sell me to the sex traffickers and I'd grow up to be a—a—"

Mark heard her voice break. His heart felt like it was cracking along with it. "Asha," he breathed out, hearing the raggedness in his own voice.

"I could have been living the lives of all those women in the red light districts. I could have been right there with Rani, only I would have grown up there. I would have been sold off to the highest bidder once I'd gotten old enough to . . . They would have . . ."

He could hear her crying, and would have given anything to be able to put his arms around her right then.

"Asha, I—"

"Wait, wait, I'm okay." He heard the words, but did not believe them. How could she be okay, hearing she was nearly sold into the horrifying world of prostitution as a child?

"So Cindy felt like she had no choice but to pay the guys and take me, but if she bought me it would be considered child trafficking, and that was illegal." Asha continued, her voice growing stronger the more she spoke. "So she told the guys to wait while she got some money, and she ran to the clinic to get help. But the guys must have figured out what she was doing because when she came back with some of the male nurses, the men were gone. She was standing there, worrying, when she heard a baby crying. It was me."

Asha sniffed. "They had left me there, in the grass, right outside the fence. Like a useless orange peel or an empty water bottle. Cindy said she never did understand why they did that—if they had gone to all the trouble to steal me, why just leave me? Maybe they were worried Cindy had called the police and they would be looking for two men with a baby?"

The phone connection crackled. "Mark? Are you still there?"

Mark nodded, then remembered she was on the phone. "Yes, I'm here."

Asha continued. "At first she had no idea what she was going to do with me, but then she remembered a couple she had met the last time she visited America with some of the American doctors to raise funds. A couple wanting to adopt a child from overseas."

"She took care of getting me to an orphanage, and then got in touch with the couple and eventually worked things out for me to be sent to America and adopted by them. But first, Cindy found out who my real family was."

"How did she do that?" Mark was finding this story more unbelievable at every turn.

"She was doing rounds at the clinic and checked on a woman from a Muslim village who had come in after delivering twins. Mark, I have a twin brother. Can you believe it?" Her voice rose in excitement, and she kept talking without giving him a chance to respond. "I'm a twin! It's no wonder I've always had this need to come back and find my family. They say twins have a real connection, even if they're separated."

Mark was shaking his head again, though he knew she could not see it.

"So Cindy is checking this woman, who was having complications after the births, and she finds out the woman is also grieving because one of her new babies was stolen from her—the very night the guys had brought me to Cindy! So Cindy rushes home, gets a photo she had taken of me, and brings it to the clinic. The mother doesn't recognize it because she never saw me before I was taken—my own mother had never seen me!" She stopped again for a moment, her voice catching. "But the aunt who was with her did, because she helped deliver me. So everybody's all excited, then Cindy remembers I'm already at the orphanage ready to be adopted. She tells my mother all about it, and when my mother hears the whole story, especially the part about the bad guys, and the one having the scar, she panics and says I have to be sent away."

Mark felt himself leaning forward, on the edge of his seat. "Why?"

"Well, Cindy says she thinks my mother might have been scared that if she took me back, I'd get stolen again or something. So she tells Cindy to send me to America to be adopted, where I will have a better life and be rich and grow up to be a great lady."

Silence. Mark waited for more, but after several moments passed, he asked, "So what are you going to do now? Will you still try to find them?"

He heard a sniff. "Oh, Mark," her voice was breaking again. "Of course I have to find them! Don't you see? All these years, all my life, I thought they had given me away because they didn't want me. Now to find out my mother gave me up for my own safety, because she thought I would have a better life in America—I just have to find her. I have to see her and somehow, I have to—I don't know. She gave up so much. I need to give something back, or something."

Her voice was full of feeling. He felt relieved, if only for the fact she had stopped thinking about how close she had come to being sold into the sex trade. But a nagging concern was spreading across his chest at the tone of her voice when she spoke of giving something back. "What do you mean?" he voiced. "Will you go looking for them soon?"

"Tomorrow." Her voice held such hope. "Cindy isn't going with me. She says it will 'clutter things up,' whatever that means.

She's sending me with a Bengali who can show the way to their village."

"And when will you come back?" He left the question vague, allowing her to decide whether he was asking when she would be coming back from the village, or when she would be coming back to him.

The silence this time sent a chill down his spine. Mark did not put much stock in premonitions or gut feelings, but his gut was churning on this one.

"I don't know," came the soft reply. "Cindy plans on me only being there for the day, but . . . I don't—I just don't know."

What about that guy with the scar? he wanted to ask. *What if he's still around?*

"Asha, I know you aren't going to like this, but I think you should consider not going, especially on your own."

"What?" Asha's voice held surprise. "How could you even think that? I've come so far and I'm so close!"

"I know, but you're a single woman on your own. That might make you a target."

"A target for who? Like robbers? I'm only taking a little bit of cash with me, so I'm really not worried about that."

Mark could tell she was only half-listening. "No, not robbers." How could he say it? "What about the guy?" he asked, his voice tight.

"What guy?"

"The guy who stole you in the first place. What if he's still around?"

"Mark, don't be silly. That was twenty years ago! Besides, it's not like I'm a baby anymore."

Mark's self-control was being tested to the limit. "Asha, this whole thing just sounds dangerous. I really think—"

He heard her sigh with impatience. "I can tell you still think I shouldn't be going." There was silence at both ends for a full minute, but Mark did not take the opportunity to refute her statement. How could he?

"Well, I am going, Mark. I need to find them."

He swallowed the rest of his objections, knowing they would not be heeded. "I'll send you a text with my cell phone number on it, in case you want to talk again." He paused. "Promise me you'll be careful, okay?"

"Of course." She paused, then said tonelessly. "I—I have to go now. We're getting an early start in the morning."

He could think of nothing to say to bring her back. Nothing that would not push her even farther away.

"I just wanted you to know what'd I'd found out." Her voice was soft now, and sad. "Thanks for listening."

As if he had done her a favor. As if they were barely friends, and she had only called him because she could not think of anyone else.

"I'm glad you called," he said sincerely. "I've been thinking about you." That was an understatement. She had filled his thoughts every waking hour, and some of his sleeping ones, too. "I hope tomorrow is all you are hoping it will be."

"I know you don't think it will be," she said, her voice low with resignation, "but thanks for saying so just the same."

They both sighed into the phone at the same time. Why was this so hard?

"I really need to go," Asha said again. "I guess I'll talk to you . . . whenever I get back . . . ."

Mark rested his forehead down on his fist. "I'll be thinking of you." He would not be able to help it.

"Thanks." Her voice had dropped to almost a whisper. "Bye."

He wanted to think of something to say that would bring them back to a good place. A together place, despite the distance.

But nothing came. "Goodbye, Asha. I'll be praying for you."

Mark closed the phone. Wearily, he put his head down on the table and began to pray.

For now, and for possibly a very long time, it was all he would be able to do.

CHAPTER FIFTEEN

This was it; the day she had been imagining for as long as she could remember.

Asha was in the village. Her village.

It looked rather nondescript, as villages go. She had seen several just like it in her recent travels.

But this one held her family. Her biological parents. Her twin brother. Perhaps even some grandparents or cousins.

Asha tried to still the wild beating of her heart. It was possible, she reminded herself, that they no longer lived in this village, though it was unlikely they would move. A burning sensation crept its way through Asha's chest. She wanted to run down the slope and into the cluster of bamboo huts, calling out her parents' names. Only she did not know her own family name, did not know her father's name at all, and the fear that overshadowed even her impatience kept her rooted to the spot where she stood.

"Are you ready?" the Bangladeshi nurse at her side asked.

"Yes, I think so, Mrs.—I'm sorry, I don't know your name."

The nurse smiled. "My name is Shabnam, but here in Bangladesh we do not use first names for married women. I am called 'Deepak's mother.' Deepak is my oldest son."

"Oh." This was news to Asha. So once she found out her twin's name, she would have to remember to call her mother by his name instead of hers.

The nurse—Deepak's mother—began her descent down the rough dirt path, parting the overgrowth that sought to cover and conquer it again. Asha followed.

A small tea shop stood at the entrance to the village. Perhaps "stood" was too sturdy a word, Asha thought. It looked more like an old, stooped man ready to topple at the first heavy wind. Several men sat under its awning, drinking tea and smoking cigarettes.

They all stared openly at the two women passing by, though not one said a word. Asha felt the sensation of what she used to call the creepy-crawlies slithering over her skin. The men's clothing, particularly their white caps, reminded her she was in a Muslim village, and in their eyes, though every part of her skin was covered except her head, hands and feet, she was still exposed and immodest.

Asha felt the men looking at her as if she were strolling through their village in a bikini. She wished she had thought of buying a head-covering for herself. But then again, would that label her as a Muslim?

This was not a good start. There was so much she already did not know. And if Bangladeshis were as indirect as Cindy said, how would she ever find out?

With swift, tiny steps, Deepak's mother hurried her along past the tea shop and through the center of the small village. Around a bend along the dirt path, finally past the watching eyes, they saw a woman squatting over a cooking fire.

"Excuse me," the nurse said in Bengali, pulling back a little when the woman stood and looked at her with great surprise. "Does the woman Shazari still live in this village?"

Asha hoped beyond hope the woman would say yes. That one name was all they had, the only clue to finding her entire family.

The woman's eyes darted back and forth, as if unsure whether or not to answer. Deepak's mother stepped forward again, introduced herself, then began explaining that Asha was visiting from America and wanted to see Shazari. That Asha had a gift for her.

The woman's eyes lit up when the nurse mentioned America, and with sudden deference to Asha, she began leading the way toward a row of small, rickety huts, giving slight bows along the way that made Asha decidedly uncomfortable.

"What did you mean—I have a gift for her?" Asha asked as they walked.

"Did you not bring a gift?" came the befuddling answer.

Asha moaned. "No. I wanted to, but I didn't know if that would be appropriate or if it would make it look like I thought I was rich and would offend them or something. And on top of that, I had no idea what anyone would want. What do you give someone who lives in a bamboo hut in a village?" She ended the conversation mostly talking to herself.

The Bengali nurse shook her head as she walked. "I have worked alongside foreigners for many years, and know many of your ways, but I still do not understand you."

Asha was racking her brain. She had only brought one small bag with her, not wanting to appear ostentatious. In it was one change of clothes, one travel bottle of body wash, one notebook and pen, ten dollars worth of *taka* coins, her small travel Bible, and a few other insignificant things. There was only one other item that mattered, the only possibility of a gift, but it was something Asha had never wanted to part with.

Wrapped carefully inside her change of clothes, Asha had packed a small, somewhat ragged blanket—the blanket that had wrapped her the night she was born. It was the only piece of her family she owned, and she had kept it close always.

Now, as they neared the hut where her family lived, Asha considered the sacrifice of giving her precious possession as a gift to her mother. Surely it would mean a great deal to her mother to know she had kept it all these years.

Yes, Asha decided, it would be a perfect gift, one that would show Asha's feelings of love for her family, and her desire to be reunited with them. She would be sad to part with the treasure, but it would be worth it.

The village woman stopped outside a small hut and removed her sandals. She turned to them. "I am Shazari's aunt," she announced before dipping her head to enter the small dwelling. Asha and the nurse also removed their sandals and stepped inside.

Covered in stripes of shadow and light from the bamboo and sun, two women squatted at the far edge of the small hut, weaving baskets from what looked like long blades of grass. One was older, her face creased by years of sun-damage and toil. The other, at her side, was a much younger woman, a teenager if there was such a term in Bengali. Could this be a younger sister? Asha's pulse raced. She felt the excitement bubbling within her like a shaken-up can of Coke®.

A man followed in behind her, and Asha recognized him as one of the men from the tea shop. She saw the surprised look on the two women's faces. They rose and welcomed the visitors who filled to capacity the small structure. The younger girl spread a woven straw mat on the floor.

Asha waited, expecting a chair or stool to be set on the mat, but then realized quickly there were no chairs or seating of any kind in sight. Careful not to step on the mat, she approached and seated herself on it, remembering from *Bangladesh at a Glance* to curl her legs under her so as not to point her feet in anyone's direction.

Whew. So far so good. Asha wondered who was who as the three hut occupants, the two women and the man, sat across the hut and stared at the three visitors, the woman who claimed to be Shazari's aunt being one of them. Asha assumed the aunt must be finding this unusual occurrence interesting, and was waiting to see what gift the American had brought.

The younger girl stood, excused herself, and soon returned bearing small cups of tea and tiny cookie-like snacks. The guests accepted out of politeness, the nurse making small talk while Asha fidgeted and wished they could get to the reason she had come.

Everyone was treating her like a queen, offering food to her before the others, smiling and nodding toward her, asking her if she wanted anything else. Asha wished the Bengali nurse had not mentioned America at all.

She smiled and nibbled at her cookies, trying to ignore the flood of questions waiting to burst forth. Was this her mother and father and sister? Were they even in the right house? How were they going to find out anything if they spent the whole time talking about this year's crops and when monsoon season would start?

Finally, just as Asha was near to bursting, the nurse gestured toward her with a flattened palm, the Bengali version of pointing, and again mentioned Asha was from America and had come to visit them.

Three pairs of blank eyes looked her way. It was clear no one could imagine why an American would come visit them. It was also clear they had no idea how they were supposed to act in this untoward situation.

In the lengthening, uncomfortable silence, Asha decided it was now or never. Reaching into her bag, she said, "I have brought a gift for you."

Encouraged by their pleased response, she pulled out the treasured blanket and carefully unwrapped it, holding it out for them to see.

The blank stares became confused, uncertain, though the smiles remained in place.

"Do you recognize it?" Asha asked hopefully. "Do you remember where this is from?"

The man scowled, mumbling rapidly, something about why a rich American would bring an old used blanket as a gift.

Asha was feeling foolish, foolish enough to barely notice how crestfallen her facial features had become, when the aunt sitting on the nurse's side suddenly grabbed the blanket with both hands. "I know this blanket," she said, her eyes wide. "I wrapped your baby in it the night she was born."

At the word "your," she had looked toward the older woman. Asha felt tears stinging her eyes. So this must be her mother.

Asha looked toward the older woman and said words she had been waiting to say her whole life. "I am Asha. I am your daughter."

CHAPTER SIXTEEN

Again, three pairs of eyes stared. Blank. Confused. Then the woman Asha had just called mother jerked a little. Her eyes went wide and her hands flew to cover her mouth.

Asha thought she saw tears in the woman's eyes. There was so much Asha wanted to say, but where could she even start?

The only one not stunned into silence was the woman still holding Asha's precious blanket. She let out a barrage of questions all at once. "What are you doing back in Bangladesh? What is it like in America? Can you buy rice there? Do you know any famous movie stars?"

She was jabbering at such a speed Asha had no time for replies, even if she had been inclined to talk about rice or American movie stars.

The woman smiled widely, showing a collection of blackened teeth. "I am your auntie. I helped deliver you that night. I was the one who wrapped you in this blanket." She held up the piece of material like a prize.

All this time the younger woman, as well as the man she assumed to be her father, had not moved. They seemed as confused as she felt. There must not be a protocol for this type of situation, Asha decided, and without protocol, no one knew how to act.

Not able to stand the stillness any longer, Asha said, "I am so happy to finally meet you." Her words felt stilted, almost farcical. She wanted to feel genuine warmth, but it was difficult when being stared at like a strange creature at the zoo. "I've been thinking about you my whole life. Wondering who you are and what your life is like."

Plastering on a broad smile, she finished with, "So I came back to Bangladesh to find you, and to meet you, and . . . well, here I am!"

The grand finale was not met with hugs or cries or even words of welcome. Her father, who had yet to actually speak one word in her direction, took a quick, almost wild look in several directions. An expression crossed his face that looked like . . . fear? He mumbled something quickly to his wife then walked out the door and was gone.

Asha was dumbfounded. Surely that had not just happened. What did it mean?

As she tried to decipher the impossible scenario happening all around her, the woman Asha had spoken to as her mother also rose, gave a gesture of excusing herself, then she too left the hut.

Tears were welling up in Asha's eyes. "What is happening?" she asked quietly to the Bengali nurse at her side.

The nurse gave a small head nod, which meant nothing to Asha. "She will cook a meal for us," was the maddening reply.

"But I mean, why did they not say anything about me being their daughter? Coming all this way? Why is everyone pretending I'm not who I am?" She heard herself almost whimpering and bit down on her tongue to control it.

"They are probably wondering why you have come so far. Why you are here. If you are wanting something from them."

"But I just want to know them!" Asha declared passionately. "Can't I just say so?"

The woman smiled. "It is a very strange thing you have done today."

The auntie had continued her chatter off to the side while Asha and the nurse were talking. Asha looked over to see her rifling through Asha's bag, curiously inspecting every item.

"How much did this cost?" she asked of Asha's extra salwar kameez. "Is this English?" She held up the Bible, then returned it to the bag.

Her aunt continued digging through the bag, though it was now empty, asking with disappointment where her other things were. Was that all she brought from America? She held up the money Asha had packed. "Is this all you have? I thought all Americans were rich. You don't even have any gold jewelry on!" Much disappointed, the auntie stuffed everything back into the bag and thrust it back in Asha's direction.

Asha swallowed. This situation was getting stranger by the minute. "Are you my sister?" Asha asked the younger woman across the hut, who had been staring silently at her the entire time.

The huge eyes widened. The girl giggled, hiding her face down behind her hand.

Not shy, the auntie grunted. "Your sister? Hah! This worthless one is your father's second wife."

Asha heard a squeak come out her throat. "His second wife?" Okay, she knew that was permissible in the Muslim world. She would leave that one to think through another time. Turning her attention to the one woman who seemed willing to give her information, Asha asked, "Is my brother here? My twin?"

As if a curtain dropped, the woman's attitude changed completely. Her mouth clamped shut, her eyes dropped down. The grin disappeared. Slowly, she rose and, like the others, exited without a word.

Forgetting the young woman still watching, Asha threw up her hands in frustration. "What in the world is going on?" she said loudly in English. Why bother keeping her voice to a soft, feminine level when no one was sticking around to talk with her anyway? "What kind of family is this?"

The girl had crossed the hut to kneel at Asha's side. She looked into Asha's face, as if looking for any features that would prove her claim of being born to the man she called husband.

"Are you really their daughter? Was their son really your

twin?" Her voice held a kind of awe. When Asha nodded, she shook her head. "They never told me there was a daughter." Her long eyelashes fluttered upward as she looked at Asha. "How did you get to go to America?"

Asha began explaining that she had been stolen away as a baby when the young woman gasped and scurried back away from her. "It is the curse!" she whispered, her tone full of terror.

"What?" *This is the strangest place I have ever been.* "What curse?"

The girl only hid her face and trembled. Giving up on information on that subject, Asha asked her if she knew where her twin was. If Asha could meet him.

Slowly, uncertainly, the young woman looked all around, and Asha wondered if she was checking to make sure no one was listening. "Your brother was with his second auntie, Sumi. This is not the auntie here today; her name is Alia. They were in a canoe ferry, crossing the river. Many years ago. Your—your mother and father," the words came out stilted, as if the woman had not yet decided to believe if Asha was, indeed, their daughter, "they were riding in another canoe. They were all on their way to a relative's funeral. The boat tipped over and your brother and auntie fell into the water, with the canoe driver. Your mother and father's canoe could not reach them in time."

Shocked, her mind not accepting the indirect application of this woman's story, Asha asked, "Why didn't anyone jump in the water and rescue them?"

The girl seemed surprised Asha would even ask. "No one could swim."

No one could swim? They were crossing the river in boats and none of them could swim? Asha shuddered. What a horrible way to die. What a horrible death to watch.

How did her mother bear it? To lose a daughter in such a traumatic way, then to lose a son in an equal tragedy. "Did—did they have any more children?" Asha asked hoarsely.

No, the girl motioned. She looked in sympathy at the tears now running down Asha's face, recognizing her grief.

Hoping to find a family, Asha had only found another loss to mourn.

CHAPTER SEVENTEEN

"We've given you much trouble."

"Oh no, you've given me no trouble."

Dinner was nearly over and Asha was ready to burst from the tension. Her mother had served them, then retreated before Asha could ask any questions.

"Why is she avoiding me?" Asha asked her Bengali guide.

"She is showing you hospitality," the nurse responded.

Before Asha could voice her protests, the nurse continued, "She is allowing us to enjoy the meal as guests. She will eat when we are finished."

Asha felt her jaw clenching. She looked across the small hut to where her aunt had carelessly thrown her precious blanket. Since then no one had bothered to pick it up. It lay abandoned and forlorn: exactly how Asha felt.

Listlessly, she used the fingers of her right hand to scoop up the second-to-last bite of curry and rice in her bowl. She knew to leave a tiny bit to show she had been given enough. What she did not know, however, was why everything had turned out so opposite her expectations.

When her mother returned with a small jar of water, Asha watched as she poured some over the Bengali nurse's fingers where she held them over the bowl. The woman rubbed the water around, washing her right hand. Once her hand was nominally clean, Asha's mother removed her bowl, then used her own hand to rub the used water around the bowl before pouring it out, thus washing it as well before placing it behind her on a small bamboo shelf weaved into the wall.

Asha's turn was next. She looked down as she washed her hand, wanting so much to ask the questions on her heart. Did her mother have no questions to ask her? Weren't they curious at all about her life on the other side of the world? Weren't they curious about her?

Before leaving the hut, Asha's mother glanced back once. In her eyes Asha saw the confusion she herself felt.

Deepak's mother spoke. "It is time to return, so we can arrive back at the clinic before dark."

Asha shook her head. "I can't. I can't go back yet. I don't—I haven't gotten to know any of them at all yet. I have so many questions. I want to know about their lives, about who they are."

The nurse shook her head. "You can't just stay here. You don't have one of the GCC cell phones in case you have an emergency, or a contact set up to check on you, or money to pay the family for feeding you. And our clinic team would not want you to stay in a village with a family no one even knows." She looked outside, then back to Asha. "This just isn't done. We have a whole protocol set up for short-term visitors."

Asha bit her lip. She couldn't go back already. "Don't worry, Deepak's mom," she said, her voice conveying more confidence than she truly felt. "After all, I came out to Bangladesh on my own. I'm not officially with GCC, so you don't need to feel responsible for me."

She could see from the nurse's knitted brows that she did, indeed, feel responsible for her. "And I'll try to get back to the clinic station soon to get more money to pay them for my stay, and get the emergency phone or whatever else you think I need. Okay?"

The nurse sat still for a moment, thinking. Then, silently she rose from her position on the floor mat and walked softly from the hut without a word.

What have I done wrong now? Asha's frustration mounted. Nothing since her arrival was making any sense.

The woman returned and sat next to Asha. "I approached your mother and have gained some information for you," she said to Asha's pleased surprise.

"Most of the men in this village are farmers, harvesting barely enough rice to feed their own families. Your father—do not ask his name because it would be shameful for your mother to speak it aloud—he is a cigarette-seller at the *dokhan* near where we entered the village. He is proud not to have to work hard in the fields like others. You will see this as the fingernail of his smallest finger has grown long to show he does not do manual labor."

Asha was not sure what to think about that piece of information. "Does that mean he has more money than the others?"

"Not likely. It is probable he is in debt, but many would rather be in debt and have an easy, higher position than to have to work hard for just enough."

"I see," Asha said, though she really didn't.

The woman rose and motioned for Asha to follow. They ducked through the small doorway of the hut to the cooking area just outside the room where they had been eating. The younger wife was stirring something in a large tin pot that sat directly on the cooking fire, smoke billowing out around it. Nearby, Asha's mother was calling the young woman lazy and useless, instructing her to stir the contents of the pot more carefully.

"Mother." Asha used the word and hoped it was the correct one. If it was inappropriate for a woman to speak her own husband's name, who knew what she should or shouldn't call anyone?

At the sound, the woman named Shazari rose quickly. Asha started to speak, but a quick touch on her arm by her guide communicated she should refrain.

Instead, the nurse spoke on her behalf. Asha guessed that must be more polite.

In poetic words, the nurse communicated Asha's gratefulness for her mother's kindness, and her desire to remain with her Bangladeshi family for awhile.

"You didn't explain why," Asha whispered to help her out. "I want to learn their ways, to learn the culture, and get to know them."

The nurse shook her head no. "It is not our way to be so direct," she replied in English.

That was being direct? "I am so not going to make it in this culture," Asha said under her breath, even as her face retained its pasted-on smile.

Two hours later, Asha was convinced she had been right.

The Bengali nurse had returned to the clinic, shaking her head at Asha's irrational decision to stay in the village. "I suppose it was irrational," Asha said to a curious bird as she made her way down a path to where some kind of bathroom was supposed to be. "I left my phone at the clinic station since it doesn't work in this country anyway. I don't have any way of getting in touch with anybody from civilization. I did have the sense to bring extra anti-malaria pills, so at least I won't have to worry about that."

At the large forked tree, she made a left turn, as she had been instructed by Neena, the young wife. Neena had offered multiple times to accompany her, but Asha refused. Surely she could get to the bathroom by herself, not to mention she really needed to get away and process for a minute.

Any hesitations she might have had fled when Neena spied her roll of toilet paper and asked what it was for. Asha's answer made her laugh out loud. "You waste such nice pretty cloth that could be used for so many things on that? You Americans are so silly!"

Now traveling alone despite her new family's objections, the extravagant roll of toilet paper gripped tightly under one arm, Asha spied the area the entire village used as a restroom. She had been informed there were two separate holes. She asked if one was for men and one was for women. Again, she was laughed at for having such a ludicrous thought.

Close enough now for her sense of smell to differentiate the separate uses of the two holes, Asha directed her steps toward the correct one. The hole was indeed that, just a hole dug into the ground. A thatched screen stood around the small area for privacy. There was no way to lock or latch the screen from the inside, so Asha hummed loudly in hopes that anyone wanting to use her particular hole would refrain from opening the screen while she was inside.

Now she knew why it was a good idea to go in pairs.

Finished, feeling wasteful even though she had used the least amount of toilet paper possible, Asha made her way past several bamboo huts along the flat dirt-packed path to arrive again at the one her family called home.

She looked around the village before entering the dimly-lit hut. This place would certainly never feel like home, but maybe a few days here would turn out to be good. Maybe once they realized how much she wanted to get to know them, her family would open up a little.

She hoped her mother especially would become more comfortable around her in time. What was the point of coming all this way to meet her family if they would only ever see her as a stranger?

Mark sat at the computer and read the e-mail for the third time. It was from Cindy Stewart; she had written to give him Asha's message.

Checking again to make sure he had gotten every possible piece of information from her vague note, Mark shut the computer down and pushed away from the desk. He ran over the facts in his mind. Asha had decided to stay in the village with her family. She did not know when she would return. Could he please pass along her note to her adoptive parents?

Oh, and he should not try to contact her, as there was no way to reach her in the village.

"Well, if that isn't being given the axe, I don't know what is," Mark muttered. She had left him with just enough information to make him miserable.

He had the benevolence to hope she was having a great time in her village with her family. But as far as Mark was concerned, that was as far as his thoughts needed to go from now on. He needed to stop thinking of her, stop missing her, stop waiting for her to come back and care. There were a lot of important things for him to be doing. She had made her position clear and he was through holding out for more.

"Have a nice life, Asha," Mark said, jaw tight, focusing on the sound of his teeth grinding so he would not hear the breaking sound in his heart.

CHAPTER EIGHTEEN

"She must be here to make an American movie."

"Maybe she works for the president, and is scheduling a visit for him to our village!"

Asha bit down a smile as she drank her tea and resisted the urge to remind these latest guests, the fourth batch that day, that she understood Bengali.

She had been in the village three days now, days filled with curious visitors coming to see for themselves the strange American who had come into their world. They gossiped and twittered back and forth about why she could possibly be there, assuming since she had grown up in America, she surely knew only English.

It was enjoyable to watch the bustling, busy community filing in and out of the hut at all hours on all sorts of pretexts: one wanted an onion, another to tell juicy details about a neighbor's recent marital spat, yet another began lecturing on how rickety bamboo fences are no good at keeping goats out of the garden.

The first time guests had arrived that first day, Asha had greeted them warmly and started to introduce herself, but was quickly, almost urgently cut off by her mother, who presented her as a guest visiting from America.

Just that. Not their daughter. Only a guest.

Why? Why not tell people who she was? Asha remembered her father's second wife's earlier response, that what happened to Asha was part of some curse. Did that explain her mother's abnormally high-pitched tone as she spoke? Her quick glance, almost a plea, toward her father when the first visitors had approached the house?

Since then, every time new guests arrived, Asha was presented to them in that same manner. Just a visiting guest, though every guest was demanding to know why a rich American had come to their village and chosen to stay with such an inconsequential family.

Knowing the uselessness of directly asking what was going on, Asha racked her brain trying to think of how she could find some answers.

The solution arrived only a few minutes later in the form of her talkative, uninhibited aunt, who swept in right after the most recent guests had left. "Do you really think they won't figure it out?" she said callously.

Asha's mother responded with a caustic sound that was not really a word.

The aunt countered with the same sound in response, and Asha's mother marched from the hut, lecturing to no one in particular about nosey relatives.

Asha motioned for her aunt to sit. "Please, Auntie," she tried to sound only mildly curious. "Why are my parents introducing me as only a guest and not their daughter?"

Again, that same throaty sound. Asha assumed it was a way to voice frustration. It certainly sounded that way.

"No one, except the second aunt and me, knew that your mother had two children instead of just one. When you were stolen away, your mother grieved, but your father said they should not tell anyone about the second child. They still had a healthy baby boy. They should not show their shame to the village."

"To the people of our village . . . all these years . . . you have never existed."

Asha felt a void expanding deep within her, but was distracted when her aunt peeked out the window, then sat close enough to make Asha uncomfortable. "So how did you come back?"

The woman was practically licking her lips with anticipation. This aunt was a very strange person. "What are you talking about?"

The aunt leaned far into Asha's personal space. "I know you were taken, stolen away by the Evil Eye," she said. "But how did you escape? How did you find your way back here?"

Asha inched to her right. "What are you talking about? Didn't you know I was stolen as a baby?"

"Of course I know that!" The woman threw her hands up. "I was there the night it happened, remember?" She lifted Asha's baby blanket and waved it in her face.

"And later at the clinic you found out the truth."

"I didn't go to the clinic. It was your second aunt that took your mother." The woman's eyes became slits of suspicion. "Why? What happened at the clinic?"

Asha looked down at the frayed blanket. "That's where my mother found out I had been stolen by two men, one with a scar on his chin, and then they tried to sell me to—"

The woman let out a loud, shrill scream. Asha lurched backward, completely shocked as her aunt wailed a stream of words in rapid staccato, like machine-gun fire, so fast Asha could not understand the Bengali words.

When her mother ran into the hut, Asha could only look, wide-eyed, as her aunt rose and shouted into her mother's face, "It was no Evil Eye at all! All these years! How could you not tell me what really happened?"

Fear glazed Asha's mother's eyes for a moment, but then it vanished and she gave a noncommittal shrug. "Tell you? And have it all over the village by nightfall?"

The feigned indifference went unheeded. Asha's blanket became a worn ball in her aunt's clenched fist. She shoved it forward before Shazari's eyes, then threw it to the ground.

It hit the dirt in the far corner of the hut. Dust particles bounced up all around it, as if in celebration, but Asha could only wince at the sight.

"All these years! All these years!" Her aunt was practically delirious with anger. She marched from the hut, still shouting and waving her arms. When a neighbor rushed forward to ask her what was wrong, she shouted, "Nothing! Go away!" and continued toward her own hut.

Shazari's eyes met Asha's. "I'm sorry," Asha whispered, though she was not sure what she was actually sorry for.

For a moment Asha thought her mother was going to speak, perhaps explain something. Anything. But the moment passed. Her mouth closed and she turned away. Asha felt tears sting her eyes as she watched her mother gather up tin pots and utensils for another long meal preparation.

Why didn't you tell anyone about me? Why didn't you tell your own aunt that I was stolen away?

A hollow emptiness filled Asha. None of the villagers knew anything about her birth or her existence at all. No one had grieved her disappearance. No one had even known.

No, that was not true. Her mother had known. Her mother had cared.

When the older woman left the hut in silence. Asha decided her mother must still care, deep down underneath the bitter covering she wore. Maybe it was like the long black *burkah* the Muslim women wore when going outside among others. It covered their clothing, their hair, even part of the face. It hid them, but did not remove them.

Maybe behind the harsh façade, her mother's heart still felt love, and was only waiting for the covering to be removed and her true self to be brought to the light.

"Worthless thing!"

Asha winced as her mother called for her father's second wife. Then again . . .

It will be worth staying to find out, Asha decided, determined not to leave until she had unearthed the mother that this stranger used to be.

Seeing her mother once again supervising Neena at the cooking pot the next day, Asha felt the urge to offer her help, but knew if she tried she would only humiliate herself by her incompetence. Instead, she snuck into the small hut and spread her mat over the packed-dirt floor.

Lying down on the scratchy, hard surface, Asha pondered this strange relationship—or lack of relationship—she had with her birth mother. She didn't even know what to call her. Was it okay to call her mother? Or was she supposed to say her brother's name? How could she, when she didn't even know what his name was? And how could she ask without being too direct?

When voices touched her senses, curiosity overcame cowardice and Asha rolled onto her left side to peak through a slit in the bamboo wall. She saw her father pull out the cooking spoon, taste the sauce, then toss the spoon back into the pot.

His gesture was angry. Sauce spilled out over the edges of the pot, bringing a quick, sizzling response of fire and smoke.

Neena drew back from the fire but remained silent. Asha inched closer to the wall when her father walked from her line of vision. She curved her head to see him stand beside her mother.

"What are you going to do about this problem?" The question filtered through the bamboo barrier.

"What can I do?" Asha's mother was squatting and did not look up. Her voice was equally irritated. "She came. She is staying. How can I do anything about it?"

Asha noticed Neena's eyes were down on the ground. The two adults completely ignored her as they argued.

"Everyone in the village is coming to our home to see our visitor from America. Do you know how much money it costs to feed everyone in our village?"

Her eyes remained lowered in deference, but Asha could see her mother was angry. "And what do you want me to do? Refuse to serve tea and snacks to our guests?" She said this as if the thought were incomprehensible. Her father's response confirmed it was.

"I know. We cannot lose face with all our relatives and friends. But people are asking me very difficult questions. And she has given us no money. Everyone thinks we are rich now because we have a guest from America. But we will end up poor because of her instead!"

The conversation continued. Her father was now berating her mother for telling Alia that Asha had been stolen. Asha rolled back over and scooted away, as if distancing herself a foot from the wall would somehow make their words go away.

She had wanted them to be happy to finally meet her. But it seemed they saw her only as a foreign curiosity, and even that had harmed her family rather than helped them.

"You need to send her away. Get her to leave."

Her mother's voice washed over her. "How would I do that? You know she will stay until she wants to go."

Asha heard steps cross very near the bamboo wall where she lay. Her father's voice was forceful. "Then make her want to go. It is dangerous having her here."

"Dangerous for who? For her, or for you?"

The questions remained unanswered and the footsteps faded away.

When another set of footsteps headed toward the hut, Asha curled up and feigned sleep. When the steps entered, paused, then drew closer, Asha forced herself to breathe deeply.

The figure retreated to the other side of the hut. Asha allowed one eye to open slightly and saw her mother kneeling several feet away.

She was facing the opposite wall. Asha craned her neck and saw her reach down and retrieve something from the floor of the hut.

It was Asha's baby blanket, still lying where it had been discarded by her aunt. Asha sucked in a breath. What would she do with it?

The woman cradled the blanket in worn hands. She smoothed the dirt from it, then folded it slowly, carefully, before slipping it beneath her own rolled-up sleeping mat as she whispered, "Stay. It has been so long since you left me. Stay."

When she rose and turned, Asha quickly shut her eyes. She heard her mother walk across the hut and out the door. Asha then rolled over to look through the crack in the wall again to see her mother resume her squat near the cooking fire as if nothing had happened.

What did it all mean?

CHAPTER NINETEEN

I'll never take a washing machine for granted again!

Asha groaned; her back and shoulders ached in complaint. She wanted to stop and take a break, but then noted with chagrin that Neena at her side had not paused for a moment, her arms swift as she dipped another six yards of sari material into the scummy pond water, then rubbed it against a rock to grind the soap in.

Feeling her gaze, Neena looked up with a smile and the wide-eyed innocence of a child. Asha fought the revulsion she felt every time her awareness grasped upon the fact that this young girl, younger than her by years, was wife to her father. Neena still carried a youthfulness, as smooth and pure as the young skin of her face. The huge, trusting eyes only accentuated the appearance of naivety and helplessness.

It was strange. Here Asha was, unmarried, unaware of the secrets of marriage, yet she felt ages older than this girl at her side.

Neena was looking at her shyly. Quickly then, with a nervous giggle, Neena looked all around, then leaned to whisper so conspiratorially Asha could not help but feel she was back in middle-school hearing the latest gossip. "Now that we are away from the others," Neena said with another look around, "we can really talk."

Her eyes held an eagerness that made Asha nervous. "I've heard rumors about Americans," she said. Asha swallowed. "About American men and women." Asha swallowed again. What was she going to say next?

"I heard someone in our village say once that American men and women meet in public places like cafes and they sit right there in front of everyone and talk to each other!"

Asha felt herself coughing and almost gagging on her relief and the immense desire to laugh that came alongside it. "Yes, that's true," she admitted, trying to sound appropriately solemn.

Wide eyes stared at her in fascination. When Neena asked, "What is a cafe?" then "What do men and women have to talk about?" Asha could not stop the laughter from bubbling out.

"Don't you talk with my father?" Asha countered the question with her own.

Neena's face became pure puzzlement. "Talk?"

As Asha stared in disbelief, Neena's hands returned to her washing, running the sari up and down on the rock even as her eyes remained vacant. "Talk?" she said again. "About what?" she finally said, looking to Asha as if she carried some great wisdom beyond her world.

Asha sighed. She had read once that humans used only three percent of their brain capacity. It seemed certain Neena had been raised to use a totally different three percent than she had.

"I have a friend—an American friend," Asha began, wondering how much she should reveal and how much to hide. "His name is Mark."

At the masculine pronoun, Neena squealed, and Asha's thoughts were again taken back to her middle-school days—talking with her friends about their latest crush, or giggling over whether a certain boy had talked to them in the hallway that day or not.

"You know a man you are not related to?" Neena asked breathlessly. "And you talk with him?"

Fearing she was treading on scandalous territory, Asha wanted to retract her words, but it was too late now. She nodded, and when Neena asked in true, undiluted curiosity what they talked about, Asha felt herself drifting back to memories under a banyan tree. "We talk about everything. Our hopes and dreams. Our disappointments and our successes. I can talk to him about things I'm confused about, and he listens and tries to help. I can tell him when I'm scared, and he prays with me.

"He prays with you." The words were breathed out in holy reverence, as if this was too great an intimacy to be spoken aloud.

Asha nodded, suddenly missing Mark with an ache that would not recede. "He is my best friend."

Hands had stilled. The sari lay forgotten at the water's edge, its fringed border dancing in swirls as the water ebbed toward them then away, as if unseen fingers played with the threads. Neena sat in complete awe, her huge eyes reaching far into the distance, imagining being best friends with a man—a thought as incomprehensible as man flying to the moon, or a box called a computer that sent messages to people on the other side of the world, or a machine that washed your clothes for you.

Feeling a stab of guilt, Asha reached for another dirty shirt, and bent over the task of washing it with vigor. She should not have said so much. Why tell Neena about a world she could never experience?

She was berating her lack of conscientiousness when Neena's whisper floated over the water like a breeze. "Since I was a little girl," she said softly, wistfully, and in the voice Asha heard both a woman and a child, "I have always had the hope that one day—" and here her face ducked down as if she were embarrassed to have any hopes, much less express them. "I have dreamed of a man looking into my eyes with love, of his hand touching my face softly, with gentleness."

Less than a minute passed before Neena's eyes lost their faraway glisten, and she picked up the forgotten sari and scrubbed it hard, as if it held forbidden dreams that she could somehow scrub away if she tried hard enough. "It is a foolish thing," she said with resignation. "I am married now. This is my life. This is how I will live until I die."

Asha, too, returned to their tedious, arduous task, her mind grappling with the grim likelihood that Neena's assessment of her future was correct. Never once had Neena made a choice about her own life, and if things continued as they almost certainly would, she never would.

"How old were you when you married my father?"

"Sixteen maybe?" Neena shrugged. "My father wanted to arrange a marriage for me once I turned fourteen, but no man wanted me."

Asha let out a choked sound. "What?"

Another shrug. "My family has little money for a dowry, and no man in our village wanted me. My skin is too dark."

She had spoken with an acceptance that rattled Asha. "But Neena, you're beautiful!" Asha protested.

The young woman looked at Asha in benevolent disbelief. "I was going to remain unmarried and a burden to my family until your father decided he needed a new wife in the hopes of having another son."

Neena ducked her head suddenly, avoiding Asha's gaze. "At first he did not mind that my father could only pay half the dowry he asked for," she continued, her voice trailing down to a whisper of shame. "Because I am from another village, everyone hoped the curse would not affect me."

Asha felt a chill. "What is this curse?"

Neena's voice remained a whisper. "The curse of the babies. We must not speak of it." She hurried on. "I have not been touched by it yet, because my belly has carried no child. As time passes and I do not produce a son, my husband is becoming more angry. He demands the rest of the dowry money."

She shrugged and bent back over her washing. "He beats me sometimes, and tells me to pressure my father to give the money. But beating me does not make my father any less poor."

Asha rubbed her fingers across her now aching head. A hundred questions cluttered her mind, but none seemed to formulate into anything she could actually ask. How was it possible people still lived this way?

And what is this village curse no one will talk about?

Neena stood and began to swing the cleaned clothing into the air and onto the rock, making a harsh, slapping sound as water droplets burst forth from the material and flew free. Asha attempted to copy her movements, finding herself again incompetent and inept, while Neena's movements were swift and smooth.

"My father is a good and kind man," Neena said softly, throwing each newly-slapped article of clothing into a pile—on the hard-packed dirt, Asha noticed. "He wanted to give me in marriage to a wealthy, good man who would care for me." Again, she shrugged, lifting the pile of clothes. "But to have no money is to have no choices." She turned away. "And as I said, no one else wanted me."

Neena walked up the embankment as Asha fought the urge to sit down and cry, her own helplessness in the face of Neena's words filling her with pain.

Asha suddenly felt the overwhelming urge to talk with Mark. To tell him she had taken so much for granted. Asha had known what it was like to be looked at with love, to be touched with tenderness. She had experienced the highest, most unattainable dreams of the married woman standing next to her, and yet she had walked away in anger because she had expected more.

Oh, Mark, I'm so sorry. She wished she had some way to tell him, to apologize.

When Neena mentioned on their return walk, "I think being a free American must be the happiest thing in the world," Asha thought of all the miserable people she knew. All the broken relationships. All the junk on the nightly news. She was suddenly taken back to a day in a sari shop when Rani had brokenly asked her what good it was to be rescued from something bad, if you weren't rescued to something good. She would have to tell Neena that being American did not make people happy. Neither did being rich, or free, or even loved.

But there was no time. They had reached the outskirts of the village, and life beckoned with its relentless duties. Asha spread the wet saris across the bamboo fence to dry as Neena began preparing for dinner.

However, from that evening on, Asha prayed for the right time to tell Neena where true happiness could be found, and the wonderful news that it was attainable for her, even in the life she now lived.

CHAPTER TWENTY

Normality had finally woven its path into Asha's consciousness. The daily routine had become less difficult, the strict rules and customs more familiar. Even the basket Asha was weaving was looking less like a haphazard child's craft attempt and more like something that might one day be useful. Maybe even pretty.

When outspoken Aunt Alia rushed in saying, "Your cousins are coming," Asha thought nothing of it. People had been coming since her arrival. What were a few more cousins?

It was a bit odd they had chosen that time of day to visit. Normally, no one left their homes during the hottest part of the day. But that still did not account for her mother's strong reaction.

As soon as the words were spoken, Asha watched in surprise as her mother bolted from her sitting position and rushed toward the window. She looked outside, then moved quickly to the opposite side of the hut to where their small horde of possessions were kept.

"Where is it?" Alia asked, joining Asha's mother as she scrounged through the pile. "Sabir's mother, where did you put it?"

So Sabir must be her brother's name. Asha started to ask a question about her brother when her mother quickly pulled out her long, black *burkah* and thrust it toward Asha. "Put this on," she hissed.

Asha stared at her, too startled even to speak.

"Found it!" Alia declared, and to Asha's surprise and increased confusion she lifted her baby blanket from under her mother's sleeping mat. "What were you doing keeping it there?"

"Put this on." Asha felt the heavy weight of the long *burkah* thrown around her shoulders. She could barely murmur an objection as her mother covered her hair with the head-covering, then her face with its veil.

"I can't see a thing," Asha complained. Why was her mother doing this?

Shazari gestured toward Neena. "Go with her," she commanded. She snatched the blanket from Alia and shoved it into Neena's hands. "Take this. Take her to the toilet, and do not come back until they have gone."

Neena knew fear when she saw it, and did not hesitate to obey. Grabbing Asha by the arm, she half-dragged her from the hut and away from the coming visitors.

"What's going on?" Asha asked, tripping over something. She could not even see whether it was a tree root or the edge of the black robe. The veil covering her face was black, and although technically it was sheer, the density of the material, while completely hiding her from prying eyes, was also succeeding in hiding the outside world from her own vision.

"How do people walk around in these things?" she muttered, trying in vain to gather up enough of the flowing material into her hands so she would stop feeling like a walking tent. The sun beat down upon them and Asha felt the added layers of black collecting and containing the heat. By the time they reached their destination, Asha was drenched in her own perspiration.

Neena paused to catch her breath before speaking. "I don't know what just happened," she admitted, a hand to her heart.

"But ever since I came to live here, whenever those two men appear, your mother shows great fear. I do not know why."

"Afraid of them? My father's cousins?"

Neena nodded. "The eldest son has a reputation in the village. It is not a very good one, but the family is not openly shamed because no one knows if he is really bad. He leaves the village for days and sometimes weeks, and whenever he returns the family has more money than anyone else in the village. Their house is made of mud, and they have a satellite for television, and they even have a tin roof that keeps out the rain!"

A laugh almost burst out at the thought of a TV and a tin roof being the ultimate signs of wealth. "Do you think the cousins are bad?"

A shrug was Neena's initial answer. "The younger son, he works hard in the rice fields, though I don't see why since his family is rich. The eldest, however, he is . . . I don't like him."

"Well . . ." Asha's interest in the mysterious reputations of her father's cousins was being stifled by the weight of the heavy *burkah*. "Do you think they're gone yet? Can we go back?"

With a knowing smile, Neena lifted the sheer front on Asha's veil. Even that tiny bit of freedom brought an appreciative sigh. "I remember when I first started to wear the coverings. I felt so hot, so trapped—like a bird walking around in my own cage."

Asha nodded. That could adequately describe the claustrophobic feeling she was battling at the moment. "How old were you when they started making you wear this stuff?" she asked.

"Eleven," came the reply, and Neena barely noticed Asha's shocked intake of breath. "That is when I became a woman. After that my father was busy trying to arrange a marriage for me. It was important to keep protected by wearing the *burkah*."

"Protected from what?"

Neena's reply was confident, as if well-practiced. "The covering protects my family's reputation, and protects a woman from men's eyes. Men are basically good, but weak when it comes to temptation. A woman might tempt a man with her hair, or her voice, her ankles, or her eyes. If a man is tempted, he cannot help his weak nature, so we must keep from being a temptation. This is for ourselves and for the honor of our families."

Letting the veil drop again, Asha used the covering to hide the disgusted expression on her face. Several acid remarks came to the tip of her tongue, begging to be let out. Instead she prayed for strength to curb her fleshly response of anger.

"We must protect ourselves. We must wear the covering, and never walk alone." Neena touched Asha's hand. "This is why I want to go with you when you are going to the toilet. I had a friend once, my first friend in this village. She was brave like you—too brave. She said she would not live her life hiding and being afraid."

Asha had a feeling she did not want to hear the rest of this story. "Do you think we could go back now?"

Neena ignored her request. "One day I told her, like I tell you, that she should not go out alone. She laughed at me and then dared the evil spirits to follow her. She said out loud she was not afraid of them."

The chill, now a familiar response to the frequent talk about evil spirits, rushed up Asha's back. "What happened?"

"I told her it was not the evil spirits she should fear, but the weakness of men. But I was wrong. One day she went alone to the toilet . . ." Neena took in a soft breath.

Asha leaned forward to hear better.

"She never came back."

The chill spread to cover Asha's body. "What do you mean, she never came back?"

"That is all." Neena's eyes were pools of regret. "She disappeared. I never saw her again."

"Did anyone go looking for her? Did you ever find a—a body?"

Neena's shudder betrayed that her feelings ran deeper than the perspective she communicated with words. "It is what was ordained for her. She should not have gone out unprotected." Then she lifted her eyes and revealed her own heart. "But I wanted to go look for her! I know she did not mean to invoke bad men or a bad spirit. She was only young and foolish . . . She was my friend."

Asha was again biting her tongue, but this time in emotion. She had no words to say.

"You will be more careful now?" Neena clasped her arm. "You will not walk alone? It brings fear to my heart."

Asha's own heart clenched. "I will be more careful," she said.

The responsive sigh of relief went unnoticed as Asha closed her eyes and again began praying. Praying for the people of this terrorized village, who lived in superstition and fear. Praying for the others in Bangladesh, and in India, and in so many other places, who faced unknown fates like Neena's friend simply because they were women and had not submitted to their own vulnerability.

"What are you doing?" Neena asked with curiosity.

Shaking herself, Asha opened her eyes and smiled. "Sorry. I was praying."

"You were praying?" Neena's eyes were huge. "Right now? Using your own words?"

Asha felt her anger evaporate. She spoke gently. "I can pray to God at any time and in any place. The Holy Book says God wants me to pour out my heart to Him. I am His child and He wants to help me live right." Her comments ended wryly. "I can't live right without His help, that's for sure."

Still looking around as if they were being spied upon, Neena's voice lowered to a whisper. "Your holy book says this about women? God wants to listen to women?"

Asha wanted to cry. She sat and gestured for Neena to join her. "Sit down, please. I want to tell you a story."

Beginning at the beginning, Asha told of creation, of Adam in the garden, and how even though Adam had a perfect world, God saw he was alone, and it was not good. So God made a woman. And God declared that both were made in the image of God.

"Neena," Asha spoke with assurance, noting Neena's eyes had not left her face since she had begun. "You being a woman is not an accident or a mistake. God made you a woman on purpose. He did it because He wanted to. He made you exactly who you are, exactly how you look." Asha smiled. "The Bible says He even knew you before you were born, and He knows how many hairs you have on your head!"

Neena's hands flew to her hair, as if attempting to cover it from God's sight. "But—but our hair is a temptation to men. How can God be looking at our hair and thinking about it, without—well, without it being bad?"

"Oh, Little Ma." Asha could not decide whether to say her name, or use a family term out of respect. "God is pleased with you—how you look. He is the one who made your hair to be beautiful, and your face to be attractive, and even your body to be pleasing."

Neena drew back in shock, pulling her arms across herself and curling her knees up to her chest.

"In God's original plan, there was no sin. Men did not lust after women's beauty, or use it for wrong purposes. God intended you to be beautiful, to be pleasing to your husband. Your beauty is not evil. When God made the man and the woman, He said what He had made was very good."

Asha was not sure it was the right thing to say, but felt compelled. "God likes you, Neena." Then she said words Neena had never heard before. "God loves you, Neena."

Looking up and all around, as if this new revelation of God might produce His image in the sky, Neena's voice whispered toward the heavens, "God cannot be known. He cannot be understood. He gives us rules to live by so we can be holy. He is most merciful and forgiving. If His rules for women seem unfair, it is because we do not understand Him. We can never understand Him." Her voice became fearful. "And we must never question Him or His ways. We must never say He is not right."

Biting her lip, Asha again prayed for wisdom. Then, feeling a sense of irony that she, the one covered in a *burkah*, was speaking words that throughout the centuries had set the captives free, spoke the truth in love. "Little Ma," she said softly, "it is true God's ways are higher than our ways, and His thoughts higher than our thoughts. But my holy book says God is not just holy. It says God is love. It says He loves and takes care of His children like a good shepherd watches over his sheep."

She then told Neena of the shepherd who left his herd of ninety-nine to go find the one lost sheep. She told Neena that love was why God sent Jesus, the promised Messiah, to rescue people from hopelessness and sin. She spoke of how much Jesus loved her, that He loved her enough to die for her. Then she watched as tears formed at the edges of Neena's large brown eyes and spilled out.

"Except for my father, no man has ever done anything out of love for me." Neena's voice was hoarse. Her eyes were filled with pain. "I have been commanded all my life to never believe anything a Jesus-follower says, but your words are so beautiful, they tear into my heart. If what you say is true, if Jesus is who you say He is—I can't—"

She seemed unable to articulate the flood of emotion that continued to escape in the form of tears. Asha reached out to take her hand, and Neena grasped it with force. "I want to hear more about your Jesus," she said with conviction. "I don't care if we have to sneak out and meet in secret to talk about Him." She looked around her again, but this time with resolve. "If there is hope in the world for women, for me, I want it. If there is love—I—"

Asha gripped Neena's hand tightly as she bent her head and let the tears flow.

"If there is love, I would give anything to find it."

Tears of her own were running down Asha's face as she replied, "My dear friend, you don't have to find it. Love has come to find you. Jesus is as close as a prayer. Why don't you try talking to Him, asking Him to show Himself to you? To show that He loves you?"

Like a flower bud opening to the sun, Asha watched the smallest flicker of hope open in Neena's eyes. She smiled. Soon, for Neena, the world was going to change completely. Love would change everything.

Asha could not wait to watch the hope unfurl and burst in bloom.

CHAPTER TWENTY-ONE

"I think Sabir's mother might be sick."

Asha looked toward Neena. "Yeah, she must be—she let me cook lunch today and didn't even stick around to tell me everything I was doing wrong."

Asha tried to hide her disappointment behind her smile, not ready to tell Neena she had approached her mother to ask some real questions, but her mother had simply handed her the cooking spoon, told her to stir, then retreated to lie down in the hut, not stopping even when Asha called out to her.

Neena's responding smile was distracted. "This was a surprise, indeed," she agreed. "But I wasn't teasing. I think she really is sick."

Asha looked across the hut to her mother's sleeping form. "You know, you may be right. She has been lying down a lot more the past few days. I thought maybe she had finally accepted I wanted to help and was letting me do more."

Neena shook her head. "When I first came, I was required to do most of the chores, but she did not leave me to do them as I pleased; she followed me to tell me exactly how to do each thing." Again she shook her head. "What happened today was not normal."

Now concerned, Asha crossed the small space to her mother's side. "Mother?" When there was no response, Asha reached out to touch her mother's forehead. "Neena, she's burning up! She definitely has a fever."

Neena's face was grave. "Pity on her," she whispered, then began moving her lips, eyes closed. She was not speaking Bengali. Asha wondered if she was speaking in Arabic, recognizing the sing-song tones as the same from the call to prayer that rang out from the mosque each day.

Asha felt her mother's forehead again. Her mother groaned and, never opening her eyes, pushed Asha away with a weak hand.

"She's really ill." Asha turned to Neena. "We need to get her to a doctor."

Neena began to speak when Asha's father entered the room. Immediately, Asha rose to her feet and, being sure to keep her eyes down at the floor, said in her most respectful tone, "Father, my mother is sick. We need to take her to a doctor. If you give me directions, I will take her myself."

The man, seeming to ignore Asha, continued on to the back section of the hut and rummaged through a small pile of possessions. He pulled out a small bottle and handed it to Neena before exiting the hut.

"What was that all about?"

Neena approached and handed Asha the bottle. "Here is some medicine we will give your mother for her fever."

"But what if it's more than just a fever?" Asha voiced. "What if it's malaria or typhoid or something?"

Neena shrugged. "Who has money for doctors? To go to the doctor is far. Too far to pay."

"Well, what do people do here when they are sick? What about when women have babies, what do they do then?"

A hand swung to the side indicating the two questions were vastly different. "Women have babies with the help of family members or village midwives, of course."

"Okay, but what about if someone gets really sick?"

"I heard your aunt took your mother to the clinic once because the bleeding from childbirth would not stop. But usually sick people either get better . . . or they die."

Asha gasped. She had read about the common fatalistic attitude in the booklet about Bangladesh culture and customs, but her first encounter with it felt surreal.

She looked back at her mother. "We can't just leave her like this," she protested.

Neena looked at her with sympathetic eyes. "We will give her this medicine, and then we will wait and see what Allah ordains."

Three days passed. The sickness which began as just a fever quickly digressed into chills, then delirium. Asha had no idea what the sickness was, but she knew it was serious.

Unable to wait silently, Asha had reported on her mother's condition each day to her father, hoping if she communicated how quickly the illness was progressing, he would see the need for action. Finally, exasperated with her "nagging," he left to summon a doctor.

Asha was deeply relieved, until he returned with a village doctor. Knowing she dared not protest, she watched in helpless silent prayer as the man chanted incantations over her mother's form. Curiosity kept her eyes on the man as he blew "good spirits" onto some herbs, then wrapped an amulet—verses from the Koran wrapped inside a capsule on a string—around her wrist for protection from the sickness.

The man left with the promise that Asha's mother would be well by nightfall. The herbs seemed to improve her condition, but only temporarily. By early afternoon, she was worse again. Her father was mumbling about wasting good money on a doctor when Asha approached him once again.

"My father." How could she broach this in a way that would get through to him? "I respectfully request permission to take my mother to the clinic. Please."

"The clinic? The one with the foreigners? Impossible. It is too far to pay for the trip and too expensive."

Asha bit her lip, praying for wisdom. "I have money, Father. Money I brought from America. I will happily pay for the trip and the expenses."

Her father turned his head and looked with skepticism in her direction. "All of them?"

With lowered eyes, Asha nodded quickly. *Please, God, let him say yes*! "Yes, Father. I left my money there at the clinic station. If I go back, I can get some extra money to bring back for our family."

She could see that had sealed the bargain. "Okay, you can go."

Asha quickly bowed at the waist—this wasn't China, but she figured it couldn't hurt—and thanked her father profusely before rushing inside.

"Neena! He said yes. Can you help me get my mother into a baby taxi, please?"

"He said yes?"

"After I agreed to pay for everything."

"Everything?" Neena's jaw dropped. "Do you know how much money it costs to take a taxi so far? That is a lot of money!"

Asha started to get nervous. "How much will it cost?"

Neena gave a number in *taka*, the local currency, and once Asha had mentally translated the number into American dollars, she nearly laughed. This huge amount of money it was going to cost to take her mother to the clinic was a mere two dollars.

"That's two whole days wages!"

Well, if you put it that way, it does translate to a lot of money. "It's okay, Neena. Mother is worth it."

For the third or fourth time that day, Neena shook her head at Asha in astonishment. "It is not a question of whether she is worth it, but whether you have the money, and if you must use that money for other things, like food."

And for the third or fourth time that day, Asha sighed with incomprehension. When Neena explained it that way . . . With no credit cards, no insurance, and no money to spare, it made sense that money could not be spent on something like medical care when there was no money to be spent at all.

"Neena," Asha said with renewed purpose. "I am going to take my mother to the clinic. I will pay for her to get help. And then I will return, with enough money to pay the rest of your bride price, so you will not be beaten anymore."

Neena was speechless, then without warning, she dropped to the ground and began touching her fingers to the top of Asha's feet, then to her own head in the ultimate sign of showing honor.

"No, no, Neena please." Asha was decidedly uncomfortable at the unexpected display. She pulled a sobbing Neena to her feet, wishing she could give her an American-style hug instead.

Unable to bear the idea of the woman prostrating herself before her yet again, Asha asked her to go find a baby taxi, then busied herself with packing up her small bag of possessions for a return to the clinic.

Excitement began to find spots within her and fill them. She thought of all the small luxuries she would soon enjoy: getting her clothes actually clean, using running water to take a shower, and going to the bathroom in real, closed-door privacy.

Her heart sped up when she thought about getting to e-mail Mark. Maybe there was even an e-mail or two from him waiting for her.

Asha felt a renewed sense of purpose. Paying Neena's bride price would be real, legitimate help for her family. It would take away Neena's shame and make her father happy. Maybe in the end this would help her parents see her as a blessing instead of a burden.

Hope hurried her actions forward as she and Neena lifted her mother onto the taxi Neena had summoned. It took some coordination, as they certainly could not ask the driver for help as that would be touching across genders.

Finally, they were settled and the taxi lurched forward across the bumpy dirt road. Asha held tight.

Lord willing, they would reach the clinic before nightfall.

CHAPTER TWENTY-TWO

Dear Mark . . .

Asha sat and stared at the internet screen for a full five minutes, wondering what she could even say. How could she explain all that had happened? All she felt?

Did he even want to know?

I'm glad I have the chance to send you a note. I've really missed you. The days in the village sometimes pass by slowly, and I catch myself thinking about you at the strangest times, wishing I could tell you about everything that's happening—when I make a complete fool of myself, and the extremely rare moments when I actually get something right.

When I first came, well, let's just say I made a lousy village girl. They teased me and wondered if I was good for anything. Couldn't cook. Couldn't wash clothes. I didn't even know where to go to get water. And I don't even want to talk about the bathroom situation.

But little by little I've learned, and my opinion about so many things is changing completely. I used to think of their lives as simple, and yet when I joined them, I was the one who didn't know how to do anything and they were the smart ones.

I'd like to tell you all about it, sometime, if you'd like to hear. But at this point I wonder if you really want to hear from me at all.

Here Asha paused again, wondering if she was making any sense, or if she should just push the cancel button and walk away.

But she could not pass by the opportunity to talk to him, even if it was one-sided.

My family isn't what I expected at all. My father is . . . well, I wonder who I would be if I had grown up here in the tiny bamboo hut in this village in Bangladesh. I would know how to cook over an open fire. How to wash clothes at the edge of a dirty little pond. I would be able to haul water, and have really strong arms. And I would not be able to comprehend the idea of a city, or running water inside a home, or a million other things that are normal life to me. Two dollars would be an amazing amount of money, and getting sick would just mean I was sick—and I wouldn't have the option of going to the doctor if my life depended on it, because nobody would have enough money to take me. And I would have grown up religious, but being told I could never really know God because He is far away. I would cover myself up whenever I left the house, and I guess, in a way, that covering would represent being covered in a whole lot of ways. Life would be full of work, and a whole host of expectations, and little else. I guess I would be covered in a shroud, like the burkah I wear here, shrouded intellectually, emotionally, not free to be any different than exactly what is expected of me.

I have never in my life so much appreciated the kindness that has always been given me—by my parents in America, and now especially by you. You have lived in India all your life, but you never decided life should be this way. That women are just property. I look at the way my father treats my mother . . . I see this young girl my father has married and doesn't even know . . . I feel so—oh, I wish I could talk to you in person—I feel so . . . I always respected you, but my respect for you has grown so much since I have met my real father, and it is mixed with gratitude because you not only listen to what I say, but you care about who I am.

I realize now that—in cautioning me about coming here—you did that out of care. I'm sorry I didn't understand before. I want you to know, while I have the chance to say so, that I really hope you haven't decided to give up on me. I know I need you in my life. I keep wishing you were here, or

I was there. Seems everything that happens to me, good or bad, you're the first person I want to tell about it.

Right now I wish you were here, to ask your advice about all this stuff that's going on.

Asha chuckled to herself as she wiped one stray tear from the corner of an eye.

I'd even take criticism at this point if it would help me figure out what to do!

Pushing her elbows up onto the desk, Asha rested her head onto her hands, rubbing eyelids that had suddenly become very weary. After a few moments, she looked at the computer screen again. The words slurred together as tears filled her eyes.

Please pray for me. Pray God will show me what He wants me to do. And that I'll have the courage for whatever it is. I've never stood in a place that had so many unknowns before. It scares me.

I hope you are well. Please write me soon.

I miss you.

Asha

A hesitant finger hovered over the mouse, then, biting her lip, Asha clicked send and watched the e-mail disappear. She leaned back in the chair, took a deep breath, and sighed.

"Oh God, please help me. I need You so much. I've never been so confused." Asha wiped the moisture from the edge of her eyes and almost smiled. "You know, God, that I like to have a plan and know which direction I'm supposed to go, and sometimes I've followed my feelings instead of waiting on You. So . . . this time, I want You to know I'm going to let You have everything. Not just the easy stuff. Not just the stuff I don't want to be in charge of. Everything."

Asha stared at the computer screen again, now blank. "I give you my feelings for Mark. I give you my situation with my family. I give you my future. And I ask You to show me what to do. I am going to wait." She stopped and smiled, looking upward, knowing God was probably smiling too. "Even though You know that is so hard for me to do. When my mother gets better, I will take her back to the village, and I will serve my family as best I can. I will try to be like Jesus, so they can see You in me. And I will wait for You to show me what You want me to do. But please make it very clear, because You know I sometimes have a hard time recognizing Your voice over my own emotions."

Asha stood resolutely, feeling an unexpected, unreasonable peace.

"In Jesus' name, Amen."

CHAPTER TWENTY-THREE

Dear Asha,

Your Dad and I were so happy to get an e-mail from you yesterday! You know what a worry-wart I am in general, and after weeks of not hearing from you at all, I was starting to think maybe something had happened to you, or you had decided to stay in the village forever! You know I'll always be concerned about my baby girl—and I'm so glad to hear I can still call you that. I've always had this fear that if you ever found your birth family, you wouldn't really think of us as your parents anymore, and it was a gift to my heart that you still do. I've always thought God gave you to us and made you ours, just as much as if I had carried you around in my own body before you were born. Maybe even more so, because we picked you on purpose.

I know I've never been good at saying things to you in person. I have a hard time sharing my heart sometimes. But I want you to know if I had to do it all over again, I would still choose you. You have been such a blessing in our lives, and we love you very much.

It's been so quiet around here since you've gone. Your friend Amy has called a couple of times to say how much she misses you dragging her off on some hiking trail, and how she's gained ten pounds since you left because you aren't there to make her do anything. =) I hope you're not working too hard in the village. I hope they are spoiling you! And I hope you're learning all the things you have needed to know for so long.

Write again when you can and tell us what it's like roughing it in the village! Do you ever get to take a bath? Do they feed you snakes?

We're praying for you every day.

All our love,

Mom and Dad

P.S. You didn't mention anything about that guy you've been writing all year. Did you get to see him in India? What's the latest on that? I know I sound like I'm itching for a good dish of gossip, =) but I am your mother, so I think I'm allowed!

After writing a long response to her parents, then a quick note to Amy, Asha checked to see if any new e-mails had come through while she had been typing.

Nothing. Three whole days and not one word from Mark.

As soon as they had arrived at the clinic and gotten her mother settled with good care, Asha had found Cindy Stewart and asked if she could use the computer in the nurses' lounge. Her initial hope of having an e-mail from Mark in her inbox was quickly dashed. Now after checking her inbox at least three times a day since then, she was starting to get the message.

Her mind said maybe he was too busy to write, or maybe the internet was down, but her heart sank with the terrible likelihood that she had pushed Mark too far, and he was finished with her.

"God," Asha prayed as she left the computer behind and headed down the hallway back to her mother's bedside, "this is an awfully big test right away. I know I told you I'd be content, but . . . I love him, God."

Saying the words out loud for the first time brought immediate tears to Asha's eyes. Unbidden, the memory of their shared kiss a year ago flashed into her mind, with it a deep pain.

"I love him," she repeated. "But will I ever get the chance to tell him?"

She wiped her face with her *orna*, not wanting a clinic full of people to see her distress. Did this mean God wanted her to stay in the village, because there was no future for her in India?

Asha turned the corner into the patient ward. Two lines of white-sheeted beds ran parallel down the long room. Nearly every bed held a patient. Asha suddenly hurried her steps when she saw that her mother's bed, down toward the end of the room, was empty.

Relief spread through her heart when she realized her mother was in the middle walkway, being aided by a nurse. She took small, hesitant steps.

The nurse looked up and smiled at Asha. "She is weak, but well. If she continues to improve, you will be able to take her home tomorrow."

Home. Asha's heart once again felt pain. Home was Mark, and India, and her adoptive parents in America. Here in this place, and to this woman, she was still a stranger. Would that ever change?

With great effort, Asha set aside her own heart and her own desires. She stepped forward to grasp her mother's hand.

This for now was her purpose, and God would have to take care of the rest.

Leaves rustled above the village as the two brothers left the tea *dokhan*.

"It will be easy enough to convince them the Christians are to blame." Ahmad's smooth voice floated across the narrow path.

"It's not right, *Dada*. No one from that village has ever wronged any of us."

"No, Little Brother," the man sneered. "But they have so many children there. Many boys. Enough to feed the idea that perhaps there is no village curse—that perhaps the babies are taken by people." He chuckled. "Evil people."

The younger of the two was sweating again, despite the breeze tugging at his clothing and hair. Rashid hated everything about the life they led, and his regret and shame had only multiplied with the arrival of the Bengali American who, after just the right amount of pressure from Ahmad at the tea *dokhan* just now, they now knew for certain was the cigarette-seller's daughter.

"Look." He did not even bother to keep his voice to a respectful tone. "I was thirteen years old the night you forced me to steal that girl. In all the years since then, you know I've kept as far away from what you do as I can. What you do is wrong."

All these years he had said it by his actions, his quiet resistance, his back-wrenching work in the rice fields to earn his own money—honest money. Now he was finally saying it out loud. But what difference would it make? Ahmad would only enjoy his misery.

As if reading his thoughts, Ahmad let out a deep, throaty chuckle. "You are such a coward, Little Brother. You think you are better by not getting involved. But you are involved. Your silence helps keep the family business running."

Shame washed through Rashid's body. His brother was right. Though he hated it; he had done nothing to stop it. How could he, when doing so would dishonor his entire family, particularly his parents, who were blissfully unaware that the luxuries they enjoyed came at such a terrible cost to so many others?

Chest heaving, Rashid focused his anger. "This is too much, *Dada*. If you do this, if you cause an entire innocent village to be attacked just to hide your own sins, I will . . . I will—"

"You will what, Brother?" Ahmad's voice was taunting, laughing. "Expose the crime you helped commit?" He picked up his pace and snarled, "Stop whining. I need to get home and think about what to do about that girl. She'll be coming back soon."

"You-will-not-harm-that-woman." Rashid stood still in the midst of the path, declaring the stand he should have taken twenty years ago.

"Wanting her for yourself, are you?" Ahmad gave Rashid a small shove, knocking him easily from his firm stance. "She is quite pretty, I'll agree. But not pretty enough to separate two brothers, is she? Of course not. Nothing is big enough to break up a family."

Ahmad pivoted in a slow circle, rubbing his hands, his gaze taking in the collection of huts that made up the small village.

"Perfect," he whispered. "Why didn't I think of it before? If another child was taken, the very night I plant the suspicion about the Christians . . . and then the American girl disappeared too . . ."

Rashid shuddered. "What are you going to do?"

Ahmad ignored him. Laughing again, the low, deep laugh Rashid hated most because it meant Ahmad had a plan he liked, the eldest brother sauntered away toward home, leaving behind a boy who should have been a man, but had never taken the risk.

Part Two

Speak up for those who cannot speak

for themselves; ensure justice

for those being crushed.

Yes, speak up for the poor and helpless,

and see that they get justice.

Proverbs 31:8-9

CHAPTER TWENTY-FOUR

Mark sat down at the computer with a sigh of relief. It had been a wearying but satisfying few days. He had just returned from accompanying his father to several churches in outlying villages, discussing the mission's future involvement as partners with the national believers. A lot was going to change over the next year, and Mark saw the changes as good ones.

The missionary presence would lessen and the Indian leadership would increase. Mark and his father set up national liaisons to act as mediators between the resources the missionaries could provide and the needs the different churches had. That way, as time passed, fewer and fewer people would even know about the American involvement, thus releasing the national pastors from several burdens they had carried—especially the assumption villagers made that because the pastor was associated with Americans, he had access to great wealth.

As most of the pastors were poor farmers, working to feed their own families while also shepherding small flocks of believers, the problem could become devastating, as the pastor was expected to maintain a higher standard of living, and in general thought stingy for hoarding all the money he was surely getting from his Western friends.

Within the next few years, that problem would fade and likely dissolve completely. At least Mark hoped so. He hated the idea of their work, intended for good, to be in any way a harm or hindrance to the Gospel ministry in India. He felt a deep sense of satisfaction that he had been able to help engineer a solution to this problem that had plagued missionary-national relationships for years.

Best of all, his father was the one who had not only listened to Mark's suggestions, but implemented them.

"You've got some good ideas, Son," his dad had said, not even adding a joke to his comment. "I think what you want to do is actually a good continuation of the work your grandfather began. I was so stressed out when your grandpa died . . . I never—I didn't see that before, and I'm sorry."

The long drive back had continued in silence for at least half an hour. Mark did not quite know what to do with the serious person his father had become over the past weeks.

"Dad . . . how, um, how have you been doing with things now that you're in charge of the compound?"

John Stephens had smiled. "Better than people thought, right? I know everybody expected I'd have botched up the whole thing by now."

"Now, Dad . . ."

His father's chuckle turned to a laugh. "It's okay, Son." Then he sobered. "Truth is, I figured on that, too. It's been so long since I expected anything of myself, I got just plain scared at the idea of people depending on me again."

"What do you mean?"

"Well, I suppose I should just spit it all out. No sense keeping it in anymore. Like when you get a bug in your curry—no sense chewing on it awhile before you get rid of it!"

Mark laughed. Now that was his dad.

"The plain facts are—well, I grew up seeing my dad, your grandpa, so revered and honored, I knew I could never measure up to the hero he was. So I never bothered to try. I was so sure I would prove myself a dud that I never asked for any real responsibility."

Silence again reigned for awhile. Then John Stephens spoke again. "You know how sometimes the kid with the most to hide turns into the class clown as a cover-up?"

Mark shook his head. "Uh, no. I was homeschooled, remember?"

"Oh yeah, that's right. Well, anyway, I noticed growing up that dad got all the attention for the good stuff, like caring about people and rescuing children and talking all serious about people's souls, and well, I learned that if I came in and cracked a good joke, I got some attention, too. People would look at me all surprised, and then with admiration. It felt good. Like I mattered."

A huge pothole loomed ahead, and Mark's father swerved to miss it. "By the time I'd grown up enough to call myself a man, everybody knew me as the funny guy. Then I met your mother. She was the only one who saw into who I really wanted to be."

Mark watched in silent surprise as tears pooled in his father's eyes. "When she died, for a long time I didn't even care anymore. I stayed at the mission, but only because I had nowhere else to go. Nothing else I was good at."

"Then a few weeks ago when dad died and all the questions that had been piling up the past few years got dumped on me, I panicked. People have been saying we need to change the system for a long time now. Even you've been wanting to leave for years."

When Mark began an apology, his father raised a hand to silence him. "Things do need to change, Son. And they will. We're going to have several meetings over the next few weeks, deciding whether we should keep the compound system or eliminate it entirely."

At that he chuckled—it was the first sign to Mark that his father had not completely transformed into someone else. "Boy, is that going to give some of the old ones a shock. We'll have to be sure Dr. Andersen is present in case any of them faint away."

Now back on the compound, the bouncy, jolting car ride over, Mark headed for the computer room, looking forward to catching up after nearly a week without any outside contact.

What would happen to the compound and the group of missionaries, Mark had no idea, but he knew he would stay as long as it took for them to come to a consensus. He was part of a team, a great team, and now he was convinced his father would be a good leader of it.

He tapped his fingers on the desk, waiting as the internet brought up his inbox page with the speed of a snail on Benadryl®.

As to when he would be free to follow his own path outside the compound, Mark was leaving that firmly in God's hands. He would not bring it up to his father or the other missionaries again.

Scrolling down through his inbox, deleting spam and advertisements along the way, Mark found himself humming an old hymn. It had been a successful week. Not only was he able to help the Indian churches in a tangible way, but he had finally managed to spend a few days where Asha had not been in the forefront of his thoughts.

Being off the compound had helped—in the village there was no empty swing, no empty yellow-shuttered house, no vacant seat at his grandmother's table to constantly remind him of her absence.

Yes, he was finally getting a grip on his emotions. Finally gaining ground in his fight to keep the haunting thoughts of her at bay.

Mark continued to scroll down through his e-mails, opening several, responding to a few.

Then his hand froze on the mouse. There, at the bottom of his screen, her name appeared and in a flash his hard-earned victory shattered to bits.

The cursor hovered over her name, hesitating. Why was she interrupting his world now, now when he was finally starting to break free?

Mark held his hand back from clicking on the message, wondering if he should open it, knowing he would. What could she have to say? Was she coming back? Or was she only writing to say she was staying in the village longer, driving the knife deeper into his gut?

Excitement and dread churned in his stomach, an unpleasant combination.

Well, whatever she had to say, and however it would make him feel, he might as well face it. Mark opened the e-mail and read it. Once, then twice.

Quickly, pulling up a reply page, he typed a short response and sent it back to her, hoping she was still at the computer and they could e-mail back and forth. Just in case, however, he also copied his message to Cindy Stewart's e-mail, on the chance Asha had returned to her mother's bedside and Cindy was on the computer instead.

That done, he began typing another longer e-mail to Asha when he glanced and noticed the date and time on the message she had sent. It had come four days ago.

Just then the phone rang. Mark noticed the number was from Bangladesh and quickly answered it. "Asha?"

"Sorry, Mark. It's Cindy Stewart."

Mark felt a hot flood of embarrassment. He sounded like a love-sick school boy.

"I just got the e-mail you sent to Asha," Cindy said matter-of-factly. "I'm sorry to tell you she left to return to the village just this morning. You missed her."

Missed her is an understatement.

"I called to tell you that one of our Bengali male nurses is going out tomorrow to a Christian village that is near Asha's family's village," Cindy continued. "He would probably be willing to take your note to her, if you'd like him to."

Mark thought over the words of his small, quickly-typed note. They were important. Important enough. "I'd appreciate that," he responded. "I'll gladly pay him for the extra time it takes."

"Okay," Cindy agreed. "I'll let you know if he brings back any reply from her."

"Thanks."

Once off the phone, Mark sat in thoughtful silence for several minutes. In her e-mail, Asha sounded confused and alone. And with him not responding at all to her message, she would likely be thinking all sorts of unhappy things about him, too. He hoped she would consider the very real probabilities of the internet being down, or him being out of town, but knowing Asha as he did, her thoughts likely dwelt on the most emotionally traumatic possibilities her mind had surely conjured up.

Mark stood. This had gone far enough. He had tried forgetting about her. Tried staying on the reasonable side of things. It wasn't working.

He might as well admit that, for better or worse, his heart was wrapped all around this woman, and her struggles were his struggles. He wanted to share them with her, even though, if given the choice, he would rather avoid them altogether.

But he was not given the choice. If she was hurting, he was hurting with her.

And it was time to tell her that.

Pulling the cell phone from where he had pocketed it, Mark called an Indian friend who was also a travel agent, grateful that in India he could get plane tickets a mere day in advance. He told his friend he wanted a flight for tomorrow from Kolkata to the capital of Bangladesh, then from the capital to Chittagong. From there he would catch a bus to Hatigram, and hopefully be in Asha's village before nightfall tomorrow.

Thus resolved, Mark went to inform his father, who, though surprised, responded it was high time Mark took a vacation, though going out to a village in the middle of nowhere did not sound like much of a getaway.

Mark had never had any desire to get away. And now, he was not getting away either. He was going toward. Toward her. Toward the woman he loved. He would tell her that. And he would pray with her about what God wanted for her future.

Mark packed as lightly as possible, fitting everything into one backpack. Tomorrow he would leave India. If all went as planned, he would be returning soon.

And, if things went as he hoped, he would not return alone.

CHAPTER TWENTY-FIVE

Asha brought a few small treasures back from her visit to the clinic station where she had left most of her belongings. First, she pulled out an umbrella, which she gave to her mother to use when it rained—both inside and outside the hut.

Next, she gave Neena her small travel pillow, enjoying Neena's childlike delight as she blew into it and watched it inflate, then deflated it so she could blow it up again. It took several attempts to explain what the pillow was for.

Finally, Asha demonstrated by lying down and placing it beneath her head. Neena laughed at the oddity, but Asha's mother grunted and remarked about Americans giving useless presents.

Undeterred, next Asha pulled several photos from her small bag to show them a glimpse of her life on the other side of the world, enjoying Neena's curious questions about snow, about the strange hats men wore called ball caps, about why Americans always showed their teeth in pictures.

By the following morning, Asha's mother was feeling much better, and Asha was as well. The walk from the well to the hut seemed to be getting shorter every day. Asha felt her muscles adapting to the physical rigors of her new life. Her mind followed at a slower pace, but it, too, was coming along.

Every once in awhile, she even forgot to think of herself as a "foreigner." She was thinking and even dreaming in Bengali now, and the only time she ever switched back to English, even in her thoughts, was when she imagined talking with Mark again.

She hefted the jar filled with water from its place on her hip to rest up on her left shoulder. *Wow, I didn't spill anything that time. I'll have to tell Neena.*

The thought of Neena caused Asha to quicken her steps. Asha's mother had asked for Neena's help just as they were leaving to collect water, and as only women walked the path to the well, Neena had relented when Asha suggested she go to the well alone, just this once.

Asha was smiling to herself, thinking of Neena worrying over her like a mother hen, when a shadow crossed her path. She stopped and looked up, then quickly down again when she realized the shadow belonged to a man.

There were two of them, and one was blocking her way. Asha suddenly wished she had borrowed her mother's *burkah.* Its oppressive weight would have been a welcome barrier between her and the eyes which continued to regard her openly. Though her gaze remained on their feet, she could feel their eyes on her. A tingle ran down her spine. She felt a premonition of danger.

Was it just her imagination, over-applying the strict rules and the reasons for them? Was it the stories Neena had told of friends who had been accosted when out alone?

Willing her body to stop trembling, Asha tried to speak in the meek, unassuming voice expected of her. "Please let me pass."

She thought of the self-defense tactics she had learned in America. Hold your keys between your fingers to use as a weapon if need be. Not helpful—no keys. Walk with your shoulders back and head held high to show confidence. Not helpful—it would be seen as a challenge. Scream, make noise, assert yourself. That might be useful, though she had no legitimate reason for screaming as of yet.

Maybe they would just throw out a few inappropriate comments, like those she had often heard yelled at her from the streets when she had walked in the city, and then move on.

"Please let me pass," she said again, this time a little more forcibly.

A male voice responded, and Asha thought it as slippery as a snake. He used the Bengali equivalent to "What have we here?" and chuckled without mirth. "The little foreigner from America who has come back home. Isn't she beautiful, Little Brother?"

A hot wash of anger filled her. The mention she was beautiful was no compliment. She could feel his eyes running over her and wanted to run, but the path behind her only led to the well, and even more solitary places. The path ahead was firmly blocked with his presence. If only she could get past him and run the twenty or so yards into the village!

"Leave her alone," another voice followed. A less intrusive voice. Less arrogant. "Let's just go home." Asha felt her hopes rise. If this second man did not wish her ill, maybe she could appeal to him for help.

"Go home?" The first voice laughed. "But we have found the very thing I have been searching for. The elusive guest of our cousin. And as uncovered and free as if she were in America."

Asha felt a shudder run through her. These must be the very men her mother feared. She was starting to understand why. "You do your family no honor by speaking to me in this way," she said, with as much courage as she could bolster at the moment. It was hard to speak confidently while concentrating on keeping her eyes down and at the same time keeping her hands from showing they were trembling.

The man laughed with real pleasure. "She's a feisty one, isn't she? Like an American. Thinks she's better than the rest of us." Footsteps drew closer, and Asha stepped back. The voice lowered. "Maybe she is like American women in other ways, as well."

Asha saw a hand reach out toward her. Her carefully guarded restraint broke in two. "Don't you touch me!" she yelled. Her eyes flew to confront him. Forget the rules, she thought, she was facing this guy head on.

The face was attractive in a menacing way, like the bad man in the movies that the sweet, naïve girl wants to tame. Thick eyebrows arched over eyes full of an awareness Asha did not understand. Full, dark hair framed a long face, angular cheekbones, a solid chin.

Asha's gaze froze. She stopped breathing. There, deep into the skin along his chin, was a scar. As if he had been in a knife fight.

"Ahmad, let's just go."

For a split second, Asha's frightened eyes found the second man, for all appearances a smaller version of the first, but far less intimidating. Like a spectator at a disaster who is equally horrified and captivated by the gory scene, Asha could not keep her eyes from shifting back to the man called Ahmad, and his scar.

Cindy Stewart's description of the men who stole her came into full clarity. Two men. One calling the other an older brother. The older brother having a scar running along his chin.

How many men connected to her family had a scar like that? What were the chances it might have been someone else? Someone else with a younger brother?

The thoughts clanged and jolted inside her mind, like people in a panic trying to escape from a small room all at once, while the man with the scar continued to look down on her with a terrible mixture of disdain and desire.

Then, as if the world stopped, Asha suddenly recalled her mother's face when she had heard they were coming. Her mother's voice when she insisted Asha put on the *burkah* and leave the house until they were gone.

These two men were the ones who had stolen her away. Tried to sell her.

And her mother knew it.

The horrifying truth resulted in action without thought. Flinging her water pot forward, she doused the unsuspecting man, who drew back with a curse. Then she ran. Past the younger brother, who stepped aside to let her pass without hindrance, even as the elder shouted at him to grab her and stop her from getting away.

She ran all the way to the hut, stopping only once she was inside and the door was firmly shut. Though it stood a flimsy barrier against any would-be attacker, it was the only measure of protection she had.

Breathing heavily, her back against the closed door, she saw her mother and Neena both rise in surprise.

"I saw them," she choked out, looking only at her mother. "The older one is Ahmad, and he has a scar across his chin."

Her mother's look confirmed her worst fears, but she had to hear it in words. "They are the ones, aren't they?" By now her body was trembling violently. "They are the ones who stole me. You knew all the time, didn't you?"

Shazari grabbed her by the arm. "Did they speak to you? Do they know who you are?"

Asha ignored the questions. She did not even try to frame her words in something that sounded indirect. "How could you live all these years knowing they were right here in your village? Why didn't you do something?"

The woman's anger was obvious. "Do what?" she asked loudly. "What could I do? I did the only thing I had power to do. I sent you away, to safety."

Deflated, in tears, Asha slumped to the ground. She put her head into her hands. "He looked at me so—so evil," she whimpered. Her eyes rose to her mother's. "I'm scared," she admitted. "If they were willing to steal me and sell me back when I was a baby, what would they be ready to do to me now? I'm sure they see me as a threat, being back here. And now after today, after what happened, they'll be angry, and what will they do?"

She sent pleading eyes upward toward her mother's anxious face. "What will they do?" she repeated.

Neena had been standing in silent horror, but at that she approached to kneel beside Asha and take her hands. Rubbing them, she said with surety, "You have told me many stories about how big and powerful and good God is. If God could protect Joseph and Queen Esther, and stop entire armies from harming His people, won't He take care of you? Is He what you say, or isn't He?"

Asha reached out and hugged her, not caring if it was a cultural thing to do or not. "Thank you," she whispered, her voice ragged. "I was letting fear overcome my faith. You're right, God will take care of me."

She heard her mother's snort of disregard. "God may do whatever He chooses, but I am the one who is going to protect you," she said with a strength Asha had never heard in her voice. "I'm going to go speak with your father. I will tell him what I know about his cousins and the night you were born. I should not have kept it a secret all these years. Now he will know, and he can expose them for what they are."

She marched from the hut with full purpose, Neena following close behind, not allowing her to walk alone. Asha wanted to cheer them on. Then, wondering suddenly if approaching her father unasked for might be akin to Esther's entering the court of the king without permission, and thus risking her life, Asha began again to feel afraid.

"I think I'll just follow her," she whispered into the empty hut. Dusk had fallen without her notice. Soon the night would come, and with it, the protection of darkness.

Asha wrapped herself in the suddenly-appreciated black *burkah* and left the hut, careful to stay out of sight.

Out of the hut and down the path, keeping far enough behind that her mother and Neena never noticed, Asha followed down to the tea *dokhan*, where it seemed every man in the village had gathered. Their voices were jumbled, raised in heated anger over something. Asha could not distinguish enough words to figure out what, nor did she bother to give it much of a try. Her thoughts were full of the fact that Ahmad and his brother were both there, under the awning, one standing on each side of her father.

Suddenly with a shout of "*Allah akbar*!" the band dispersed. Asha ran to hide behind a large tree, watching around its curve as her mother and Neena also retreated from the path to let the men pass by. Once they had, Asha emerged, then backed behind the tree again. Her father's two cousins were still there, talking with her father. Now Asha wished she had crept closer to the flimsy structure. What were they talking about?

Finally, the two brothers left and only her father remained, smoking a cigarette. Slowly, Asha slipped from her hiding place and continued toward the small, rickety shop.

She tried to stop wondering where Ahmad had gone. If he was nearby. If perhaps he was searching for her right at that moment. All that mattered was that her mother was okay, she told herself. When she saw her mother walk to stand beneath the awning without resistance, or even acknowledgment from her husband, Asha breathed a sigh of relief.

She could go back now. Everything seemed safe enough.

But a question had risen as Asha stood there. How would her father react when he found out that the men who had stolen his daughter were his own relatives? Had been living in his own village the past twenty years?

She imagined his fury. She envisioned him storming from the shop, finding the men and dragging them to the community leaders, demanding justice.

A hint of a smile surfaced beneath her heavy veil. She would wait and watch, see how her father responded to the opportunity to defend her, to rescue her, to come through as brave and courageous. A man.

Stepping through the deepening shadows, Asha crept toward the *dokhan* and the conversation they had taken inside, holding her breath, knowing this night would define forever in her heart how he truly felt about her. His daughter.

CHAPTER TWENTY-SIX

Asha huddled outside like a mischievous child. Crouching under the awning just outside the door, she gripped her knees with trembling hands and pressed her ear against the bamboo wall, straining to hear.

At first, only muffled sounds came through. Asha could make out her mother's voice, but no words, then her father's response, but again, no actual words could be distinguished.

Frustrated, anxious, Asha crept around the small structure, searching for a window or an opening somewhere that would allow her the guilty privilege of eavesdropping. *Does it count as eavesdropping when it's my life they're talking about?*

The voices rose, at first back and forth. Now they were both talking at once. Arguing.

Asha had walked all the way around the *dokhan* and reached the open doorway again, nearly walking past it and exposing her presence. She took a step back and hunched down, the darkness covering her like a protective blanket.

She had been so startled by nearly walking right into the doorway, for several moments her only thought was stilling the wild beating of her heart. Then she heard a shriek of emotion. Anger? Disbelief?

What had happened? Restraint set aside, Asha, now on her knees in her crouch beside the doorway, curved forward just enough that one eye could see inside. A tiny kerosene lamp illuminated her mother standing to her feet to hover over her father, who still sat, his eyes down. Neena sat in the corner farthest away from them, shoulders hunched and face purposefully turned away from the scene, as incongruous and unnoticed as a piece of furniture.

"You!" Asha heard her mother's shrill voice, and saw her point an accusing finger. The gesture was shocking. Asha knew she was seeing her mother openly dishonor her father with it. "You are the one who caused all of this?" She rushed upon him as if, after years of self-restraint, something inside finally burst free. "You told them they could steal away my baby and sell her?"

Asha gasped.

"Why?" the scream came. "Why?" The voice was at once both as desolate and threatening as a wounded animal.

Asha held her breath to hear the man's response. "What good is a girl?" he said in lame defense. "We couldn't afford a girl." He never once looked up at his wife. "Did you want your husband to be a lowly rice farmer?"

"She is useful now because she is an American and is rich," Asha heard him say, his words piercing her heart, "but I can't go against Ahmad at this point. You know he would expose me, and I would lose everything."

His indifferent shrug was the final snap of the whip. Asha watched, open-mouthed, as her mother picked up a clay jar and threw it toward where her father sat. His diffidence dissolved immediately. He ducked and skittered across the room. The jar missed his head to crash and shatter behind him.

Another jar came flying across the store. Then a teapot. Cups. Saucers. Asha winced at the sound of objects flying, breaking, at her father's meager attempts to restrain a lifetime of repressed wrath.

When there was nothing left to throw, no objects left to break, Asha heard her mother's hollow voice. "I despise you!"

Asha grieved to see her father huddled at the edge of the shop. Her mother's words gave him no mercy. "You used me without love when we married. You let your cousins steal away my daughter. When my son died, you gave me no comfort. And after all that, you took another wife. I have been your slave. Your property. And now you will do nothing to protect your daughter, who is in danger because of you! They stole her once for money. Now she is a rich American—do you think they would not steal her again and hold her for ransom?"

Asha covered her mouth to keep from gasping in fear.

"You pathetic, selfish man!" The woman pointed again. "I am taking her to safety. She will go back to America, where she is free to be no man's slave." Her words spit venom. "And when I come back, I will tell everyone what you have done. I don't care if we all get sent away from the village—you will be dishonored and shamed by everyone."

At that, the man stood. "You can't talk to me like that, woman!" His hand reached out and with a long, hard sweep, he struck her across the face, knocking her to the ground.

Involuntarily, Asha cried out. Her father, hearing the sound, looked around in fear. Asha quickly realized it was not in fear that someone had seen him slap his wife, but rather in fear that someone had heard his wife's accusations. Accusations that were true.

He was coming toward the door, too quickly for Asha to retreat unseen. She stood, tears streaming down her face, yanking away the head covering so he could see her face. His daughter's face.

When his eyes found her, standing just outside the doorway, for a moment his face contorted into shame, regret, apology. Asha did not lower her gaze in respect. She stared. Who was this man? What force had guided his life choices; what lies had convinced him to give in to such evil?

Only a breath of a moment passed. The man—father, husband, betrayer—flinched, and for the first time, his eyes lowered first. When he walked away, shoulders bent in despair, Asha could feel only pity for his inability to love anyone other than himself, even as her own heart tore with pain at his rejection.

A movement brought her attention back to where her mother groaned as she stood. Neena rushed to her side and offered help, but was pushed away.

Asha took a step forward, but then she paused, knowing somehow it would only add to her mother's pain to see that her daughter also had come to know the awful truth.

As the older woman walked heavily toward the door of the shop, broken shards of teacups cracking beneath her sandaled feet, Asha backed away slowly, keeping out of sight as her mother's retreating form was enveloped by darkness, followed by Neena, until both were covered and silenced within the secrets of the night.

Asha waited until all was silent, until even the women's footsteps on the grass-strewn path could no longer be heard.

Then she, too, fled into the darkness.

The wind had picked up. A storm was coming. Asha barely noticed except to acknowledge that even the weather seemed to be rising in tempest along with her heart. The hut Asha returned to was a whirlwind of activity. Her mother was throwing things, wrapping clothing into one unrolled sari, mumbling half-insanely even as tears ran through the crevasses of her wrinkled face.

Asha's own pain brought a totally different reaction. She dropped to her knees over her sleeping mat and poured out her heart to her God. She gave Him the pain, the fear over her own safety, the terrible grief of losing a father she now knew she had never had.

"Do you dare to call on God now?" The acid voice behind came from her mother. "Do you think He cares? Do you think He is anything different than your father?"

Grief extinguished any possibility of a reply. Asha squeezed her eyes shut and continued praying.

"Well while you pray," came the bitter words, "I'm going to actually do something about this. God won't bother to save you. But I will."

An arm reached down to roughly pull Asha to her feet. "Get up," her mother snapped. "We're leaving. Now."

"Leaving?" Neena, who had been watching in silence, eyes wide, now rushed to Asha's side. "Going where?"

Indeed, where could they go? Asha wondered. Where did Muslim women flee when in danger? Their whole world was wrapped around whatever man was their present authority. No one would act without his approval.

"Will you go to the community leaders?" Neena asked. "You can tell them what happened. They stop wrongdoing and care about justice."

"No." Shazari's answer was abrupt. "I would have earlier, but after tonight I don't trust anyone anymore."

Uncertainty crept across Asha's shoulders. "Let's take a minute and think this through," she offered. "We could get a rickshaw or a taxi and go to the clinic station. I know they would help, and—"

"No! I won't have anyone know where we are going."

Her mother was tugging her toward the door, impatient as Asha reached back to give Neena a tight hug. "God willing, I will see you again," she whispered quickly, wishing for an hour, even a few minutes, to talk one more time with her.

No time was granted. "We have to go *now*," came the harsh order.

A spattering of rain had begun to fall as the two women, from separate generations and separate worlds, joined only by blood and birth, set out into the night, searching for safety.

CHAPTER TWENTY-SEVEN

Mark hung up the phone, stunned. He sat, then stood. He paced, then sat down again.

She was gone. She was in danger.

And he was stuck in the capital city, a nine-hour bus ride away.

What was he going to do?

He had called Cindy Stewart the moment he arrived at the guest house in Dhaka. Her voice was strained, and she had gotten straight to the point. The Bengali man she had sent to Asha's village with his note had just returned. He said he had been delayed on his journey, and by the time he arrived, it was already dark—maybe around six or seven that evening. He had found Asha's home, but Asha was not there. Not in the village at all.

"I don't want to concern you unnecessarily," she said, "especially since your flight to Chittagong got canceled because of the cyclone coming . . ."

A sliver of fear climbed up Mark's spine.

"What are you trying to say?"

The nurse was silent for interminable seconds. When she did speak, her words shot through him. "There have been rumors. It's happened once before, but that was over twenty years ago."

Mark waited, refraining from speaking, hoping the silence would urge her on.

"We have been hearing rumors that the Muslim village across the way may attack the Christian village nearby . . ."

Heart pounding now, Mark's mind scanned through the possible dangers to Asha. She was in the Muslim village, not the Christian one. No, the man said she was gone. Gone where? Did someone take her to safety? Or—Mark's heart stopped. Was she in the Christian village for some reason?

"What—" Mark's voice betrayed him. He cleared his throat and tried again. "You said all this has happened before. What happened the last time?"

Again, silence. Then the soft voice spoke. "They burned the village to the ground. They beat the pastor and several others. They didn't beat anyone to death, but two people did die in the fires."

Now it was Mark's turn to remain silent. His mind was pacing between panic and prayer.

He had to rescue her. But he couldn't. He was trapped by the weather of all things.

"Normally, we would have sent—people from—to—search for her already." Mark could barely make out Cindy's words. The connection was breaking up. "Contacted—police about rumors—but—storm coming—too busy—bad night ahead—don't know—"

The connection died and Mark stared down at the silent phone. There was no sense even trying to call again; the encroaching storm had wiped out any possible signal.

He had not yet unpacked, had not even taken his one backpack to his room before making the phone call.

Now, unable to imagine enduring an entire night of not knowing, he grabbed his backpack from the floor where it leaned against the chair leg, jotted a quick note to explain his departure, then left.

He quickly summoned a taxi, glad he was fluent in Bengali. "To the bus station, please," he said, his voice filled with urgency. "As fast as you can go."

Surely there was a bus somewhere in the city that drove through the night to Chittagong. If there was one, he was going to be on it.

Cyclone or no cyclone, Mark was going to find the woman he loved.

CHAPTER TWENTY-EIGHT

Asha could not have felt more surprised had her mother told her they were going to trek up to China.

They had been walking for what seemed like hours, the storm increasing with each step, hindering their progress—if they were making any at all, Asha thought.

Now, as the storm beat upon them like the fury of the Almighty, Asha could see her mother would not be able to continue much longer. They were already soaked. With all the rain, there was no need to worry that they were leaving a trail behind them. Even if someone had begun following them, surely they would have given up in this storm. Couldn't they stop and rest awhile?

Then again, where could they stop? No tree could give shelter against this kind of rain. It swirled around them in circles. Asha had removed her head-covering so she could see, but it did not help. Only darkness and rain met her gaze. At this point, she could not distinguish anything more than a few feet away.

Shazari turned and spoke, but Asha heard no words. "What?" she shouted into the storm.

"We have to stop!" Her mother's voice penetrated through the rain. Asha could tell she was yelling, but she barely heard the words over the shrieking of the wind. Shazari came closer, bringing her face only inches from Asha's so Asha could hear her words. "The storm is only going to get worse," she shouted. "We are going to the Christian village, but the rain is too thick. I can't see where to go."

The Christian village? There was a Christian village nearby? Asha was stunned beyond words. But then the logic of the situation filtered through. Of course. Her mother's Muslim village would not offer help to them. The women would want to, but they were powerless against their husband's will—just as she and her mother were powerless.

So of course her mother would think to take her to fellow believers—her mother would assume people of her own religion would take her in.

Asha's mother was shouting, but the wind tore her voice from her. "The storm is too bad to get there tonight. We have to wait it out."

How did one wait out a storm like this—outside?

For an hour or so, Asha and her mother huddled together at the base of a large tree, futilely attempting to shield themselves from the worst of the storm by holding an unused sari over their heads. When the wind picked up to an astonishing speed, knocking them over where they sat, Asha's concern grew to fear. She could not see her mother's face through the downpour. Like a child, she tugged on her mother's sleeve, her gesture asking questions.

Her mother clutched her arm, pulling her down until Asha's ear was near enough to her mouth that she could be heard over the torrent. A flow of words came, but only one was strong enough for Asha to hear. And that word filled her with terror.

"Cyclone."

Dear God, what are we going to do? Asha had studied enough about Bangladesh to know a major cyclone was deadly.

And they were outside in it.

"God, help us!" Asha screamed into the wind, knowing God heard though she could not even hear herself at this point.

Her hair whipped around her face, slapping her with painful pricks. The rain beat down relentlessly. It came from every direction. The wind had become their enemy, carrying with it fallen twigs and leaves that stung as they slapped up against her face, even dirt from the ground that had broken loose.

The wind again knocked them down where they sat, pushing them into the dirt with violent fury. Asha tried to pull herself up, but found the force of the wind greater than her strength. A grave sense of danger pressed down upon her. She felt her mother struggling beneath her and rolled away to give her room to breathe.

This storm was trying to kill them. If they did not do something soon, Asha feared the wind would tear them from each other and fling them through the jungle like two abandoned rag dolls, throwing them through the air until they crashed into one of the trees. If that happened, would either of them survive? Especially her mother, still weak from her bout of fever?

The sari they had been using as a flimsy covering flew up in Asha's face and pushed against her skin. She jerked it away, but then an idea came.

Quickly, before fear could overtake her again, Asha pushed with all her might and was able to rise to her knees. She felt blindly to her left until her hand reached the trunk of the tree where they huddled. Falling against it, unable to walk or even crawl against the force of the wind, she flattened her back against the hard tree, then used it for leverage as she struggled to pull her mother the few inches needed for them both to be set against the tree's strong base.

Her mother's body was dead weight. Either she had fallen unconscious, or had just given up, accepting with fatality that God must have ordained their deaths out there in the darkness.

Asha was not ready to accept death. Not yet. Working furiously against the storm, she twisted the sari material into a strong coil, like a thick rope. Then, with the little strength she had left, she wrapped it around the tree, securing it under her mother's limp arms where she sat, then under her own. Lastly, she tied and knotted it several times, until she was certain no amount of wind could dislodge it.

Finally secured, Asha felt her body give in to weakness, submitting to the power of the storm. A deafening crack sounded above her head, followed by a terrible rending sound, as if a huge tent was being torn in half. Asha looked up to see a thick tree limb tear away above her, falling toward the ground a mere few feet away.

Right before it hit the ground the wind swooped under it, flipped it, then sent it flying straight toward Asha. Her slim arm reached up to protect her face, but was little barrier. The branch swung in an arc, punching against her face with such force it smacked her head back against the tree. Asha saw flashes of light spark behind her eyes. She tried with meager effort to roll the branch off her form where it had finally fallen, but found she had no strength left.

Would they live to see the morning? Asha begged for life for her mother, who did not know Christ and was not ready for death. Then she allowed her head to fall back against the tree, and surrendered to unconsciousness.

CHAPTER TWENTY-NINE

Mark exited the large bus with relief. It had been a long night. He had managed to get an hour or two of sleep despite the incessant blaring of the bus' horn and the torrential rains beating down upon the bus roof. The rocking back and forth that came from frequent slides into oncoming traffic to pass slower vehicles had felt like a ship on the high seas, which was also less than relaxing.

Not that Mark would have been capable of relaxing. He kept taking his anxiety to the Lord, giving Asha's safety into His care. But he found himself frequently, unconsciously taking it back again, the fear flooding him, the inactivity a torment.

Wind swirled around him as Mark took a look across the bus station, getting his bearings.

He needed to find the ticket counter and get a seat on whatever bus was going north from Chittagong to Hatigram the soonest, immediately if possible. He swung his backpack off his shoulder, reaching in to get five dollars worth of *taka* bills to pay for the trip.

"Excuse me, are you Mark Stephens?"

Between the noise of hundreds of shifting passengers, the barking of several conductors, and the whipping of the wind through the trees, Mark barely heard his name being called. He looked up from his backpack and was surprised to see a white man standing there. The man was dressed like a Bengali, and his dark hair and beard made him look almost like he belonged, though not quite. Mark was surprised the man knew his name, as he had never seen him before.

At his nod, the man approached, his hand out. Mark shook it, then out of habit also gave the traditional Indian greeting, holding his hands palm together to lightly touch his forehead.

The man smiled. "My name is Rick Jones. I work at the clinic with Cindy Stewart."

Mark nodded again, unsure of what he should say. He wiped a layer of sweat from his brow. The heat felt heavy, as if the air itself was dense with it. The sky was dark as midnight, despite the morning hour.

"I came to Chittagong a couple of days ago to pick up supplies," Rick said. "Cindy called me this morning and asked me to come and meet you. They got your note at the guest house in the capital and passed on the news that you were coming in today."

The man was considering the sky with a frown. "We'd better get going," he said to himself, then focused on Mark. "I'm sorry to tell you this, but I've been asked to take you to the guest house in Chittagong where my wife and I are staying."

Before Mark had the chance to argue, the man held up a hand. "I know your situation is dire, but I'm afraid it will have to take a backseat for a few hours. See that?" Mark followed his outstretched hand to view ominous, swirling clouds, dark and threatening.

"A cyclone is headed straight for us. It has likely already passed through or around Hatigram at this point. Regardless of how much you want to get there, it is even more urgent we get to shelter, and soon, before this thing hits."

Mark had no choice but to follow the man to his vehicle. Helpless frustration raged through him. He knew enough about cyclones to know they were deadly, and the tiny country of Bangladesh, arcing around the Bay of Bengal, was particularly prone to them. He remembered hearing of one ripping through

Chittagong back when he was a kid that killed over a hundred thousand people.

What now? Mark tried to visualize Hatigram on a map, see how close it was to the water. Bamboo huts could not withstand a cyclone's fury. Had Asha been in even more danger from the storm than from an attack? What if she had been hurt, or was right now trapped under debris?

He would have given anything to be with her right then. To face danger together would be so much better than this. Even being on his way to her would be better than this awful waiting.

But he was stranded until the storm thinned out or moved on. That could be hours.

By then, would it be too late?

Asha woke, looking around groggily. Where was she?

She struggled to rise, but found she could not get up. Her head hurt horribly. A massive tree branch lay sprawled across her lower body. Reaching up, Asha felt along her aching forehead, pulling her hand away to see caked blood and dirt. Looking down, seeing the sari tied securely beneath her arms, awareness came flooding back.

The cyclone. They had made it. They were still alive.

At least she was. Asha leaned over her mother's form and checked for breathing. As the rise and fall of her mother's shoulders assured her she was sleeping, Asha breathed a prayer of thanksgiving and relief, then looked around to ascertain their present situation. Light filtered in through the leaves above them, so the sun must be above the trees already. Rain continued to fall, but thankfully it lacked the violence of the previous night.

Again, Asha sighed with relief. She was drenched, with steam rising from her clothing as the warm, humid air promised another day of sweltering heat. Her entire body ached from being flung about throughout the storm.

But none of this really mattered. They were alive, and Asha was grateful.

Once her mother woke, they could continue on. To the Christian village.

To safety.

CHAPTER THIRTY

Fierce winds whipped with violence, pulling trees up from their roots and throwing them across roads and yards, slamming them into houses and cars and the unfortunate pedestrian seeking shelter.

Mark had to keep busy. He would go crazy if he did not. Asha was out there, just sixty-five miles away. In a village made up of bamboo huts. In danger.

And he was stranded here. So close, but completely unable to help her.

Mark ran a hand through his hair. It was wet already, despite his position of safety on the third floor of a Chittagong guest house.

Oddly enough, more rain was coming in through the screened-in area on the third floor than the two levels below. In circles, the rain whipped in and around him, Rick, and Rick's wife as they swept the flooded tile floor using handmade straw brooms.

"Open the door!" one of them shouted. Mark could barely see who it was. His bare feet sloshed across the front entrance. Outside the door was a small landing over stairs leading down to the first floor exit. Fortunately, as the entire area was made of concrete, they simply swept the water onto the landing and watched as it became a waterfall down the steps.

By the time Mark returned, the newly swept floor was a pool of water again.

How was she? Was she okay?

Not even a raging cyclone could distract Mark's tormented thoughts. Was there a cyclone shelter near Asha's village? Had the nation's warning system contacted them, and in time?

It was a full hour before the worst of the storm passed, and several more until the rain finally stopped.

"I'm amazed at how quickly the roads get cleared after a storm like this," Rick said as they swept the last layer of water down the stairway. "People rush out and start chopping up the fallen trees and branches and taking them home for firewood."

They went down the stairs and Mark paced the courtyard of the guest house, hating every minute that kept him inside the courtyard gates. "But for awhile a bus and even a car will have a hard time of it. My dirtbike would be your best bet on the roads today," Rick added, "if you knew how to ride one, that is."

Mark's head shot up. Why hadn't he thought of that before?

Ten minutes later, Rick Jones's dirtbike shot through the gates. Mark tensed over the handlebars, every muscle focused toward one goal: to get to Asha as quickly as humanly possible.

Years of driving in India's chaotic traffic served him well. Mark dodged tree limbs, fallen brush, people gathering and chopping wood, and the few vehicles braving the roads.

If he only knew how to get straight to her village. As it was, he would have to go to the clinic first, find the nurse who had mediated Asha's adoption, and then be taken to Asha's village. Every wasted moment stretched before him, filled with potential danger to the woman he loved.

Sixty-five miles away, Neena sat huddled in the farthest corner of the battered hut, a paper lying open on her lap. She stared at the foreign marks, not able to understand even one of them.

Her fingers traced over the incomprehensible words:

Dear Asha,

I understand.

Whatever you decide,

I love you.

Mark

Neena fought the temptation to envy her husband's daughter. This man Asha called her best friend must be wonderful. To have a man care enough about her to send her a letter was almost unimaginable. But far more amazing was the certainty Asha had that she was loved by God Himself. This was beyond anything Neena had ever dared to dream.

Neena held her hands out, palm upward in the traditional Muslim fashion, and with the letter resting open on her hands called out to the God Asha worshipped, asking Him to protect her new friend.

She asked nothing for herself, not because she withheld her wishes from being spoken aloud, but because there were no wishes to be said. Instead, the young woman hesitated even to ask on a friend's behalf, not sure it was permissible to request help for a woman.

The soft rain settled into a quiet sprinkle. Neena sighed. Now would come the long and arduous task of repairing and cleaning what had been damaged in yet another storm.

She carefully folded the paper and tucked it securely inside her salwar kameez top, the only place she could be certain to keep it dry until Asha's return.

If she returned at all.

Resolutely then, with a practiced acceptance, Neena stopped her prayers to return to the never-ending work awaiting her.

CHAPTER THIRTY-ONE

When the clinic station came into view, Mark breathed out in relief. After two hours of swerving and dodging on the potholed roads, his muscles were screaming with exhaustion.

He pulled inside the gate, parked Rick Jones's version of a motorcycle, and before doing anything else dropped to his knees. Not caring who might be watching, he clutched the bike beside him and prayed, giving up his immediate desires to fear, to panic, to fight. He thanked God for his safety and asked for Asha's. He placed the next critical hours in God's hands and asked for guidance and wisdom.

When he stood, he found himself facing a middle-aged Western woman. She wore scrubs and was removing a pair of latex gloves. "You're Mark," she stated simply, not bothering to ask. "I've been watching for your arrival."

"You must be Cindy Stewart." Mark mentally thanked God for sparing him the minutes he expected to lose while tracking her down.

She waved across the path, and in less time that it took for Mark to turn around, a young Bengali man stood at his elbow, a huge grin showing off very white teeth.

Mark placed his palms together in the usual greeting, noting the man looked about his own age, though he was over a foot shorter.

"This is Ratan," Cindy introduced the man, who returned the greeting at the mention of his name. "He is the one who volunteered to take your note to Asha. Since she was not there, he feels he did not complete his task and has been waiting to take you to Asha's village and help you find her."

Mark expressed his gratitude in Bengali.

"Oh, you speak Bangla!" Ratan sighed with relief. "I am so happy about this, for I do not know any English at all!"

Suddenly his smile disappeared as quickly as it had come. He leaned in toward Mark, his nose nearly touching Mark's shoulder. "We should go as soon as possible, you know. The cyclone was bad enough here to postpone the attack, but not to stop it. I want to get there and get your woman out before they start burning houses, you know?"

Mark waved in thanks to the nurse, who nodded before turning back toward the clinic.

Then he straddled the dirtbike and kick-started it. Ratan hopped on behind him with the eagerness of a little boy. "I've always wanted to ride one of these, you know!"

It was dirt roads most of the way, made soggy and slippery from all the rain. After several stops to pick the bike out of mud-filled potholes, Mark was beginning to wonder if walking would have proved faster.

Finally, one more turn took them to the edge of Asha's village. The presence of a white man was cause enough for a stir. A white man and a dirtbike drew people from every direction to touch the vehicle and ask curious questions about the tall foreigner.

When Mark asked in fluent Bengali where Asha was, the chatter ceased immediately. People began backing away, murmuring to each other. Then, in a flash, everyone scattered, retreating into whichever hut was closest.

Mark realized as they ran that they were all women. Not one man was in sight. His heart twisted.

Ratan must have been coming to the same conclusion at the same time. "We are too late," he said soberly. "They have already gone to attack." He looked at Mark sorrowfully. "We may never find your woman."

Your woman. Mark's throat closed up. That was what he wanted, for her to become his woman. His forever.

Where had she gone? It had been a night and a day, and dusk would be falling again soon. Was she lost? Hurt? Alone?

A flash of orange caught his attention. A woman, very small, stood at the door to a hut to his left, waving urgently.

As soon as he looked her way, she shut the door.

What did that mean?

Ratan was already moving forward. "She has information. Let's go."

Mark followed. As they neared the hut, the door opened from the inside. The woman's face could barely be seen behind the door.

Ratan stopped two steps from the door, and Mark stopped behind him. They were close enough to hear her voice.

"Is the foreigner the man who is Asha's best friend?"

Mark felt his eyes sting. "Yes," he said hoarsely.

He swallowed, ready to ask if the woman knew where Asha had gone, when she spoke first. "Her mother took her away. There are bad men in our village, men who are afraid of her. Angry with her."

"Afraid of Asha's mother?" Mark clarified.

Mark saw through the cracks in the door that her head was shaking in the negative. "They are afraid of Asha, that she will expose their shame. They are the ones who stole her as a baby, and now they are angry she is back. Asha's mother is afraid they will harm her to protect themselves, or they will steal her again to hold her for ransom."

Adrenaline ran through Mark's entire body. The very thing he had warned Asha about; now it was real.

The woman's face peeked out from around the door. She looked in Ratan's direction, then his, managing somehow to see them without looking either of them in the eye. Her hesitation and fear were obvious.

Mark took a step forward. "Please," he said softly. "I love her. I want her to be my wife. Please help me find her."

The woman's eyes had widened and for the briefest second a soft smile played around her lips. She stood thinking for a moment more, then, as if deciding to trust him, she spoke. "They went to the Christian village. Asha has told us that people who follow Jesus are all part of one family. They love each other and take care of each other. So her mother took her there, where she could be safe."

Safe. A shudder rocked Mark's body.

The woman's eyes filled. "I did not know about the attack until just about an hour ago. We were all busy cleaning up after the storm, then as we finished the men gathered together and began shouting. They said the Christians are the ones who take our babies—I don't know what lies Ahmad said, but they believed him." She reached a hand out, imploring. "There is death in their eyes, but they left just awhile ago. If you drive there on your motorcycle, you could reach the village before them."

A tear escaped and trickled down her cheek. "Please rescue my friend," she implored.

Mark barely heard her words. He had already turned to retrieve the dirtbike. "Do you know where the Christian village is?" he asked Ratan.

Ratan swung his head to the side, indicating yes, as they both climbed on. Mark looked back at the woman in the hut. "Thank you," he called out, hoping he would have the chance to thank her again once he brought Asha back safely.

They tore out of the Muslim village, taking care to avoid the path the men had likely taken. Ratan directed Mark down small footpaths, barely wide enough for the bike. Water-filled potholes slowed their progress. Mud from puddles splattered their clothes. Reeds and tall grass slapped against their legs on both sides. Mark did not notice.

"Stop!" Ratan suddenly called out, and Mark put on the brakes so quickly they were nearly thrown to the ground.

"What is it?" he asked breathlessly.

Ratan pointed with his chin. "Down there is the village. Let me walk ahead and look down the hill. If the men are there, riding in will only get the motorcycle stolen and us likely killed, you know."

Mark waited as Ratan ran ahead and out of sight. When he returned, Mark could tell it was good news. "Not there yet, and I see no one in the village. Maybe they heard of the attack and got away!"

That would be great, Mark thought, starting up the engine again and heading down the hill. But where would they go? And how would he find Asha if they had?

As they rode over the crest of the hill and then down toward the village, Mark assessed the situation. The village consisted of twenty or more bamboo huts, most of them in shambles, due to the cyclone, Mark assumed. In the center of the village stood one sturdy mud building. Its tin roof was curled upward in one corner, exposing a portion of the building to the elements, but other than that, it looked like it had securely weathered the storm.

As Mark neared the village, his eye caught a small movement at the door of the mud structure. It had opened just a crack, then quickly shut again.

"Someone's there!" he called back to Ratan, steering straight toward the building. In less than a minute, Mark had parked the vehicle just outside the door and was about to knock when the door suddenly opened and a frightened-looking man faced them.

"I don't know why you are here," the man's Bengali words were a rapid staccato, "but we need help. Come quickly!"

He turned and was halfway across the building, headed toward a separate back room, when suddenly he pivoted on his feet to face them again. "You are Christian?" he asked, the fear back on his face. Mark wondered if he had just thought about the fact that, if they were the enemy, he had just let them in.

"We are Christian," Mark answered quickly. "I'm looking for—"

As soon as he had heard the word Christian, the man turned again and rushed toward the farthest open window. He spoke loudly. "Pastor Bishash! There is a man with a motorcycle!"

Mark heard heavy footsteps sloshing around the building toward the front door. A stately Bengali man entered from outside. At the same time, Mark heard crying and soft voices from within a room behind them, inside the building. How many people were still here?

The man Mark assumed to be the village pastor was covered in sweat. His clothing was streaked with dried mud and even blades of grass. He looked worse than haggard, and when he held up his hands in greeting, Mark noticed they were shaking.

"Thank God He sent you to us. They will be attacking soon. God must have sent the storm to hold them back and give us a chance to escape to the hills until the attack is over." The man was gasping as he spoke, as if he had been running.

"Why didn't you escape with the villagers?" Mark wanted to ask where they had gone and if Asha was with them, but he refrained. This man obviously was in great need.

The pastor slid his back down the wall to squat, leveling his elbows on his knees and folding his hands to rest his head on them for a moment.

Just then a moan from inside brought all their heads up in alarm. The pastor rushed toward the room, stopping just outside the door. He put his hand on the doorknob. "I have been praying outside. I convinced everyone in the village to go up into the hills." His voice was agonized. "I didn't know at the time . . ." His hand dropped from the doorknob. "I was going to take her to the clinic once the rest of the villagers were safely away. Now the only help we have is women I don't even know . . ."

Mark and Ratan turned to the man who had let them in, their eyes questioning.

"As the village was evacuating, the pastor was helping everyone climb the hills through the storm. It was very difficult.

For awhile, the entire village was hiding here inside the church to be safe as the cyclone was very bad. We all stayed for many hours, but then when the storm was a little bit better, a friend from another village came and told us about the attack coming today. The pastor told everyone to go into the hills and hide until after the attack was over."

Usually Mark did not mind the Asian way of talking for some time before getting down to the subject at hand, but today it nearly drove him mad. Enraged men were heading straight toward them, and this man was telling a story with as much detail as if they were casually enjoying a cup of tea together.

"So why are you still here?" he said slowly. His words were calm, but his hands kept clenching.

"Just as the last of the villagers were leaving, the pastor's wife began to . . ." Here the man stopped, hesitant. "She is with child, and her time has come," he finally said. "We had planned to take her to the clinic, but like everything else, including getting police help for the attack, the cyclone washed away our plans."

Another groan from inside the room confirmed the man's words. Mark groaned as well. What timing! What were they going to do?

Ratan touched Mark from behind. "I think I know which path the men will take. I will go around through the jungle and see how far they are, so we will know how much time we have."

Mark thanked him in great relief. Knowing if they had any time to spare would help greatly. They could not move a woman in labor, but then again, she and the baby would be in even more jeopardy if the attack came while they were still here.

God, what do we do? Mark's prayer was agonized. He desperately wanted to find Asha. For a moment he felt the temptation to just leave them all and go. But he knew he could not even consider it.

With another silent prayer—this time for Asha's protection, for Mark had no idea how long it would be before he could be free to look for her again—Mark started pacing the room as he thought through their options.

Once the baby was born, the mother would be too weak to travel up into the hills. The baby may need care, as well as the mother. Mark could carry the mother up into the surrounding jungle, but if they had to stay for days, her life may be in danger.

He was thinking, weighing the ramifications of each idea, when the pastor knocked on the door that barred him from his wife. It was opened by a Bengali woman.

"Is she all right?" the pastor asked, his voice hoarse.

As the woman responded, for a moment the door swung wide open.

Mark saw a woman lying on the floor in obvious pain. He was turning his head to respect her privacy when he saw a familiar sunshine-yellow salwar kameez, covered in grime and dirt, worn by a woman sitting to her side, her back to Mark.

Just as the pastor caught the door and began to shut it, the woman in yellow turned to look out the door.

Mark's heart stopped. He watched her face freeze in shock. She mouthed his name.

The pastor shut the door.

CHAPTER THIRTY-TWO

Asha was having trouble breathing. Had her eyes just deceived her? It could have been a different white man. One of the doctors from the clinic coming to help? Surely she had just imagined it was the person she wanted to see most in the world, like a desperately thirsty woman in the desert sees cool pools of water not actually there.

Again grasping the hand of the woman in labor, Asha tried to focus her thoughts. But someone had been there. And the person was white.

Could it—was there any chance at all Mark had come for her?

Her mind resisted the certain disappointment of even hoping it. Even if he had come to Bangladesh to find her, he would have gone to the clinic, and they would have directed him toward her family village across the way.

There was no reason for him to be here. None. Her mind insisted the man must be just one of the clinic doctors, but her heart kept crying out, *It's him*! *He's here*! *He's come for you.*

Unable to bear the uncertainty any longer, willing rather to face the disappointment than the pain of hoping, Asha stood and flung open the door, not certain she could believe what her eyes revealed to her. He was still there, in the exact same spot.

"Mark?" Had he really come to find her? "Oh, Mark."

Their eyes reached out and held. Asha felt tears slipping out and spilling down her cheeks. How desperately she wanted to reach across the void and cling to him. Never let him go. Her body ached with the strain of physically holding herself back from touching him.

She stepped forward. Opened her mouth to speak. But the woman inside cried out and, with one long regretful look, Asha turned away from Mark to the need greater than her own.

Again, the door was shut. Mark stood in stunned silence. He tried to process the past few moments, how he had gone from giving up his need to find Asha in order to help another, only to find after all these days and all his fears, she was right here. Right behind that closed door. So close.

Close enough to touch, though he knew he could not. He ached to wrap muscled arms around her and pull her toward his heart.

The culture, however, demanded they remain apart, and the situation demanded they set aside their own wishes for the sake of others.

He was thinking through these things when the door opened again, this time with less fervor, Asha remembering to guard the woman's privacy and only provide enough space to slip through.

Then she was standing before him, in tears. His eyes traveled across her weary features, her bruised and bloodied face, and he tried to guess at her feelings.

He could not. His own kept getting in the way.

"I love you," he said. The words refused to wait for a more opportune time. The fear of losing her, the danger they were in even now, propelled his heart forward, even as his body had to remain several feet away.

She covered her mouth with her hand, and he watched her eyes close and tears wash down over her fingers.

"Mark," she whispered, and his name from her lips sent shivers down his back. "Mark, I—"

Again, her words were stopped by a cry from inside the room. The door opened and an older woman gestured toward Asha. "The baby is coming."

"I have to go." She turned, then quickly as if a fear overtook her, she pivoted toward him again. "You won't—you won't leave me?"

"No," his voice was husky with emotion. "No, I won't leave you."

Her eyes held his for one brief second, then she slipped back inside.

"I don't know what to do!" Asha was cringing at the very idea of helping deliver a baby. This was worse than not knowing how to cook over an open fire or draw water without spilling it. This was a child's life that might soon be literally in her hands.

On top of that, she was having an extremely hard time concentrating, knowing the man she had longed for all these weeks was standing only a few feet away. And he loved her!

"Pay attention!" Asha's mother swatted her arm harshly. "I'll tell you what to do." Shazari continued working with the woman to push the baby into the world. "At least she will not need fear that someone will take her baby from her."

It was the most revealing comment Asha had heard from her, and helped bring her focus back into the room where they worked. "Mother," she broached the unspoken subject. "I keep hearing about the village curse, about babies being taken . . ."

Her mother's face was bathed in sweat. Keeping the door closed protected privacy, but gave no air flow. Heat and humidity swathed them all. "For a long time now, women have lost their babies. Many babies in villages die at birth or soon after, but this is different. They would say the baby died, but no one would see a grave, or have a prayer service for the child." Asha held her breath. "It was as if the child just . . . disappeared."

A scream ripped into the dense air. "Almost," Shazari urged. "Keep pushing!"

"Do you—" Asha hated bringing up the idea. "Do you think other babies are being stolen—like I was?"

Asha's whole body tensed up, fearing the answer.

There was no time for a response. The baby's head emerged, and Asha helped bring a beautiful baby boy into the world. She cried at the miracle of birth as she helped her mother clean the squalling infant.

"You're a loud one," Asha said with a laugh, holding the baby. "Are you calling your father in the next room? Letting him know you are here and ready to meet him?"

Pastor Bishash's eyes filled with love and wonder as Asha exited the inner room and handed him the new baby. He murmured to the infant, as if he had forgotten everything else in the world but the beauty of this new life.

Asha silently returned to her mother's side.

As they worked together to bathe the new mother, Shazari kept her eyes averted from Asha's. "I have thought what you said about the curse, but it cannot be. You are a girl. The curse is that the ones who disappear must all be boys."

"How do you know that?"

"I watch in our village, and I see. This is also how I know it cannot be the normal infant mortality."

Asha wanted to know the truth. "Mother, what do you see?"

Her mother looked off into the distance with longing before she spoke.

"All the children in our village are girls."

CHAPTER THIRTY-THREE

"They are coming! They are coming!"

Ratan was running. He stopped and spoke sporadically as he tried to catch his breath. "I saw them—many men—angry. We must go soon. We have only a few minutes."

Mark had been trying to think of a plan, trying to put his heart behind his head long enough to consider the very great danger they were all in.

He skipped the congratulations as he approached the pastor and got straight to the point. "I want you to take your wife and baby to the clinic station. Use the dirtbike I brought."

Pastor Bishash looked at Mark in silence.

"I know it will be difficult for your wife so soon after delivery," Mark said. "But she is in too much danger here to even think of staying, and trying to travel into the hills would be too much of a risk."

When the pastor glanced in concern toward the baby, then back toward the door which shielded his wife, Mark tried to think how to convince him. They had so little time! "They think your village has been stealing babies from their village. They want vengeance, and if they see your wife with a healthy baby . . ." He left the rest unsaid, but could see his words had hit their mark. The pastor's face paled and he nodded.

The other Bengali man, who had just introduced himself to Mark as Daniel, the pastor's cousin, approached and laid a hand gently on the pastor's shoulder. "I know you are torn by your desire to shepherd the village people," he said. "Do not worry. I will help our people as you would."

Mark left the two men and rushed into the room where the women were helping the pastor's wife stand.

"I apologize for intruding," Mark said quickly. He looked only at the pastor's wife, sure that if he looked at Asha he would pull her to him and protect only her.

"We must get you out, now," he continued. "The attack will come very soon."

The woman nodded, willing, but her body rebelled and slumped to the ground. A crimson bloodstain spread beneath her.

He opened the door and called the pastor. As quietly as possible, he spoke. "She is still bleeding. You must get her to the clinic right away."

Nodding, the pastor handed Mark the baby and rushed to his wife's side. Tenderly he lifted her into his arms and carried her toward the waiting vehicle. "You and our child are my first ministry," he whispered when she objected. "God commands I love you like Christ loves His church, and He would never abandon His church when in need."

Pastor Bishash gently lowered his wife to sit on the makeshift pillow Asha had quickly created from worn blankets and set on the back of the dirtbike. The woman winced in pain, but kept silent.

"Quickly," Mark reminded. He handed the baby to his mother as the pastor revved the engine. "God be with you."

"And with you," the pastor replied. "I will return when I can, tomorrow if possible."

The noise of the engine filled the air and again Mark winced, knowing the attackers were likely close enough to hear it.

"We have to move. Now."

Ratan was instantly by his side. "I'm ready," he said. "I'm sure not going to stay here and give them someone to beat on, you know!"

The pastor's cousin, Daniel, was also near. Where were Asha and her mother?

Mark found them back in the room, Asha's mother packing, of all things.

"There's no time!"

Asha sent an exasperated look his way. "I'm trying!" she mouthed.

Setting aside all protocol, using the only method he could think of, Mark reached out and touched the older woman's arm.

"Asha's mother," he said respectfully, calmly, "I am Mark, son of John, from India. I am here because I love your daughter and want to see that she is safe. She will not be safe if we stay here one more minute. The men from your village will come, and they will not be happy to see you here. We must go now!"

Whether the touch or the news shocked the woman into submission, Mark did not know or care. He ushered the wide-eyed woman from the room and out of the building, glancing back to be sure Asha was following.

She was, and despite all the danger they were in, she was grinning at him. Then to his shock, she winked!

He almost laughed when, in the distance, they heard shouting.

"Hurry! They're coming!"

Now running, the small group rushed behind the mud building, then down the path through the village and away from the approaching attackers. At the edge where the village ended and the jungle began, Mark asked the only one in the group who lived there, "Where would everyone go from here?"

Daniel did not hesitate. "This way." He pointed with his chin toward the left. "There is no path, but several miles through the hills there is a small stream and trees for shade. I know this is where they would go."

As soon as he pointed, Mark had unquestioningly begun ushering them all up the steep hillside in that direction. Though relatively in shape, Mark noticed the Bengali men were still comfortably climbing when he began to run out of breath. It was then he noticed Asha and her mother lagging behind.

He retraced his steps to join them. Asha was struggling to climb and support her mother. "She's been sick and is still weak," she said.

When his eyes questioned her, Asha tried to smile. "I'm feeling pretty worn out myself," she admitted. "It's been a rough couple of days."

Though his feet propelled him toward Asha's mother's left side, so he, too, could help her up the hill, his eyes were only on Asha.

He could see her clothes were stiff from having dried in the sun, and several rips in the cloth testified of some kind of trauma. Her face was smudged with dirt and dried blood. A huge, dark bruise covered the entire right side of her forehead. He ached to think what she might have been through since they had left the village. Where had they been when the cyclone hit?

Silently, channeling all their energy into cresting the hill, the three walked together as one toward the stream, the other villagers and safety.

The two Bengali men had stopped at the top of the hill. Turning toward the angry sounds, the three new arrivals looked through a break in the trees. Asha gasped.

The village, what was left of it, was on fire. From that distance the men looked like children playing as they ran from house to house, arms in the air, waving victoriously. But they were no children, and the fire no toy.

"God have mercy on us," Daniel whispered. The rest looked toward him in sympathy, except Asha's mother, who lowered her head in shame.

Slowly, the small group turned and began the descent down the other side of the hill, away from the noise of the crackling fire and a village being destroyed.

CHAPTER THIRTY-FOUR

Asha lay down to rest soon after arriving at the little clearing where the escaped Christians had gathered. She watched from her position under a large tree while Mark and Daniel gave the sad news to the villagers that their homes were gone.

Her mother had backed away as they spoke. She looked in a panic for Asha, rushing to hide behind a tree nearby. "They will kill me!" she whispered fiercely. "They will hear I am from the village that attacked them and they will take out their anger and vengeance on me!"

Asha shuddered. She wanted to reassure her mother, but, realizing she had no idea how they would react, she remained silent.

"Our homes!" "Our village!" For several minutes, people huddled in groups, mourning their loss. Women put hands over their faces, wailing out in deep grief. The sound made Asha wince.

Then softly, sweetly, through the sounds of sadness came a song. One lone villager sat cross-legged on the ground and began a gentle melody Asha had never heard before. The notes were arranged in a distinctly Bengali way.

ওহ জেসুস ইউ আরে মিনে *Oh Jesus, You are mine.*
থে রিভার ইস দ্বীপ থে বাত ইস স্মল *The river is deep; the boat is small,*

লর্ড কারী মে অক্রস *Lord, carry me across.*

Minutes passed as the man sang alone, the beauty of his words bringing the voiced grief down from wailing anger to muffled crying. Then Daniel sat alongside and joined in the man's song. Mark followed.

ইন ইউ ই আম ভিক্তরীয়ুস *In You I am victorious,*

কমে লর্ড গিভে মে স্ট্রেংথ *Come, Lord, give me strength.*

Gradually, slowly, one by one the villagers sat with the man near the stream and lifted up their hearts together.

Chills covered Asha's body at the sight. She watched as her mother slid from her hiding place and sat beside her, her face a mask of disbelief.

"What are they doing?" she asked, staring.

Asha gave a tired smile. "My guess is they are giving their sorrow to God."

"I have never in all my long life seen such a sight. Why are they not shouting? Why are they not vowing to exact vengeance?"

At that moment, one villager rose to his feet, the physical anger on his face a testament that at least one wanted to do exactly what she suggested.

"Why must we suffer like this? Why must life be so hard?"

Daniel responded. "Jesus told us we would face tribulation in this world, but not to fear, because He has overcome the world."

"It doesn't look like He's overcome anything!" came the passionate response. "Give me one example that God's goodness is in this somehow. You can't, can you?"

Others murmured in agreement to the man's feeling. "Now they will rise and attack me in anger," Asha's mother said with conviction. Asha could see her bracing herself, her body stiff and hard but her limbs visibly trembling.

Shockingly, the pastor's cousin smiled at the man. "I have an answer for you," he said calmly, the confidence in his voice catching the attention of all. Several leaned forward.

"We all know a cyclone is likely to come to our village once every three years. This is a fact." Many heads nodded. "What we cannot know is when those who think us enemies will find reason to attack."

His smile widened. "Wasn't it kind of God to arrange to have them attack us right after the cyclone hit? Many of our houses were already destroyed by the storm. This way we only have to rebuild once, not twice!"

At this, one man laughed and several women smiled.

Again, Asha's mother sat speechless with amazement.

When Daniel spoke again, Asha noticed even her mother leaned forward.

"My beloved ones, we have faced a hard loss today. It would be easy to allow anger to fill our hearts, but God says if we do that, a root of bitterness will grow within, and we know in time it would destroy not those we wish to hate, but ourselves."

A grimace showed Asha her mother was listening.

"God commands us to forgive." At this several voices raised in protest.

"But it is so unfair!"

"They aren't even sorry!"

"Why should we have to forgive again and again?"

Asha's mother was nodding energetically to their comments.

Daniel put his hands up for silence. "We are called to forgive, not because those who hate us deserve it, but because we ourselves have been forgiven. Think of what God has forgiven you. Can't you forgive for His sake?"

No sound was made except for two small birds fluttering and bantering as they flew in circles around each other through the makeshift camp.

After several moments, in which time Asha had sat up, unable to rest as the scene unfolded, Daniel said softly, "And do we not have much to thank God for—that not one from our village was killed? Not one even harmed? Is this not God's grace? What would have happened had God not sent the storm, had not delayed the attack, had not sent us word it was coming?"

The crowd was hushed, thinking of lives that could have been lost.

When the song began again, many could not sing along. They were weeping. Not in anger any more, but in gratitude.

"I do not understand this," Asha's mother muttered. "I do not understand."

When two of the women rose to their feet and approached, Asha's mother began inching backward.

The women squatted in the usual fashion and grasped Asha's mother's hands. They would not let her pull away. "I didn't do it!" Shazari cried out. "I didn't know about the attack. It wasn't my fault!"

The women were both crying. One looked toward the other and nodded. "We came to ask your forgiveness," the older of the two said.

Again speechless, Asha's mother could only stare.

"We wronged you," the woman continued. "We felt anger toward you, knowing the village you are from. Even though we saw you were tired and feeling ill, we did not help because we were thinking of what we had lost, and—" the woman choked out her words. "We—I—wanted you to be punished, to suffer."

"But we were wrong," the second, younger woman chimed in. "And we are sorry. Can you forgive us?"

Asha was dismayed to see her mother nodding to the negative. Then her mother spoke. "This is impossible. No one can act the way you do. You cannot care for me, after what my village, my people, have done to you. No. This cannot be."

In disbelief, she continued to shake her head, even as the woman began tending Shazari's wounds from the cyclone with cool water from the stream.

"Impossible," she kept saying. She turned to her daughter. "They did this at the Christian clinic, too. They were kind and good. I thought it was because they did not know I was a Muslim."

"They knew," Asha said softly.

"How can this be?" her mother continued to talk, as if to herself, gesturing and arguing back and forth as she ate the small ration given to her from the meager stash of food carried away during the escape, a ration she expected to be withheld. "Who is this Jesus, who tells His followers to love their enemies? To forgive?"

Once full and drowsy, Shazari spread the edge of her sari on a nearly-dry grassy spot and lay down with her head upon it. She looked up at Asha. "I have never forgiven those who wronged me and made me suffer. And he is right." She looked toward the pastor's cousin. "My anger has harmed me more than anyone else."

When she curled up like a child, Asha felt her heart constrict within her. An unspoken prayer rose from her heart for this woman, her mother, whom she had come to genuinely love.

Then her mother spoke, and Asha's heart bled. "If this Jesus of yours is so powerful, maybe He is strong enough to give my heart forgiveness for your father."

As her mother's body quickly settled into sleep, Asha thought of her father and murmured in response, "And my heart as well."

CHAPTER THIRTY-FIVE

It was an unpleasant sleeping situation at best. Like the refugees they were, the villagers used whatever natural materials they could find to construct makeshift shelters for the night. The largest shelter was created in hospitality for their guests.

As a weary village woman escorted Asha and her mother to their spot, Asha objected. "We don't need so much room to ourselves. Please, won't you stay with us? This is one of the only dry areas in the whole clearing."

The woman would not hear of it. "We are village people and know how to live in the jungle. You are an American. Tomorrow we will send you back to the clinic where you can be safe and comfortable."

Again, Asha objected until her mother interrupted. "You do not know the Asian way," she said with a grunt. "They cannot deal with their own difficult situations until they are sure you are taken care of. You arguing about it will only make them uncomfortable, so get inside and lay down so this poor woman can get some sleep."

Squelching her lingering feelings of guilt, Asha did as she was told. As she lay down on the hard-packed earth, shifting to remove a small rock from beneath her, Asha wondered where Mark was. It looked like a similar shelter had been erected next to theirs, up against a large tree with long, thick branches that reached over them like protective arms. Would Mark be staying there?

Hours passed as the soft goodnights faded and the sounds of nature in the jungle took their place. It was nearly midnight by the time the last exhausted villager dozed off.

A soft whisper brushed against Asha's consciousness. Barely aware if she was awake or dreaming, she felt leaves rustling in the brush wall beside her.

Eyes wide now, battling fear, Asha rolled over and up onto one elbow. She dipped her head to peer through an opening in the brush.

She could not see Mark's features, but she knew it was him because the moonlight reflected off his lighter hair in a way it never would on a Bengali's. He, too, was half-reclining, leaning on one elbow on his side, easily visible as his shelter had no walls.

Asha's heart had been pounding in anticipation for hours. Several times during the afternoon Mark had caught her eye, and the love she saw took her breath away. He would look away before they could attract attention, but Asha could not keep from staring at him, watching in admiration as he helped set up camp. When darkness fell, he had helped gather wood for a fire.

Her own hands had remained busy preparing vegetables that someone wisely had thought to pack during the evacuation. Her hands prepared food, but her heart kept asking for Mark. Wanting him near. Wanting to talk with him. Hear his voice. Know his heart.

How had he come to find her? The mystery teased her patience as supper was eaten, then more songs were sung by the campfire. Had they been in America, Asha would have snuggled up to Mark near the firelight.

Here, however, if they were to talk alone, as an unmarried couple, they would have to do so in secret.

Hoping no one would awaken and disapprove of their unchaperoned moment, Asha slipped her hand under the brush wall and ran it across the bark of the tree, toward his.

When he whispered her name, soft as a breeze, her heart turned over. She spoke in the darkness toward his voice.

"Mark," she whispered. "I've been aching to find out—how in the world did you find me?"

His chuckle sent chills down her arm. "Later, my impatient one."

"Later?" She edged toward his voice. "Why—"

He pulled her hand upward to place a kiss on her palm and suddenly she forgot her question. Forgot her impatience and even her curiosity. She sat up and rested her head against the tree's mighty trunk, her hand stretched through the break in the shelter wall, cradled in both of his.

"Asha," he breathed.

She curled her fingers around his and sighed. How she longed to push aside the brush wall and nestle against his heart. She imagined him leaning down to rest his chin on the part in her hair, his arms tightening around her.

"Asha, for a year I've thought about you and waited for you to come back to India and be with me."

She edged closer to the break in the brush to hear him better.

"After you came back, and these last weeks, I've realized something."

Her heart sped up. "What?" she whispered.

She felt his hand trail up her arm and reach through the opening to cup her face. His thumb caressed her cheek and made her tremble.

"You . . ."

Impossibly, her heart increased its pace. "I what?"

After several long seconds of silence, he finally spoke. "You make me more miserable than anybody I've ever met."

"What?"

"Shhh," he reminded, pulling her hand back when she indignantly yanked away. One of the men in Mark's shelter shifted, and they waited in silence, not daring to move, until he settled and commenced snoring softly.

Mark's laugh was soft in the darkness. "I didn't mean that the way it sounded."

"Oh really?" Asha felt her bottom lip puckering out in a pout. "Let me guess, I was supposed to take that as a compliment?"

His arm shook and she knew he was laughing silently. "Well, actually yes."

Her sniffing sound of irritation made Mark's smile so wide it beamed out even in the dark. "I didn't say it the right way . . ."

"Um-hmm," Asha agreed.

"But what I was trying to tell you was that I know I really care about you because I get so miserable when we argue, or when you're unhappy, or when I'm not sure how you're feeling."

He kissed her hand again and she melted against the tree. "And when I knew you were in danger and I couldn't be with you . . . Couldn't rescue you or protect you or even know if you were safe . . ." She heard him take in a heaving breath. "I don't ever want to feel that way again."

She was writing his words in her heart, putting them someplace precious, saving them to keep forever.

Asha let her imagination snuggle them close, as she had wanted to do earlier near the firelight. For long, beautiful minutes, they sat in contented silence, listening to the night sounds.

Mark's hand tightened around hers. "I thought I'd lost you." His voice was husky with feeling. "I have never been so afraid of anything before."

His words trailed down into a whisper and Asha lifted her head from the tree trunk. "I thought I'd lost you," she said. "My e-mail . . . when you didn't answer . . ."

"I was out of town."

"Oh."

"Unreasonable woman." He was smiling. "You should know by now . . ."

Her whisper was breathless. "Know what?"

Mark reached up and gently ran a strand of her hair between his fingers. "I love you, Asha. You have become the most important person in the world to me."

Her heart overflowed. She leaned back against the tree again and set aside the rest of her questions. They could tell of their individual adventures in time. For now, it was enough just to be together.

Together. She smiled into the darkness. What a wonderful word.

CHAPTER THIRTY-SIX

From the first moment the sun began peeking up over the mountain's edge, villagers started to wake and begin the unpleasant task of packing to return to their village.

Or what is left of their village, Asha thought, stretching her aching muscles after yet another night sleeping on the ground. How did people do this their whole lives? Asha could not decide what she wanted most: a clean soft bed, a clean outfit, or clean hair. Maybe someday she would enjoy the luxury of all three again, though not anytime soon from the looks of things.

Though all the women had headed for the stream the evening before to bathe themselves and their dirt-caked clothing as much as possible, after a night sleeping on the ground, Asha again felt crusty. After checking on her mother, whose deep breathing assured she was still asleep, Asha rose and returned to the stream to wash the latest layer from her face and arms.

A glance across the way brought her eyes to Mark, who was helping the other men pack up the small collection of possessions the villagers had managed to carry from their homes before the attack.

Asha smiled. He could use a bath and a change of clothes, too.

She turned to go when he looked up from his work and scanned the small area. When his eyes found her, the corners of his mouth turned up slowly into that lazy smile that gave her chill bumps. Asha could not hide her yawn, a reminder they had sat together for hours the night before. She covered her mouth with her hand, only to remove it quickly as the dirt on it shifted to her face.

Shrugging, then forcing down a grin as Mark's eyes kept smiling that secret smile, Asha began the descent toward the stream and the other women who, she noticed, were huddled into a clump, their eyes watching her, then Mark, then her again. They whispered and pointed with their chins. Asha felt herself blushing.

Reaching into the water with both hands, Asha brought the liquid to her face and felt its coolness wash away the heat and the dirt. It felt so good. The women teased her as she washed, asking about the foreign man with hair like sunshine, who looked at her with such a smile. It was scandalous, they said, but then they giggled and wished aloud that their husbands would brave smiling at them like that in public.

Asha splashed more water onto her skin, vowing to stop giving in to the temptation to look at Mark every thirty seconds and giving the village ladies more to gossip about.

One last time, though, her eyes sought him out, which she immediately regretted as he and all the women were still watching her. Mark was smiling. The women were giggling.

Now mortified, Asha ducked her head to hide her flaming cheeks and left the stream in search of her mother. Maybe if she focused on helping her, she would stop looking like a twelve-year-old with her first crush.

Then again . . . she caught herself glancing at Mark again, and heard the ladies giggle some more.

Then again, maybe not.

The villagers made slow progress back, waiting for word from Daniel, who had risked venturing ahead to make sure none of the attackers remained, as well as dreading the sight sure to appear once they crested the last hill. Asha's mother kept clucking her sympathy as they walked. Asha wished she did not find it thoroughly annoying. She was so tired.

As they passed a certain tree, several men and women reached out to pull off a small section of branch. Asha waited to see what they did with it, but no one seemed to be doing anything but carrying them.

"What are those for?" she finally asked.

Her mother looked at her as if she were daft. "Those are for brushing our teeth, of course! Do you think people never brushed their teeth before plastic toothbrushes were invented?"

Asha laughed out loud, and was pleased to see a hint of a smile turn up the corners of her mother's mouth in response.

"You put the edge of the branch in the water," her mother explained. "When it gets wet, the fibers spread out."

"Really?" Asha was impressed. She backtracked to the tree and broke a piece of branch off herself. "What an ingenious idea."

Asha's toothbrush was still in her bag back in her mother's village. Asha could not remember how many days had passed since then, but the thought of being able to brush her teeth was delightful.

It took several hours for the entire group to return, those with young children the farthest behind.

At the edge of the village, instead of entering, each person stopped and stared. More families approached from behind, but they, too, simply stopped to take in the sight.

Finally one man spoke. He told Mark, "That over there, the pile—it used to be my home. Now all it is good for is a cooking fire."

Charred piles of bamboo revealed where each house used to stand. The villagers did not approach their individual home areas. For at least half an hour they remained huddled just outside the village, silent.

Asha watched them in sorrow. To lose everything in such a way, how could they bear it?

Suddenly, she heard a noise. It was nothing like the natural noises of the forest around them. This was a tinny sound. It echoed loudly. A motorcycle, maybe?

Upon hearing the noise, the villagers began to scramble back into the jungle, calling out to God in their terror to rescue them from another attack.

Mark came to stand just behind Asha. She lifted worried eyes.

"It sounds like the dirtbike I used to come find you. Perhaps the pastor is returning."

"Don't worry!"

Asha looked to see Ratan, the man who had accompanied Mark from the clinic. She had forgotten about him. He waved to the villagers. "It is only the white man's motorcycle, you know!"

Pastor Bishash was riding the dirtbike alone. Beneath his hands on the handlebars hung bags of food, likely from the market near the clinic. When he crested the small hill bordering the village and saw people fleeing in fear, he called out, "Come back!"

At his voice, many turned, and in great relief rushed back into the village to surround the beloved man.

Asha was smashed from all sides by villagers trying to get closer to the pastor. Irritation bubbled at the lack of personal space, until a large hand touched hers.

Immobile except for her head, she turned it to find Mark jostled in next to her. Though everyone's eyes were on the pastor, and everyone was squeezed in so tightly no one could see much of anything inside the crowd, Asha was still surprised when Mark wrapped his fingers around her hand and held it in his.

All desire to flee the crowd evaporated. She stood quietly while people all around her asked questions.

"What are we going to do now?"

"How will we replace all we lost?"

"Why bother trying if we'll only be attacked again?"

The pastor lifted his hands for silence. Then he spoke. "My beloved brothers and sisters, what has happened to us is terrible.

It is hard to think of beginning again. But, instead of thinking of the earthly treasures we have lost, let's focus on the heavenly treasures we have in Christ that will never fade or be stolen or destroyed."

Silence reigned. Asha jolted in her small space when her mother's voice rang out over the crowd. "You have nothing now. What will you do?"

"We will build again," he said simply. "And with each bamboo shoot we cut and each portion of house we complete, we will ask God to give us a love for our enemies."

CHAPTER THIRTY-SEVEN

Two days passed as Asha worked alongside the women, and Mark worked alongside the men. There was much to do.

Initially, it took a great deal of talking for Mark and Asha to convince the villagers to let them stay and help at all. They were determined to send them to the clinic station, away from their troubles.

Finally, Mark suggested they stay long enough to let Pastor Bishash and Ratan, Mark's Bengali guide, use the dirtbike to return to the clinic station, the guide to return home and the pastor to bring back his wife and baby if both were declared stable enough to travel.

"You are a true Bengali brother!" Ratan had called out to Mark as he rode away. "But next time, I think I will just stay home, you know?"

Mark had waved and smiled his thanks as the bike rode out of sight. Now that the argument over staying was settled, he followed the village men into the outlying areas to learn how to cut and prepare bamboo to make new huts, enjoying the camaraderie the village men shared. This is how he wanted to live, among the people he was called to serve, not set apart from them.

Asha remained with the women, who spent the first evening setting up small individual home spaces inside the mud church, the only building to survive the attack.

The next day the group collectively gathered materials then worked on building one hut at a time. Mark was thriving as he learned how to build a hut using no nails, no boards, none of the materials he was used to working with. He asked so many questions the village men started teasing him, asking if he was planning to build one himself.

"Maybe so you can get married?" one younger man asked slyly.

"Maybe," Mark shot back. He looked over to where Asha and several other women were collecting dried dung patties to burn in the cooking fires. Would she even consider living in a village like this? Could she be happy in a small, rickety bamboo hut, without any of the amenities both were used to? Could he?

At that moment, Asha looked up and saw him watching her. She glanced down at the dried dung she held in her hands. Mark watched her grimace in disgust, then shrug and turn to collect more. Maybe she was more resilient than he thought.

Before he could ponder the idea, however, she turned her head to look back over her shoulder at him and made a gagging face, then calmly continued on her way.

He laughed out loud, deciding he could be happy anywhere in the world as long as she was there, too.

Asha heard Mark's laughter in the distance and a smile spread through her from the inside out. She was glad he had not noticed that her initial contact with these dried pieces of . . . yucky stuff really did make her gag.

She was wondering if anyone in the village had a bar of soap to use once they were finished, when she heard her mother's voice, insistent and rather loud.

"Why will you forgive them? Why don't you fight back? It's not fair what they did to you, and they don't even care how much pain they caused you."

Asha realized her mother was not even aware she was suggesting retribution on her own village. She kept pestering the village women, following them as they worked, asking how they could forgive when they had been treated so badly.

Her mother was not asking out of idle curiosity, Asha realized, approaching softly behind her. She was asking for herself—a woman who had been gravely mistreated, whose bitterness and anger had been her only protection for so many years.

Fearing she would start crying and make the dung patties wet and slippery—Asha gagged again at the thought—she turned and headed back to the church building, smiling at the thought that her mother had already changed from one giving commands to one asking questions. That was a huge step forward.

Who knew what might happen next?

CHAPTER THIRTY-EIGHT

"Look at how much we've accomplished," Asha said with pride as she looked over the village.

All the old burnt remains had either been removed or collected into piles of firewood to cook with. Here and there men squatted on the ground, and Asha watched in fascination as they split bamboo logs, laid them out flat, then weaved them around and through each other to create walls. The women began collecting brush for temporary roofing, but dropped the materials cheerfully when Mark arrived, along with several other men who had all mysteriously disappeared for the afternoon.

"He bought tin roofing," Asha whispered to herself as a cheer went up throughout the village. "Enough for everyone." She blinked away tears.

Shazari came to stand beside her. "I have never seen people like these. Look at them! Here they are with nothing, with everything taken away from them, and still they are joyful. They enjoy working together, helping one another." She paused, then whispered, "I have always hoped heaven would be like this."

Asha's heart sang within her. It burst forth from her mouth into song.

Hearing the sound, several others joined in, singing praise as they worked.

Yes, this really is like heaven.

Asha was smiling as she sang until she suddenly realized everyone else had stopped. Looking around to see what had happened, her own song turned to a gasp when she saw a young woman running down the hill toward the village.

The first thought that came to Asha's mind was that this *burkah*-clad girl should not be out alone. Then she marveled at herself—maybe she had learned something over the past weeks.

In black from head to toe, the stranger rushed through the village. Everyone gave her a wide path as she ran straight toward Asha. When she removed her veil and revealed her face, Asha gasped again.

"Neena!"

Her father's second wife was out of breath. Had she run all the way from the village?

"Neena, what are you doing here? Has something ha—"

Asha's words were cut off by her mother's biting tongue. "What are you doing here? Spying on us? Planning to tell everyone where we are now?"

The wrinkled face twisted in anger, then suddenly Shazari closed her eyes, took in a breath, then said, "I'm sorry. I should not speak to you like that."

Neena and Asha both choked on words that would not quite come.

"Don't stare at me as if I had just grown two more heads!" she barked out. "I have chosen to follow the God who loves, and the One He sent, Jesus, who is powerful enough to forgive even His enemies."

Neena was still gasping, but Asha could not tell if it was from still being out of breath, or just plain shock.

Mark approached and asked in English, "What's going on?"

Asha shook her head in wonderment. "I would not have believed it had I not seen it with my own eyes."

"This is the girl who helped me find you," Mark said, indicating Neena.

At his approach, Neena restrained her shock at her husband's first wife's complete personality change and dropped her eyes in deference.

"I honor you," she said to Mark. "Thank you for rescuing my friend."

"It is I who honor you," Mark responded. "Without your help I never would have found her. Thank you."

Praise from a man only widened Neena's huge eyes ever more. She stood silent for long moments until Asha approached and laid a gentle hand on her arm. "Neena, why did you come here? Is there something you need to tell us? Do you need help?"

She remembered Neena saying her husband, Asha's father, beat her sometimes. Asha felt a deep black anger fill her.

"Has someone hurt you?" she asked urgently. "Do you need our help?"

Neena was shaking her head vigorously. "No, no, it is you who are in danger."

Mark groaned behind her. "Not again."

Asha turned to him pertly. "Well, at least this time you're already here, right?"

Neena pulled on Asha's shirt sleeve, unaffected by their teasing. Her eyes were full of fear. "You remember the two brothers? The ones who stole you?"

"Of course," Asha responded. How could she forget?

"The younger one, Rashid, he came to me today and told me that Ahmad, the eldest, is very angry with you. He is going to the Christian clinic to look for you. Rashid says he is very crafty, and will probably hire someone in the market across the street to go and ask about you, so that he will not be recognized. When you are not there, he will surely come here to find you. You must leave immediately!"

Asha's brows came together. "Why would the brother tell you this? What if it is a trap of some kind?"

Neena wiped beads of sweat from her forehead. "I cannot tell you why, but I trust him. I can hear in his voice how much he hates the evil his brother does. I believe what he has said."

"But he was with his brother when they stole me as a baby! He is part of this."

Mark edged closer to Asha from behind and whispered something in her ear. Then he spoke to Neena, "If you trust his words, that is enough for us. We will go."

The entire village had gathered by this time, everyone curious about the woman in the *burkah*. Neena shrank away from their eyes. "Please," she said very softly. "I am sorry for what my people did to your village. Please don't hurt me."

At that, Asha covered her mouth with her hand and closed her eyes tight to keep from crying. Neena had come to warn her despite fearing retribution and possibly even death at the hands of those her village had harmed. "Oh, Little Ma . . ."

"Do not fear them," Asha's mother jumped into the conversation with her usual authoritative tone. "They will never harm you. Even if you had put the fire to each house, they would not take vengeance on you. Vengeance belongs to God and because God forgives us, we must forgive others."

Again, Neena stared. "What did you do to her?" she asked no one in particular.

Asha smiled. Her joy was running over and she reached out and gave Neena, then her mother, a very American-style hug.

"They gave me hope," Asha's mother answered. "They have taught me God can put forgiveness in my heart, and I can live without the bitterness eating my soul. No matter what happens or what anyone does to me, I will never be a victim again. I'm sure I will still be treated like one, but I will not feel like one from this day on."

"Hallelujah," Mark said.

Asha nodded in agreement, unable to speak.

"I have treated you badly in the past, but that will be no more. Instead of being enemies, we will work together."Asha's mother kept talking even as Neena's face paled. Asha worried she just might faint. A Christian village woman started fanning Neena with the edge of her sari.

Shazari looked at Asha. "You will give me a Bible," she ordered.

"And you . . ." She turned back to Neena. "You will read to me from the Bible every night since I cannot read."

The small return of bossiness there at the end brought Neena back to life. A smile spread across her beautiful features.

"I'd—I'd like that," she offered hesitantly.

Mark brought them all back to the problem at hand. "We still haven't decided what to do about Ahmad coming here."

All three women threw up their hands. "I forgot!" each said in unison, then laughed together. To Asha, that was a miracle in itself.

"The pastor brought the dirtbike back this morning," Mark said. "We can use it to leave right away."

Asha's heart plummeted. "Right now?"

Mark leaned in close to her ear and spoke quietly in English. "No matter how much we want to stay, we have to think of the people of this village. They have already been attacked once. We wouldn't want to risk Ahmad knowing they helped you. It might bring more danger on them, don't you think?"

She nodded, wishing she could lean back onto his hard, solid chest and be comforted.

"Tell you what," he said lightly, "if you want a bamboo hut to live in someday, I promise I'll build you one."

Asha's shoulders dropped as the tension released from her body. She smiled up at him. "Yippee," she said sarcastically. Her lips pursed together. "Okay, I'll go, but only on one condition."

"What's that?"

"That if we end up staying at someone's house that only has one bathroom, I get dibs on the shower first."

He chuckled and the crowd behind him chuckled with him, though they had no idea what was being said. Mark turned and began saying his goodbyes and Asha, pained, did the same. Would they ever see these dear people again?

The pastor brought out the dirtbike and handed it over to Mark.

"I'll have to take two trips," Mark said, looking down at the small seat. "Only two of us will fit at a time." He looked at Asha. "I'll take you first, since you're the one he's looking for. Hmm, except if he sees your mother here, or Neena, he might be even more angry and take it out on them."

Asha's mother waved her bony hand in his face. "I'm going back to my village," she said with that distinct motherly tone that allowed no arguments. "Neena will walk with me, and you will take my daughter to safety."

It was the first time Asha had heard her mother refer to her as her daughter. Tears welled up. "Mark," she said quickly, before she lost her nerve. "Mark, can we all go to the village first, then to the clinic station? There's something I need to do."

"Asha, be reasonable. There are—"

"Oh, I'm not reasonable," Asha said with a smile. "You already know that, don't you?"

Mark bit down the remark he wanted to make and instead reminded her of the danger.

"I know, Mark," Asha said, then bit her lip. She had said his name out loud—were unmarried people allowed to do that? Maybe because they were speaking in English, nobody really noticed.

As she glanced around, Mark started the engine. The entire crowd backed up several steps away from the noisy machine.

Only Asha came closer. "It would be less dangerous if we all went to the village now!" she shouted.

With an exasperated sigh, Mark shut off the engine and turned to Asha. "Alright, go ahead and try to convince me of this one."

She almost smiled. *Now who's being melodramatic*? "If Ahmad is looking for me at the clinic, that is the last place I should go. And if after that he will come to this village, then I certainly should not stay here. His own village will be the last place he goes, and by then we can be safely back at the clinic station."

"Besides," she concluded, "I wouldn't feel right letting Mother and Neena go back alone through the woods."

At Mark's raised eyebrows, she added, "And just so you know, I don't wander around here by myself any more either."

She watched him ponder, then nod his head. "You're right," he said. "That is a better plan."

Asha grinned. "Did it hurt—saying that?"

He smiled back. "You don't have to be all smug about it."

Asha turned to suggest her mother ride on the dirtbike while she and Neena walked. She was surprised at the very different reaction they were having to Mark and Asha's banter.

Neena's eyes were full of stars, like a child watching a commercial for the thing she wanted most in the world.

Asha's mother, however, had her arms crossed and her face crinkled up into a scowl. She marched right up to the dirtbike and sat down behind Mark. "I won't have you sitting so close to this man," she said gruffly. "You two—you two . . . well, you need to get married and that's all I'm going to say."

A breath choked out of Asha's mouth. She felt the hot flash of embarrassment creep up her neck and across her cheeks.

Mark just grinned, started the engine, and began driving down the path, getting immediate brownie points with Asha's mother by asking her to give him directions.

The two other women walked behind. Asha waved goodbye once more toward the village where the crowd still stood. She turned to watch as her mother gestured and barked out orders for Mark to turn left, go slower, no, not like a snail, stop stopping so much, do you want it to take all day?

Asha caught herself giggling. What was Mark thinking right then? Was he thinking this could be his future mother-in-law?

Neena caught her eye and smiled, then they both picked up the pace, trying to keep up with the dirtbike as it led the way toward the village.

And hopefully away from Ahmad.

CHAPTER THIRTY-NINE

Mark had a difficult time keeping the dirtbike upright on the muddy path while driving slow enough that the two women behind could still see him on the trail. When Neena stopped suddenly, then Asha stopped with her, Mark hefted the dirtbike around—the path was not wide enough to do a u-turn—and rode back to where they stood.

"What's the matter?"

Neena gestured toward a foot path trailing off to the left. "This is a shortcut. We are very close to the village now. We can take this smaller trail while you continue on the motorcycle."

He looked at Asha, ready to voice his hesitation.

"We'll be fine."

He scowled a little. "You say that, but history and probability can name a whole list of things that might happen to you once you're out of my sight."

His scowl turned to a smile when she put her hands on her hips, looking very American. "Now see here." She made an exasperated sound Mark had heard her mother make earlier. "A lot of things happened to me here before you came, mister. And it was God who rescued me from all of those."

Her tone turned saucy and she crossed her arms. "And since He's God and all, I'm pretty sure He can handle me being out of your sight for a few minutes, don't you think?"

Mark wanted to kiss her.

She must have read his face. He felt sheer delight as a blush crept up her cheeks. With another flustered sound, she turned on her heel and began walking down the tiny path, Neena following behind, their shoes sinking into the wet dirt with each step.

Mark waited until they were gone from view before turning on the engine and starting down the larger path, glad to be able to go a more natural pace.

He heard Asha's mother grunt behind him. Turning to glance back at her, he saw her cross her arms just as Asha had, then grab the bike again when they hit a bump.

I'd better pay attention. Mark turned his focus to the path again, only to laugh out loud when he heard the caustic comment from behind, "Humph! You two need to get married."

Did that mean he had her approval? Mark could not remove the grin from his face even as he yelled back over the noise of the motor, "Sounds good to me!"

Asha stood just outside the *dokhan*. Her father would be in the back of the shop, likely smoking or taking a break to rest during the heat of the day.

She swallowed convulsively. "God, I need Your help." Upon their arrival to the village, Asha had gone straight to her mother's home, relieved to find her bag still intact. She reached into it to find the money she had brought back to the village, a pile of *taka* notes equivalent to the very large sum of two hundred dollars. Thank God no one had decided to curiously search through her bag during her absence.

Now approaching the man who had rejected her at birth, and again just recently, Asha felt a little lightheaded. She took a deep breath, prayed once again for divine assistance, then took the few last steps to arrive at the door to the back of the *dokhan*.

"Asha!"

Neena had never used her name before. Asha turned in alarm. Seeing Neena running, without her *burkah* on, turned her alarm to real fear. "What has happened?"

"Your father," Neena gasped out. "He came back to the house. He saw your mother and was very angry. He says she shamed him by leaving the village without his permission."

Her chest was heaving. She gestured toward the hut across the village until she could catch enough breath to speak. "He is beating her!"

Without another thought, Asha ran toward the hut. Mark had headed toward Rashid and Ahmad's home soon after their arrival, determined to talk to Rashid. If only he were here now!

How was she to stop a man from beating a woman?

"God, what do we do?" she called toward the heavens as the hut came in view. Asha could hear shrieking from inside that made her blood curdle. She rushed forward.

The door to the bamboo hut was shut, but with many open spaces for air and no glass on any windows, every word could be heard from outside. "I will kill you for the shame you have brought on me!"

Asha yanked open the door and nearly fell inside. Her eyes took in her father, standing legs apart with a large bamboo shaft in his hand, bending over her mother's cowering body.

Asha flung herself across the small space and threw her own body over her mother's. When Neena joined her, Asha let the tears flow. She said nothing. Only hid her face down, tensing up her body, waiting for the first strike.

It never came. For several moments the only sounds in the room were the harsh breaths of her father and the small whimpers of her mother. Asha peeked up to see bewilderment on her father's face.

He stood stock still. Asha could not decipher what was more shocking to him, that his daughter had returned despite the danger, or that his second wife was willing to take the beating of the first.

Not wanting to waste the opportunity, Asha rose slowly, hesitantly. She looked down at his feet, forcing herself to show a respect she did not feel. Her downward eyes focused on the bag in her hand.

Reaching down, Asha pulled the large wad of cash from it, glancing up to see her father's eyes drop down to the money and widen. He had probably never seen so much money at one time in his life. Two hundred dollars was over half a year's wages.

"Father." Asha quickly dropped her eyes when her father's raised up to her face again. "This money is to pay for your second wife's dowry. If I give this to you, you have no reason to beat her to ask for money anymore. Is that not so?"

"I will do what I like with my own wives," the man muttered.

"And your own baby daughter?" Asha could not keep the anger and hurt from her voice. His head lowered, and Asha took advantage of the momentary shame.

She could imagine his mouth watering at the prospect of so much money as she held it out to him and repeated her earlier words. "If you have Neena's full dowry paid, you have no reason to beat her again, is that not so?"

"I will do what I want!"

"If you intend to continue beating your wives, then there is no reason for me to pay the dowry, is there?" Asha pulled the money back and acted as if she would put it back in the bag.

Her father's hand upon the bamboo stick shook with rage. His face puffed out in anger. Asha was certain he was fighting the temptation to strike them all.

However, thankfully, the possibility of money was more important to him than the shame of not having ultimate freedom in the control of his women.

"I won't beat her anymore," he said through gritted teeth.

Asha felt relief flood through her. She handed the money over.

An uncomfortable silence followed. Asha turned to see Neena helping her mother rise. Asha rushed to help.

Her father turned to leave the hut when her mother's voice stopped him. "Asha's father," she called out. When he turned to face her, anger still in his eyes, the bamboo still grasped in his hand, Asha again felt fear. Would he go back on his word already?

Her mother, however, showed no fear as she faced her husband. She also showed no anger. Asha watched in amazement as her mother, one eye already beginning to swell, bruises down her arms, spoke softly, "I forgot for a moment why I called you to come here."

A gasp escaped. Her mother had known Asha was going to look for her father at the *dokhan*. Had she asked for him right then, knowing he would beat her, in order to spare Asha the pain of watching? *Oh, Mother.*

The older woman swayed a little and Asha joined Neena in holding her up. Her voice was calm, at peace. "I do not hate you anymore."

Asha saw her father's body twitch a little, as if he had been touched by a live wire.

Her mother continued. "I forgive you in the name of the One who forgave me. For everything you did to me, for all I have suffered because of you, I forgive you."

The man who had been willing to sell his own daughter stood stunned for several moments. Asha watched the anger drain from his face. The bamboo dropped from his hand to the dirt floor below.

He turned to leave, defeated.

CHAPTER FOURTY

Asha knew she had to say it. But her heart cried out against it. *It isn't fair! I shouldn't have to forgive him. He's not even sorry!*

Unwittingly her mind traveled to the Christian village, where men and women rebuilt their lives with joy because they carried no bitterness toward those who hated and hurt them. It was their love and peace that had brought her mother to faith and to peace.

Asha could barely speak for the tears. God would have to change her feelings for this man, but for now, obedience to His will was enough.

"I—I forgive you, too."

Even as her father turned away one last time without response to any of them, a peace like Asha had never felt before enveloped her. It filled every empty part of her soul.

The search for her history, her worth and her family was over. She had found all of them, but not in the sources she expected. Her family was these two dear women, her brothers and sisters in Christ in the nearby village, her parents back in America waiting for word from her.

Her worth was not in the value placed on her by her biological parents, or even herself. Her worth was in Jesus Christ, who declared she was worth dying for.

And her history, even that Asha could finally accept with peace. She had come looking for answers and she had found them. Now she knew she had never been the victim she had always seen herself as. It had been God who sent her to America, and just like Joseph, He had chosen her to help her family—not only with money to buy food, but with the good news that God loved them, and they could have a real relationship with Him through Jesus Christ.

When Mark arrived, stating they needed to leave soon, Asha's heart nearly broke. She nearly begged to stay, but the sure danger she would be putting her mother and Neena in was not worth the possible help she could give to them by remaining in the village.

She was surprised when her mother's commanding voice called out to her. "My daughter."

Asha went to her side, helping Neena lower her to a more comfortable sitting position on the floor. Asha pushed her bag behind her mother's back to support her. "What is it, Mother? What do you need? Can I get you something?"

Her mother grunted. "You'd think a woman has never been beaten before," she barked out. "What I need is for you to get away from this village. Right away."

"Mother, I hate leaving. I want to stay so much. You are my family—" Her words became trapped behind tears.

For one small moment, her mother's voice gentled. "And we will always be your family," she said, touching Asha's hand softly. "But you must go. This man," she looked toward Mark, then back at Asha. "He told me of what you want to do—about rescuing women who are stolen away from their families. This is a good thing, from God, and you must not give it up to remain here."

Tears were dripping onto her lap, but Asha barely noticed. She reached down and with her right hand touched the tops of both her mother's feet, then her own head and heart in the ultimate gesture of honor. Her mother accepted the goodbye and waved her toward the door.

"Take her back," she ordered Mark. "She could not cook like a Bangladeshi anyway."

Completely shocked, Asha turned to see her mother actually smiling. "Oh my word," she said in English to Mark. "You have completely charmed my mother already."

He winked at her. "Of course I have." Then he shrugged with a smile. "It's probably the blonde hair."

Neena sighed and Asha turned to her. "The bag I brought," she directed Neena's gaze to where she had placed the bag behind her mother's back. "Everything in it is yours, especially the Bengali Bible." Then she smiled. "You have to read it to Mother every night, remember?"

Neena nodded, her own eyes wet. "Thank you."

Mark had slowly approached from behind. "I'm sorry, Asha, but we really have to go now. I don't want to take any chances of Ahmad returning before we leave."

She nodded and reluctantly rose to stand beside him.

"*Khoda hafez*—God be with you. I pray I will see you again."

Both women nodded as Asha stepped through the door, down the path, and out of their lives once again.

"I wish I had a picture of them," Asha said in English. She was sitting sidesaddle behind Mark, restraining from holding on to him for support until they were out of sight. It was taking the use of muscles she did not know she had to keep from falling off. "I didn't bring my camera so I would blend in better, but I still wish—I wish I had one."

"Maybe someday you'll get to come back to visit."

"Maybe."

"And if you do, you can bet I'm coming with you."

She smiled as they began their ride back to the clinic station. To hot showers and non-spicy food.

How was it possible to look forward to going and still hate leaving so much?

Neena had walked halfway down the trail to wave goodbye. Other villagers, outside their homes tending to gardens damaged from the cyclone, watching with curiosity. Asha saw Aunt Alia and waved. She smiled as her mother's aunt made a beeline straight for Neena, gesturing toward Asha. It was clear from Neena's guarded response that she was asking her usual flurry of questions.

Too soon Alia, Neena and the village were all gone completely from view.

Trees and foliage surrounded them for several miles. Asha relaxed in the peaceful surroundings. She wrapped her arms around Mark and leaned against his strong back.

With only a mile or two to go until they arrived at the clinic, Mark pulled to the side of the path and stopped.

"Did you leave something behind?" Asha asked.

"Nope." Mark reached into his pocket for his cell phone and started pushing buttons.

"Who are you calling?"

"Nobody."

Looking around to make sure no one was in sight, she punched him lightly on the arm. "You know I hate it when you do that maddening vague-answer thing."

He grinned, but continued to push buttons, not letting her see what he was doing.

"You're just trying to annoy me, aren't you?"

"Not exactly," he said. "That's just an added bonus."

"Rrrgg."

"Ah, there it is." He turned the phone so Asha could see.

She gasped. "How did you—when did you get this?"

His phone showed a photograph of Asha, her mother and Neena.

"Back when we were in the hut and they were both focused on talking to you. I took it quick when no one was looking. Thought you might like something to remember them by."

Something like a happy squeal came out of Asha's mouth. She threw her dirty arms around him and held tight. "Oh, Mark, thank you!" She jumped down from the bike to hug him better. "Thank you so much."

When he pulled back to look into her face, she smiled saucily. "I think you really might be the perfect man."

"What?"

She laughed. "I found it in my Bible reading the other day. It's in Psalms, chapter thirty-seven I think. It said 'Mark the perfect man . . . for the end of that man is peace.' If you take it completely out of context and put a comma right there at the beginning, well . . ."

He chuckled. "Remind me later to bring that to your attention again."

Her laughter reached around to embrace them both. This time, with no one around to object, Mark lowered his head as he pulled Asha closer to him. His kiss was soft and she melted into it.

She opened her eyes to see his head bending down once more, but he stopped himself from kissing her again, instead leaning his forehead against hers. Clearing his throat, he looked down the path. "We'd better get going. I need to get flights arranged for us to leave as soon as possible for Dhaka."

"The capital city?" Asha did not really care where they went, so long as he was with her and there was any possibility of being kissed like that again. "Why there?"

"I got some information from Rashid that I plan to deal with." His face suddenly went hard. "About the stolen babies from your village."

"Whoa." She pulled her head back to look at him. "When were you going to tell me about this plan?"

He shrugged. "Well, you're not exactly in it."

"Are you kidding? Then let's rearrange the plan so I can be in it."

He laughed and pulled his hands up to cup her face. "I love you, Asha." He pressed a kiss to her pert nose then laughed again. "We'll talk about it after we get back and get cleaned up." Looking her over, his grin widened. "You need a bath even more than I do."

Asha reached down to pick up a handful of dried mud from the path. She looked him over mischievously. "I could fix that, you know."

His laughter echoed through the trees around them. He gripped her hand until she dropped the dirt, then kissed the back of her palm.

"Come on, Beautiful." He started up the bike. "Let's get going."

CHAPTER FOURTY-ONE

Asha asked to go shopping the moment they arrived in Dhaka, the capital city of Bangladesh. They had left the clinic after hugs and prayers from the nurses, then Chittagong, so quickly, there had been no time to find new clothing, and she was eager to replace the torn, stained outfit she had worn for weeks.

She twirled over to check her new salwar kameez in the shop's mirror. "I feel so much better! It feels so good to be clean again."

A figure emerged behind her. "You look better, too."

She turned her head. "I'd think that was insulting except I had the unpleasant experience of looking in a mirror when we first got back to the clinic station." She cringed. "I couldn't even count the layers of dirt I finally got to wash off, after all that time in my family's village, then the cyclone, then the attack and 'camping out' in the great outdoors with the Christian village."

Her mention of the cyclone seemed to sober Mark. He put warm hands on her shoulders.

Asha leaned her head against the broad muscles of his chest and sighed. "I still can't believe you came for me," she breathed out softly.

Mark wrapped his arms around her in a quick squeeze before releasing her. "And I still can't believe I'm taking you with me tonight."

She bit back a smile. "You know it will help your cover to have me along."

"I know."

"And if you left me behind, just think of all the trouble I might get in before you got back."

"I know—wait a minute—"

Asha maintained her serious face for only a moment before a laugh burst through.

"I heard once that teasing is a sign of affection for some people." She approached where Mark now stood near the window and stood on tiptoe to plant a quick kiss on his newly-shaven cheek. "Figured I'd better start practicing."

For several seconds, the look he sent her way was enough to curl her toes.

A phone alarm brought Mark back to attention. He pulled his cell phone from his pocket, checked the time, then once again looked down at the traffic below.

"We'd better go." He turned to her, now serious. "Are you sure you want to be part of this?"

Asha's face held no doubt. "He stole me and others. I want to be part of shutting him down."

Nodding, Mark led them down to the main floor of the department store and outside toward the street.

"There are two things I just don't understand," Asha said as they boarded a yellow auto-rickshaw. She was yelling to be heard over the noise of the motor. "For one, how did he get all those babies from the village all the way to Dhaka without people knowing about it?"

Mark's eyebrows furrowed. "Well, I'd guess he brought them one at a time. No one would question seeing a man with one baby traveling by bus or plane. And if someone did think it odd that he was traveling with a baby but no wife or nanny, he could make up some story about his wife being in the clinic, or his wife dying and him needing to take the baby to his parents or something."

"Hmm, that makes sense."

"What is the other thing?"

"The other thing?"

"You said there were two things you didn't understand."

"Oh," Asha smiled. "I was thinking so hard I forgot." She raised her voice to be heard clearly. "The other thing was, if for the past twenty years Ahmad had been stealing only baby boys from the village, why did he kidnap me?"

Mark gave the address to the driver. "I've wondered about that, too." He looked her way as if her face held the answer. "You're way too pretty to be confused with a boy."

She melted under his gaze, then smiled. "Well, I was only newly born. I doubt I looked much different than . . . my . . ."

Her eyes opened wide.

". . . brother."

"Of course!" Mark slapped a hand to his forehead. "I can't believe I didn't think of that. Ahmad must have been trying to steal your brother and accidentally stole you."

She sat still as stone, except for her hands which were trembling. Mark reached across to grasp both her shaking hands in one of his.

"He wanted to steal him, not me." Asha's voice shuddered under the weight of the truth. "Which is why he had to take me to Cindy Stewart instead of bringing me to Dhaka. Nobody would have wanted to adopt a girl baby." Her voice trailed off. "If he had succeeded in taking my brother, I would have grown up in that village. I would have been married off as a teenager."

She shivered. "Or I could have been the one to topple over in that boat and not know how to swim."

Her eyes shut tight. The city noises pushing through the taxi's open doorways disappeared. The trembling in her hands flashed through her body as she faced the destiny chosen for her from the foundation of the world.

"It was God," she whispered. "All this time, all those years I thought I was a victim. It was all God." Her eyes opened to beseech Mark. "But why me? Why not my brother? Why not Neena, or some other girl whose heart would have been better than mine?"

"Mark . . ." Her voice broke. "I didn't deserve it."

The taxi lurched. Mark braced himself with a hand to the metal that boxed around the empty doorway. His other hand reached to run down Asha's hair.

Thankful for the darkness, Asha turned to rest her cheek against his hand. A teardrop ran across it.

Mark's voice was hushed, raw. "Asha, God's grace chose you. I can't tell you why. Maybe so you could help Rani escape last summer. Maybe so you could give the hope of God's love to your mother and Neena these past weeks."

He pulled her into his arms for just a moment as they approached the restaurant. "Or maybe it was just because He loves you."

"But I don't—I don't—"

The taxi screeched to a halt and Mark and Asha quickly separated as the garish neon light in front of the restaurant reached in and found them.

Mark paid the driver and stepped down. He looked the restaurant over. Then his eyes went back to Asha.

"Or maybe . . ." He waited until she stepped down from the taxi and stood at his side. "Maybe God knew I needed you in my life to keep it from being too normal."

Asha's tears dissolved into a gulping laugh. "Boy, you know how to say just the right thing, don't you?"

He smiled, then looked up at the partially broken sign flashing the restaurant name.

A glance around had Asha stepping closer to Mark. Across the trash-strewn road stood several shacks, if they could be called even that. Only about three feet wide and maybe four feet high, their walls and roofs were made from discarded plastic bags, a meager covering against the frequent rains. "How can anyone live like that?"

A child emerged from one of the shacks, brandishing an empty plastic water bottle as if he had earned a trophy.

Immediately he was surrounded by a group of boys. Within seconds they were playing a rousing game of soccer, kicking the bottle as their ball.

Asha was smiling at their laughter when Mark spoke quietly behind her. “Remember, we’re not going to lie, but we’re going to give the impression we’re a newly married couple.”

“I’m not sure how to do that,” Asha joked. “I’ve never been a newly married couple before.”

He rolled his eyes. “Have you been taking lessons from my dad or something?”

She giggled, then sobered as they neared the restaurant entrance. “To be honest, I’m trying to keep talking so I don’t throw up. Just the thought of what happens in this place makes me feel literally sick.”

“I know what you mean.” Mark’s voice lowered to a whisper. When they reached the door, both stopped talking altogether.

Asha reached up and covered her head with her *orna.* She remembered a night a year ago when she wanted to run away from the evil, but she had to stay for the sake of another. Now, resisting the urge to tell Mark he was on his own and head as fast as she could back to the hotel, Asha determined to see this through.

The lives of future children in her village were at stake.

CHAPTER FOURTY-TWO

"I have heard this is a good place."

Very appeasing to the white man and his young "bride," the waiter led them, with several grins back in their direction, to a cozy booth in a darkened corner of the restaurant.

Everything about the place made Asha think of the word shady. Dim lights illuminated tables without revealing the faces of the people sitting at them. Old booths, several with what looked like knife tears in the cushions, ran along the back wall across from the bar, where quite a few men were enjoying quite a few too many drinks.

Raucous laughter competed with the cigarette smoke for the most unappealing part of the establishment. Asha coughed and tried to wave some of the haze away from her face. Was it rude to do that when most of the occupants were too drunk to notice anyway?

The man gestured toward their booth with an accommodating smile, but Mark did not sit down.

Asha stood mutely behind him, trying not to breathe, her head down and her mouth closed, as she knew was expected of a wife in such a man-based setting. Inwardly she was stomping her foot and shouting at all of them to stop drinking their money away and go home to feed their children.

Mark looked around, for all appearances an arrogant foreigner used to getting his way. Then he leaned close to the waiter and said, "I am an important man, with much power in my position."

Asha coughed again, but this time it was to keep from laughing. The man nodded seriously.

"This woman," Mark gestured behind him toward Asha, "is not with child, if you know what I mean."

Asha certainly knew what he meant!

"What good is a wife if she bears no son?"

She wanted to kick him from behind. He was enjoying this a little too much, she could tell.

The man was nodding vigorously in empathy as Mark continued. "I do not wish for another wife."

Well, at least that was something nice to say, Asha thought, her eyes still down. She blinked them; they were stinging from the smoke.

"One wife is expensive enough, if you know what I mean."

This time, on his left calf where no one else could see it, she did give him a small kick.

It was Mark's turn to cough down a laugh.

The man stepped closer. He was about Asha's height and had to look up to face Mark. "So you are wishing for a child without having to get another wife. Of course, of course this is what you want."

Mark frowned. "A man wants a son to carry on his name. I have heard there are places one can get such a wish without having to . . . deal with the unpleasant delay of government paperwork. Is that so?"

Looking left and right, then up at Mark with a greedy little smile, the man bowed again. "You have come to the right place, sir." Immediately he escorted Mark farther back into the restaurant and around a small partition where two small tables sat.

Asha followed. She did not even consider staying the ten steps back required of some wives, instead keeping so close to Mark she nearly stepped on his heels.

Once they were seated at the farthest of the tables, the man excused himself to get "the boss."

Asha stole a glance toward Mark. She wanted to ask what he thought really went on in this place. Were there children being hidden somewhere in this building? Under the restaurant perhaps?

She dropped her hands and gripped the sides of her chair to keep from bolting from it and storming down the stairs after that man and forcing him to tell her where they kept the babies.

Mark put his elbows on the table and folded his hands together. He leaned forward so his hands covered the movements of his mouth. Asha assumed the action was to hide his words in case someone was watching by surveillance camera.

"Stay calm," he said softly. "We can't help any of these kids by acting rashly."

Had the man read her mind? Asha looked up at him.

"Your feelings are showing again."

His voice was loving and kind. She felt tears threatening to fall and dropped her face down as the sound of footsteps came up the stairs.

Her eyes peeked sideways to see a large man, the largest Bangladeshi Asha had ever seen, approaching their table. The waiter followed him, practically tripping over himself in his attempts to reach in front of the man to pull out his chair without actually putting his body in front of him in any way.

The man stood impatiently as the waiter apologized for knocking over his chair. Once upright again, the chair creaked and groaned under the weight as the man sat. He leaned back and spoke in English. "I do not see many Americans in my restaurant."

His tone was lazy, casual, but with a dark undercurrent of suspicion. Asha heard her gulp sound loudly into the silence. How did he know she was an American?

He didn't, of course, she realized once her mind thawed from its paralyzed fright. He was speaking of Mark, not her.

"I explained my situation to your waiter," Mark said. "I have money to pay. Can you help us or not?"

The man clicked his tongue. Asha was glad her head was down and she did not have to look into his face. Just his voice held such corruption it sent chills down her back.

"You Americans are always so impatient. So in a hurry. You think you can have whatever you want if you only have enough money."

Mark stood abruptly to his feet. "I can find another place to get what I came for." He gave the Bengali version of snapping his fingers and Asha dutifully rose to her feet, never lifting her face from the ground.

"I see you like our women's submissive ways," the man said, motioning for Mark to retake his seat. "Better than those Western women who—"

"Will you be able to give me what I want?"

Asha wondered if Mark's interruption was to continue his portrayal of an impatient foreigner, or if he spoke quickly to keep the words on the tip of Asha's tongue from spurting out.

The man chuckled, for all appearances still lazily in charge, but Asha noticed he shifted to sit more upright in his chair. He put a hand, palm open, on the table.

"What do you have to offer?"

Mark scowled at the hand. "What do you have to give?"

Asha's peripheral vision saw the man's jaw tightening. She kept her eyes on her twisting hands, praying Mark would not push him too far.

The man's hand gave an almost imperceptible gesture and immediately the waiter was at his side.

"Take this man downstairs to room two." His voice was low and cold. It changed to slippery and light when he spoke to Mark. "You may go downstairs to choose your new son."

Asha suddenly felt his eyes on her and she held her breath to keep from shaking.

"Your woman can wait here, with me."

Her breath let out and she trembled so much she had to bite her tongue so her teeth would not chatter.

"A wife should follow her husband, don't you think?"

Relieved at the undercurrent of steel in Mark's voice, Asha quickly rose and crossed around the table opposite the man to stand by Mark's side. They followed the waiter from the room into a narrow, darkened stairway.

Descending, taking care on the steep steps, Asha felt her foot catch against something. With no banister to cling to, she reached out to brace herself against the walls on both sides of the stairway.

Mark's hand reached back to steady her. For a moment, as the waiter continued on unaware, Mark looked behind him and his gaze caught hers. Asha's eyes held her fear at what they were about to see. She grasped his outreached hand and her grip was painfully tight.

He let go of her hand and softly, quickly, reached up to palm her cheek, his thumb caressing her skin, his eyes telling her to hold out a little longer.

Wordlessly she nodded and he dropped his hand. His gaze descended to the small purse she carried. The gaudy clutch was covered with brightly-colored, cheap jewels and tiny decorative mirrors, with one square missing.

When his gaze returned to hers, again Asha nodded.

"We are almost there." The waiter's voice from below signaled Mark to hurry down the rest of the stairs, Asha close behind.

Having reached the floor below, they faced an extremely narrow hallway walled entirely in gray, unpainted concrete. Several doors hinted of rooms on both sides.

Asha found herself trembling again. She grasped her purse tightly in both hands and held it directly in front of her, as if fearful of it being taken.

The man looked back at them and chuckled. "He will want a high price from you," he said with a whisper. "Americans always pay a higher price—they know he can turn them in at the embassy for child trafficking, so they pay anything he asks."

The man's bearing took on an edge of superiority. "If you give me a small tip," he offered, halting their progress down the hall, "I could possibly give you better choices then the boss would for your money."

Mark slipped a few *taka* notes toward the man. "You are wise," he said, his smile satisfied. "It is good to have a . . . friend . . . in this business."

The man reached to his left and turned a doorknob. Slowly, the door creaked open and he motioned them inside.

Asha stepped in behind Mark and immediately wished she were wearing a *burkah* that covered her face. Putting a hand to her mouth, she forced herself not to turn away from the sight before her.

Against her emotions, Asha forced herself to walk through the room like a curious buyer, then she stood directly in front of the waiter. She tried to get herself to be still; her purse was visibly shaking in front of her.

Only one child was bothering to cry. "This one is new," the waiter explained. He half-smiled. "He must still miss his parents.

Bile rose in Asha's throat. For the first time in her life she wanted to physically harm someone. She was imagining causing this man great pain when Mark spoke.

"Do you have any older children? Babies are so much trouble."

His voice had been devoid of feeling, but Asha could see his hands clenching into fists behind him.

The waiter shook his head with a few clicks of his tongue, as if sympathizing with Mark's disappointment. "We do not adopt out the older boys," he said, again motioning toward the babies as if trying to draw Mark's attention back to them. "Only the babies. There is a great demand in Dubai and the Middle East for the older boys as jockeys in the camel races."

"And girls?"

"I am sure the American does not want a girl baby." The man chuckled. "However, if you would like an older girl, to serve as a maid perhaps . . ." At this he elbowed Mark, grinning wickedly at his own joke. "We have a woman in another part of the city who deals with the girls. She is expensive, but her products are of very high quality."

Asha stepped back and nearly fell against the wall, using its hard strength to hold her upright. The room began to spin around her. Sweat dripped down her face as her chest heaved.

"Your children are malnourished and skinny," Mark said harshly. "I will leave and think about your choices." He handed a rather large sum of money to the protesting waiter and motioned for Asha to leave the room. She did not hesitate.

Mark remained in the doorway as Asha fled into the hallway and up the first few steps. When she looked down at him, tears streaming unnoticed down her face, and gave a small nod, he turned back to the waiter still inside the room.

"I want to know where I can find the woman who sells the girls," Mark whispered.

The waiter hesitated and Mark helped make him more comfortable by slipping him another handful of money.

Swallowing, then leaning forward toward Mark, he said a name and address very quietly.

It was only after he shut the door behind him and they were again climbing the staircase that Asha was aware the room they had vacated was now silent. Even the crying child had stopped, as if he, too, finally recognized along with the others that all hope was gone.

CHAPTER FOURTY-THREE

Asha was standing on the balcony outside her hotel room, gripping the railing as she waited for Mark's return.

He had left early that morning. Now, Asha wished she had asked him where he was going and what he would do. At the time she had only wanted to hide in her room with the lights out, trying unsuccessfully to pretend what she had seen yesterday could not have been real.

Children for sale. How could it be possible?

As they rode home the night before, Asha begged Mark to let her return to the restaurant and buy all the children they had seen.

He had lifted her face and waited until her eyes met his, then he asked her to trust him. She could not ignore the sincerity and genuine care in his gaze. She nodded, then when they reached the hotel, he had held her to him as they stood outside her door. The small gesture of kindness was her undoing and she sobbed against him until exhaustion finally blurred the images in her mind. She was able to release them long enough to say goodnight, mechanically ready herself for bed, then fall asleep.

Sleep, however, brought the images back as she dreamed of children, hundreds and thousands of children, all ages and sizes, being stolen from their homes and sold. Their hands reached out to beg for help, for freedom, for their parents.

The morning sun brought the small comfort of at least leaving the dreams behind, though Asha knew she would never escape the haunting memory of what she had seen the previous night.

Horns blared and pedestrians bartered at a small market below Asha's window as she watched and waited for Mark.

"Don't you know what is happening?" she nearly shouted at them. Were they truly unaware? Did they not know of the evil that thrived just around the corner from them?

"Don't you care?"

This she did shout, but no one heard her over the sounds and distractions of the everyday life bustling beneath her.

Rage and helplessness and despair propelled her inside. She slammed the sliding balcony door and looked around for anything, any way to release the pent-up feelings.

A flash of light reflecting off a tiny mirror brought Asha's attention to the purse she had carried the night before. It was hideous, but had been the perfect way to conceal Mark's small camera with its video recorder.

She lifted the purse and turned it over until she found the one missing jewel space, the small hole where the recorder's camera extension had fit through to video everything they had seen and heard at the restaurant and the room below.

Pushing fingers into the hole, she pulled and yanked until the material gave way. She ripped and tore until the purse was completely destroyed, its jewels and mirrors scattered around her feet, winking in the light cheerfully as if ignoring the shreds of cloth that surrounded them.

When there was nothing left to tear, Asha sank down among the shreds and fake jewels and wept.

Mark knocked softly on the door, hesitant to disturb Asha if she had been able to fall back to sleep.

The sound of her sobbing reached his ears, however, and brought him quickly to her side.

Mark's eyes swept the area where she sat on the floor, the jewels scattered around her, the shreds of cloth, some still gripped in the hands she held up against her face.

He felt the familiar hurt he now knew would always grip his heart when she was hurting. Kneeling down beside her, he gathered her into his arms and she quickly jerked away, then looking up to see it was him, she flung her arms around him, buried her face in his neck, and sobbed afresh.

"Mark," she choked out. "How can they do it? How can they?"

He willed his voice to be soft even as his own muscles tightened with the desire to exact vengeance against such evil. "I don't know how they can do such things," he said gently. Then his jaw clenched. "Or did such things. God willing, they will never be able to do them again."

With a gasp, she was facing him, her hands clenching his shirt in eagerness. "It worked?" She pulled on his shirt like a child. "I mean, I don't even know what you did, but—well—did what you did—well, what did you do?"

His heart turned over with love and he pulled her to him once again. Her tears had stopped and she waited, her head against his chest but her body tensed. Mark could feel the curiosity emanating from her.

"All during the day before we went to the restaurant," Mark began, and Asha pulled back to sit up on her knees and watch his face as he spoke. "I researched to see if there were any groups of Bangladeshis here in the capital city that were actively working against child trafficking."

At the phrase "child trafficking" she winced, then nodded for him to continue. "I didn't want to just go to the police. I've heard so many of them can be paid off, and that would not help anything."

She was nodding rapidly now, urging him forward in his story. He could not help but smile at the childish eagerness on her face. It suddenly sobered him to think of the weight of hope she had placed on him. The trust she had willingly and unquestioningly given, where before she would have questioned and in the beginning would have denied him completely as she sought to find the solution herself.

They had both grown and changed over the past year. Now they worked as a team, and this new sense of responsibility as being the head of that team suddenly weighed heavily upon his spirit. He would need to seek the Lord's guidance always, to walk worthy of the trust she had chosen to place in him.

"Mark." Asha was tugging on his shirt again. "You're doing that thinking-and-not-talking thing again that drives me crazy. What happened next?"

He could not help but smile as he kissed her on the forehead and continued. "Well, to make a long story short . . ."

She nodded, happy with that idea.

"I found the right group and contacted them to ask what we could do. They were the ones who told me I needed some firm evidence that trafficking really was going on there before they could act. So that's why we took the camera last night and got a video."

She was suddenly picking up the shreds of cloth that used to be a purse, her hands moving quickly over the floor all around her.

"Why are you doing that?"

"I don't know." She shrugged and continued, now gathering the jewels and mirrors. "What happened next?"

"After we came back to the hotel last night and you went to your room, I was so angry I knew I wouldn't be able to sleep."

Her eyes flashed toward his and Mark saw the understanding there. Somehow it made him feel more like a man.

"So I left and took the video right away to the rescue group downtown. They called an emergency meeting and after everyone watched the video, they made a plan to act immediately."

Asha had unconsciously dropped the jewels back onto the floor and was shifting, kind of bouncing, on her knees where she sat. "And?"

"And this morning I went back there and found out the restaurant has been shut down, the man and the waiter arrested, and the children rescued."

"Oh!" With a squeal of victory, Asha threw herself back into Mark's arms. He laughed, his own relief as strong as hers, though his outward expression of it would never be as noticeable, he thought with a smile.

As quickly as she had come his direction, she now released him and backed away. "What about the babies? The children? What will happen to them?"

Mark thought to drop his arms, which had remained outstretched, unable to keep up with her rapid changes in direction. "I'm not sure," he said. "But I did tell them about your village and they said they would contact someone at the clinic station in Hatigram to see if they could come out and help transport the children back to your village. The ones who can be claimed by their families will be returned, and any unclaimed children will be placed up for adoption."

Another squeal. Another hug. This time it was Mark who pulled away and put Asha at arm's length to face him. "I don't want you to get your hopes up, though," he warned. "They said with Ahmad still being in the village, they are not sure how to keep it from happening again."

"Why don't they just go and arrest Ahmad, too?"

"They have no evidence against him. We'll just have to pray that God will somehow expose Ahmad for who he really is."

Seeing the anger building on her face, he turned the conversation another direction. "I also gave them the name and address of the lady—well, the woman; she's no lady—who the waiter told me manages the girls' side of this operation. They will be looking into that also, hopefully soon enough to catch them before word spreads about last night and they move on."

"Oh, Mark." Asha's voice breathed admiration as if he were the hero in a great story. He wished he could think of it that way—that the story was over and he had brought them to the happy ending.

A resoluteness, a firm commitment was building in his heart. Seeing those children, knowing the woman he loved was once stolen like they were, made the need real and urgent and his own. He had always resisted the idea of Asha putting her life and future into rescuing the women and children who were stolen and sold, but now he understood better why she needed to do this. And he now saw clearly that he not only needed to be willing to support this desire, but to help her in it.

Again, he was holding her, this time as Asha cried in relief and joy. His own heart cried out to God for strength to face this dangerous future together. For now he knew, like never before, that they belonged together.

And soon, he would tell her so.

CHAPTER FOURTY-FOUR

Alia's chatter did not falter as she lowered herself to the ground, declining when Shazari and Neena asked if she wanted to help repair the fence from the cyclone's damage. "Don't be ridiculous. I can't work with this bad leg paining me so much."

She barely breathed before continuing her tirade. "Fools! All of us were fools! To let that man take our babies right out from under our noses all these years. I can't believe we all thought it was the Evil Eye when all the time it was a person right here in our midst! Unthinkable!"

"Well, I'm just glad Asha got out of here safely before Ahmad came back," Neena said, looking down at her work. She had begun to brave joining in the conversation every once in awhile, but still did not have the nerve to look at anyone while doing so.

"I am, too." Shazari smiled, then worked the muscles of her jaw. She was not used to smiling and it was beginning to hurt. "But I feel badly for the rest of the women in our village. As long as Ahmad lives here, having a baby will remain cause for fear instead of rejoicing."

"Not if I can help it!"

Shazari looked over at her aunt. "What are you going to do, Aunt? Fight Ahmad?"

Neena giggled at the joke, but Alia did not. "We women may seem helpless in this world, but I've been manipulating my circumstances long enough to know exactly what to do about Ahmad. He can stay right here in this village as long as he pleases, but his power over all of us women is over."

Her emphatic declaration was accompanied by her fist slapping into her palm for emphasis. "Over, I say!"

"And just how are you going to stop Ahmad? He's been doing this for twenty years and no one but us even knows it is him."

"Ah, yes." Alia's grin was malicious. She stood and wiped the dust from her clothing. "But I'm going to visit my neighbor this afternoon. We'll have a little chat. Talk about how Neena went to the Christian village and found out they had not stolen even one of our children. About how Ahmad started the rumor about the Christians, how Ahmad is the one who leaves the village right around the time a baby goes missing, how Ahmad always has so much more money . . ."

"There are a lot of good men in our village," Alia continued, "who will not like to hear that they attacked innocent people because one of their own deceived them. A few choice words of distrust about Ahmad is all it will take. They'll figure out the rest."

She waved goodbye and started down the path, forgetting to limp on her bad leg. "By tomorrow the whole village will be buzzing with the news." Several steps away, she turned once more with a triumphant smile. "Never underestimate the power of a well-placed rumor, especially if it's true!"

As she walked out of earshot, Shazari muttered to Neena, "Is it possible there is someone else in the village who loves gossip more than she does? Just who is she going to tell?"

Neena laughed. It was a new sound to both their ears. "Who cares? This is the best 'gossip' I've ever heard!"

Shazari nodded. Her sore mouth ached as she smiled yet again. "It is, indeed."

CHAPTER FOURTY-FIVE

Ahmad was seething. He stood in front of the restaurant, trying again to turn the knob.

It was locked. Stepping back, he looked again at the boarded-up windows, the smashed neon sign. All the information was there for him to see and Ahmad did not like it.

A boy wearing tattered shorts and nothing else, not even shoes, ran by, his sweaty skin brushing up against Ahmad's best pants. Ahmad's arm snaked out and grabbed him.

"Ouch! You're hurting me!"

The boy looked up. He saw Ahmad's business clothing and pulled away as far as he could. "I didn't mean to!" he pleaded, trying to wrench his arm from Ahmad's grip. "Let me go!"

"You're obviously from the slum across the street." Ahmad did not even try to conceal his disdain. He yanked the boy, who cried out in pain. "What happened to this restaurant?"

"They shut it down." The boy was using his free hand to try to pull Ahmad's hand away, finger by finger.

Ahmad just gripped harder. "Tell me more."

The boy winced and cried out. "Everybody is talking about it," he said. "They arrested a big man and then they found babies in the basement. The man was selling the babies."

Ahmad's voice was cold. "How did they find out about the babies?"

"I don't know!"

Ahmad gave another yank until the boy's face was near his own. "Think!" he ordered. "Did anything strange happen here before that? Did anyone unusual come?"

The boy's eyes were swinging wildly around for an escape. "No, I don't remember anything!" he cried. "Except for the white man, nothing was strange!"

"The white man?" Ahmad's face paled. "What white man?"

"I don't know! The night it all happened, a white man with yellow hair came to the restaurant. That's all."

"Was he alone?"

"No, he had a Bangladeshi woman with him. His wife, I guess."

With a shove, Ahmad released the boy. He did not even notice as the child scurried away across the street and back into the slums.

His face was toward the restaurant again, but his eyes were far away, picturing a Bangladeshi woman from America who had stood up to him that day on the village path. A visitor from the West who asked too many questions, who did not keep her eyes down as she should, who had so far managed to escape him.

The girl he had once tried to sell to a Westerner surely had many American friends, even white men with yellow hair.

Breathing hard, Ahmad felt hatred fester into something dark and alive within him. Somehow she had found out everything. She had thwarted his entire livelihood.

His eyes narrowed to slits. He would find out how she had discovered his methods. He would find out who she had gotten her information from.

Then he would find her. And he would make her pay.

He would make them all pay.

CHAPTER FOURTY-SIX

Asha rode beside Mark in the rickshaw, sighing with contentment. He would not tell her where they were going, and she did not care. They could ride around for hours if he wanted. She was just enjoying being back in India, being safe, and being with the man she loved.

When they stopped, Asha glanced lazily to the side of the road where Mark was paying the rickshaw driver. The backdrop behind him brought a quick smile to her face. It was their banyan tree, one of the happiest places in the world.

She stepped carefully from the rickshaw, sending a look of complete love in Mark's direction.

He turned toward her as the rickshaw drove away. "This way, Princess," he said, gesturing toward the path that led to their special spot by the tree's main trunk.

Asha turned toward the path and gasped. "Mark," she breathed out. The walkway was covered in rose petals—yellow and red ones strewn from where she stood in amazement to where she and Mark always sat.

Heart pounding with anticipation, Asha followed the path, stepping gingerly over the beautiful petals.

"Oh." Asha's hand flew to her heart. Around the base of the tree, in an oval, was a pile of deep red roses, scores of them, their beauty beckoning her.

He's going to propose, was Asha's next thought. No other thoughts would follow. *He's going to propose!*

Mark stood behind her to the side, watching her reaction. Looking around to be sure no one was in sight, he slipped past her, taking her hand and leading her to stand inside the oval of flowers.

"Asha," he said gently. He took her hands in his, looking down at her with all the love she ever could have hoped for. Her heart sighed. Her toes curled.

She looked up into the face she loved more than any other in the world. A drop of moisture edged her eyes. Another hit her cheek. Then her hand.

Mark's eyes went upward. "You've got to be kidding," he mumbled. He stood still, his eyes shifting down to the drop of rain on her hand, back to the sky, then to her hand again.

Asha waited as one drop, then two, then a hundred fell to interrupt her beautiful moment.

No, no, no! she was saying inside, watching Mark's brows come together. She could tell he was trying to decide whether to continue or not. *I don't care about the rain,* she tried to communicate with her eyes. *It's monsoon season; you couldn't help that. Please say what you were going to say.*

His eyes traveled over her face, reading, questioning. Finally, with the rain falling all around them, he began to speak again. "Asha, I have loved you since you walked into my world last summer. I loved you the year we were apart, and I have loved you more each day since you came back . . ."

Asha felt tears join the raindrops on her cheeks. They were both completely soaked, the roses all around them sinking into the ground from the weight of the downpour.

Mark opened his mouth, but instead of speaking, his face broke into a wide, boyish grin. He reached into his back pocket and pulled out a small, wrapped package.

Hands trembling, Asha took the small gift, her hands traveling over the paper. It was not shaped like a ring box. What could it be?

Looking up at him curiously, receiving only a wink in response, Asha tore open the paper. It fell away easily, already weakened and tearing from the rain.

Inside was a small roll of scotch tape. Asha held it up, then once again looked up into Mark's eyes.

His smile was shy. "I was wondering if . . . someday . . . you would help me tape a bunch of roses to a car. For us."

Her eyes widened. Asha clenched the tape to her heart and opened her mouth to speak.

"Oh dear, you never know when a monsoon rain will come and ruin a great idea."

Both Asha and Mark turned to see Mark's grandmother, Eleanor Stephens, approaching. Her upper half remained dry under an umbrella and a wry smile crept across her face. "I'm so sorry, Mark dear, it really was a perfect plan. I wondered about those clouds while I was setting up the roses for you. But you'd never get anything accomplished if you waited for a dry day during monsoon season."

Asha tried to smile, but she knew the attempt was as fake as a cubic zirconium. Her hands had slipped from Mark's the moment Mrs. Stephen's voice interrupted them under the tree.

Mark's hands were now in his pockets. "Yeah," he said, his whole body communicating his discomfort. "Well, thanks for helping me give it a try, Grams."

The elderly woman sighed dreamily. "Well, it was a totally romantic idea, rain or no rain, wasn't it, Asha?"

By then Asha was able to put her disappointment someplace far from sight. "It was," she agreed, then snuck a glance up at Mark. "It was perfect."

Mark's head bent down to look at her. His features were full of regret. Rain dripped from his bangs and down his nose to rush off headlong toward his shoes.

With a half smile, Mark's grandmother handed him an umbrella. "Why don't you two head back? I'll clean up here and see you both later."

"Aw, thanks, Grams," Mark said with genuine gratitude, "but we wouldn't leave you out in weather like this."

As he spoke, Asha knelt and began filling her arms with wet red roses. "That should do it," she said, rising. Despite the moisture seeping from the flowers through her clothing, she could not help but smile, remembering her dream of one day holding dozens of roses from the man she loved.

"The rain will wash away the rest." Mark took the extra umbrella his grandmother had brought and escorted both women toward the road.

He helped his grandmother into the first waiting rickshaw. "Do you want me to come with you?"

"Don't be ridiculous, dear." The elderly woman patted his shoulder. "I'm not a helpless old lady yet! Besides . . ." Her eyes slid toward Asha. "I believe there is someone else who would appreciate your attention at this moment much more than I would."

Mark grinned. "Thanks, Grams."

Asha took one hand from her roses to wave as Mrs. Stephens rode away. Mark summoned a second rickshaw. They climbed in and waited in silence as the driver drew the plastic tarp across in front of them to shield them from the rain. Once the driver climbed aboard the rickshaw and began pedaling them down the road, Mark took advantage of the covering that allowed a measure of privacy, and reached across to take Asha by the hand.

Her eyes dropped to the hands between them. She twisted hers palm up as his turned to wrap around her fingers, their skin sliding against each other's from the moisture.

"This didn't turn out the way I'd planned. Obviously." Mark's voice was at first wry, then fell to husky and low. It sent shivers down Asha's arm and into her fingers. His own fingers responded with a firm squeeze. "I especially didn't plan on this awful waiting for your answer while my set-up lady decided to show up and—um—help."

Asha was still looking at their clasped hands. She wanted to cry. To laugh. To giggle like a schoolgirl getting her first love note.

"Just in case you didn't catch it before we were interrupted," Mark's free hand reached across the space between them to lift her chin until her eyes met his. "I want you here, with me, for the rest of our lives."

She wanted to say yes. To whisper it. To shout it. It didn't matter.

Only he hadn't actually asked her anything yet.

He was loving her with his eyes. When he glanced down to their hands, his gaze drifted. Asha wondered why he was staring at her feet, when suddenly he reached down and picked up the red umbrella his grandmother had so considerately loaned them.

Asha was all confusion as Mark sent her a grin and slipped the umbrella up through the opening between the tarp and the rickshaw cover. He opened the umbrella, taking care to avoid poking the unaware rickshaw driver in the back of the head. The bright umbrella covered the entire open space, closing them into a cocoon of privacy and tinting everything inside into a hazy crimson color.

Mark balanced the handle of the umbrella to hang over the top rope of the tarp. Thus secured, his hands left the umbrella and reached to frame Asha's face. His hands urged her closer, so close their noses almost touched.

"Asha," he said. "Will you marry me?"

The world seemed to swirl around and stop all at the same time. She looked up at this man who, amazingly, loved her. Loved her enough to want to marry her.

Rain poured all around them. Their tiny, enclosed space was filled with humidity. The rain that had soaked her turned to steam.

Asha noticed nothing. Nothing but Mark's eyes.

Her own filled with light. She bit the smile that was bursting through. "It's about time you came out and asked," she teased.

Then she licked her lips, looked at him with a lifetime of love, and whispered. "Yes."

His hand brushed down her cheek softly, sweetly.

"I love you," she whispered.

He kissed her then. She melted into the hands on her face, felt herself falling toward the feelings emanating from him.

When the rickshaw stopped she did not move. She wanted to stay right there forever, basking in the feel of his lips on hers.

She was glad it had rained. Glad Mark's grandmother had come and sent them back with an umbrella. Glad for monsoon season. It was fitting they had this moment in a rickshaw, rain all around them.

When Mark touched his forehead to hers and mentioned with regret that they should go inside, Asha looked down, suddenly shy, and said quietly, "I'd rather stay here with you."

He pulled her to him again. She nestled her head into the curve of his shoulder as his arms wrapped around her. His fingers reached up to tangle in her hair. "Me, too."

But then he pulled away again and smiled. "But I have a surprise waiting for you inside."

Asha's eyebrows rose. She followed him from the rickshaw through the rain into the compound.

What could it be? She kept close to him in anticipation. Was it a ring?

CHAPTER FOURTY-SEVEN

Asha more-or-less followed Mark to his grandmother's home. He walked calmly and she skipped around him, sloshing through the puddles, trying to contain her curiosity.

The moment he opened the door and she stepped inside her mouth dropped in shock.

"Surprise!"

"Hi, honey! Oh, you're soaked! You should go change before you catch cold!"

Asha burst into happy laughter. "I don't believe it! Mom! Dad! What in the world? When did you get here? I can't believe this—I'm so happy to see you!" She looked back pointedly at Mark as she hugged them both. "Why didn't anyone tell me you were coming?"

"We wanted to surprise you, of course," her father said, his arm still around her.

"Well, you succeeded!" Asha laughed again. "I just can't believe you're here!"

"When we heard about—"

"Now, hon." Asha smiled as her mother patted her father's hand to delicately interrupt. "Let's let her get changed first. She's dripping everywhere and we don't want her to get sick."

Oh, if they only knew. Asha kissed her mother on the cheek and then excused herself, kissing Mark on the cheek on her way out as well, with only a slight blush.

Once dry, in new clothes, and back at Eleanor Stephens' home, Asha peppered the new guests with questions.

"Oh, wait a minute," she interrupted herself. "First I want to say something, so I make sure I don't forget. Mom, Dad," she reached to grasp a hand of each of them, "I want to tell you how thankful I am for you. For taking me into your family and loving me. For raising me to have big dreams. And then for giving up your own dreams for me and letting me follow my heart all the way out here to find my past. I never realized how much of a sacrifice that must have been for you, but I'm starting to understand, and I'm grateful."

"Oh dear." Manicured hands fluttered around Maryanne Rogers' face. "I was determined not to cry for at least an hour or so."

Mark smiled at Asha's mother, then his smile deepened when Asha's response held in it a hint of her former southern accent. "In the village I realized something. I found that what I had always wanted—to be loved and accepted—was something I didn't need to go across the world to find. It was something I have always had. With you. Thank you—thank you for that."

When Asha started crying as well, her father patted her hand. He reached into a pocket but his hand came up empty. "Used 'em all up on your mother already." He shrugged and Asha laughed.

"Okay, so now tell me how in the world you got here?"

"Likely by plane," Mark quipped. Asha crinkled her nose at him and his smile spread into a wide grin.

"Well, when this young man called us and told us we needed to pray for you, well, I certainly wasn't going to settle for so little information." The words came out in a slow drawl as Mrs. Rogers gestured in Mark's direction. "I insisted he tell us what was going on."

Her husband continued the story. "I had already noticed the cyclone threat—I've been keeping up with the news in that area since you left—and I was concerned, but of course I didn't want to worry your mother."

"You knew about the cyclone and you didn't tell me?" the southern voice huffed.

"Now, Maryanne, we can discuss that later."

"But, I—"

"So when Mark added the information about the threat of an attack, he wasn't even off the phone before your mother was half-packed." He chuckled. "Which worked out well, because Mark had something he wanted to say to me personally."

Asha turned to look at Mark. Was he blushing?

Maryanne Rogers scooted in close to Asha's father and sighed. "Yes, when your father told me that this young man had asked for your hand in marriage—"

Asha gasped and looked back at Mark again. He shrugged self-consciously.

"—well, I knew we just had to come out here. I certainly wasn't going to sit at home biting my nails wondering if you were safe, and on top of that let you get engaged without even meeting the man first!"

Asha's laughter filled the room. To Mark, after the harrowing past week, it was music.

"So I guess I don't have to tell you I just got engaged," she said. "Seems I'm the last to know!"

"Indeed," a new voice added.

They turned to see Eleanor Stephens walk with slow dignity into the room. She also wore fresh dry clothing and only her wet hair testified her part in their adventure. She winked at Asha, then resumed her dignified stance.

They all watched as she reached forward with her right arm. In her outstretched hand she held a piece of aged lace. Once in front of Mark, she smiled with love and opened her palm. The lace fell away to reveal a beautiful antique ring.

An appreciative murmur arose throughout the room. Mark gently took the ring and folded his grandmother in a fond embrace. "Thanks, Grams."

The elderly woman looked tenderly at Asha. "Before Mark's mother died, she called me to her side and asked me to keep her ring for Mark and the woman he was to marry someday." She folded the lace with gentleness, her thoughts upon the past, but then looked up at Asha with a twinkle in her eye. "I've had it set out and ready ever since last summer, since the day you drove those girls out to the Scarlet Cord after rescuing them."

"You knew sooner than I did," Mark said fondly, giving her a squeeze.

"No, you knew, you were just too afraid to admit it."

He chuckled, then his features softened as he approached Asha to bend down on one knee before where she sat on the couch between her parents. Asha bit her lip.

"Asha, I—"

"Hey, wasn't I invited to this party?"

Asha covered her mouth with her hand to keep from laughing out loud.

"Great timing, Dad, as always." Mark's voice held a smile.

"Well, it's not like we haven't all been waiting for you to get around to this for a year now," his dad countered, chuckling at the red that crept up his son's face. "How was I supposed to know that you'd be in such a hurry today I wouldn't have time to get into some dry clothes first? I was outside waiting for your rickshaw when this downpour started."

"Oh my." Maryanne Rogers turned toward Asha. "He really is a teaser, isn't he?"

Asha's own face was turning red at Mark's knowing look. "It's a sign of affection," she said dryly.

"A what?"

"Never mind."

"Well, hey," John Stephens put in, flopping down comfortably in the largest chair, which Asha noted caused her mother to sit up even straighter. "Before you get this all settled . . ."

Mark gave up, dropping from his one knee stance to sit on the floor. Asha giggled.

"I'd better let you know what this is going to cost."

Mark and Asha both turned his way. "Cost?"

John Stephens was grinning. He shrugged. "Well, you know how rumors fly around here," he said. "So if you two are going to get married, well, I just think you both shouldn't be living on this compound together."

Asha noticed Mark sit up straighter. "What do you mean?"

"Do I have to spell it out?" John Stephens chuckled, then said loudly, "You're getting kicked off the compound! We had our big meeting the other day while you were off chasing this girl down, and we decided the compound structure was important to our work collectively, but a hindrance to the work you want to do."

"The work God has called you to do," Eleanor Stephens put in proudly.

"Not to mention, if you two get married, and this little lady is going to be running around rescuing more women, it wouldn't be too smart having that all happening here on the compound where everybody'd know about it, right? So you'd better get some plans to move out pretty soon and start looking for a new place to live!"

Mark sat very still, but Asha bounced in her seat. She reached out to clasp his hand.

"And, my dears," Eleanor Stephens sat beside Asha's mother and reached down to pat Mark's shoulder. "There is a new single missionary coming out in a few months, and when I told her about Asha's little home, she was quite excited about the possibility of living there. It seems God has honored both of your prayers, and given you the desires of your hearts."

Asha was biting her lip again, this time to keep from crying. Mark looked around the room, still stunned. "I—I don't know what to say," he murmured.

"Well, since I got all dressed up for the big occasion, maybe you'd better do something with that ring in your hand!" This time John Stephens' remark brought a laugh from even Asha's mother.

Mark blinked, then smiled. Repositioning himself up on one knee, he again held Asha's hand in his while his other hand held his mother's ring.

"Asha," he started, then cleared his throat. "I didn't really expect to do this part in front of everybody," he mumbled. Asha could not keep her smile from spreading.

"Well, I'll save my pretty speech for when I'm not performing to a crowd. For now, is it enough to say my life is boring and colorless without you? For better or worse, richer or poorer—more likely poorer, just so you know—I want you with me always. I want us to face the future together."

He held up the ring, his mouth turned up in that half-smile she loved. "Officially this time, before all these witnesses . . . Will you?'

Asha looked down with love in her eyes. She imagined their future, serving God together, in India. She pictured a wedding. Her in a glittering red sari. Intricate designs painted on her hands and feet. A car covered in roses.

As the small, feminine ring slipped onto her finger, Asha put her heart into one word. The only one needed for all the questions of their future.

"Yes."

If you spend yourselves in behalf of the hungry

and satisfy the needs of the oppressed,

then your light will rise in the darkness,

and your night will become like the noonday.

The Lord will guide you always;

he will satisfy your needs in a sun-scorched land

and will strengthen your frame.

You will be like a well-watered garden,

like a spring whose waters never fail.

Isaiah 58:10-11

Excerpt from

STOLEN FUTURE

CONCLUSION OF THE STOLEN SERIES

Neena shrank back but Shazari stood firm. "You get away from us," she hissed.

Ahmad continued toward them, laughing off Shazari's fury. "Your husband is dead. You have no income. Soon you will have no food."

His grin was sly, evil. "You know you have no other choice."

Neena backed against a large tree. She trembled with fear and rage. "I will never marry you!" she shrieked. She flung an arm up to shield her face from his sight. "How could you even think I would want to marry you?"

"Want to?" Ahmad shoved Shazari aside. She pummeled him with uselessly small fists as he drew closer to Neena, close enough for Neena to feel his hot breath against her.

"It is completely unimportant to me what you want."

She was shaking violently. Her voice came out in a desperate whisper. "Then . . . why?"

He reached out to grab a handful of her long, silky hair. "I want to own you," he said. His chest heaved. "I want your husband's daughter to know that I won."

His voice rose. "I will exact my vengeance on her by destroying your future."

Neena slumped down against the tree. Where had Shazari gone? Where had God gone?

"Let her go."

Neena's head shot up. Rashid stood behind Ahmad, feet planted, a small pistol in his hand.

Shazari stood directly behind him. Her chin was up. Her eyes shot sparks. "We are not as helpless as you think."

Ahmad burst into laughter. "You think my weak little brother, who has never stood up for anything or anyone in his life, is going to help you?"

Rashid pointed the gun at his brother. "Let her go, Ahmad. You have made my life miserable since I was a boy, but I will not let you do that to them. I've had enough."

Ahmad's eyes blazed, but his gaze failed to force Rashid's submission.

Very slowly, Ahmad's hand released Neena. She rushed around him to Shazari's side. Both women huddled behind Rashid, taking small steps backward toward the path that led away from the village.

Rashid backed away with them. "I will take you away from here," he said. "I will stay with you until I am certain you are safe."

Neena, Shazari and Rashid fled the village. "We'll go to Asha," Shazari whispered to Neena. "She rescues women in danger. She will have a place for us."

"You will never be safe," Ahmad called after them. "Do you hear me, Rashid? I will find you!"

He slammed his palm into the tree, shouting words raw with hate. "No matter where you go, or how far, you will never get away from me."

Ahmad clenched his hand into a fist, closing fingers around a piece of bark and crumbling it into dust. "I will have my revenge."

READER CLUB/DISCUSSION QUESTIONS
PART ONE: Chapter 1-11

1. Stolen Child starts with Asha having a hard time back in the US. Do you think missionaries can have a difficult time adjusting to being back in America? What are some things that might be hard?

2. Do you ever feel like nobody cares about what you're passionate about? Should everyone care as much as you do about what you are called to do?

3. What do you think of Asha's parents and their attitude about her going overseas? (Reluctant support—is that reasonable? Have you ever felt that way with your own children? Why?)

4. Asha has some ideas about Mark that are untrue (like he never gets stressed). Do you think she sees these things because she wants them to be true? How do we sometimes do that in relationships?

5. Now we can fly around the world within days, where before it used to take months on a ship. How do you think missions has changed because of that? For better or worse?

6. What do you think about the no touching across genders rule in that culture? Good or bad? What do you think of arranged marriages? Would you have trusted your parents to choose your spouse?

7. Arranged marriages tend to last for life, while marriages by choice have high divorce rates. Why do you suppose that is? Can we learn something from them?

8. Asha argues that what happened to her in the past is who she is now. Do you agree? Have things in your past shaped who you are? Should they define you?

9. Do you believe God orders our destiny? We talk about Jeremiah 29:11 for our future, but what about our pasts?

READER CLUB/DISCUSSION QUESTIONS
PART TWO: Chapter 12-23

1. How did you feel when you found out Asha was trafficked as a baby? Were you surprised or did you suspect?

2. What would you struggle with if you were required to be a second wife?

3. Asha talks about dreams and hopes. Neena has shut hers away. We tell kids they can do or be anything. Is that really true? According to the Scriptures, what should we teach children?

4. In the village setting, would you have a hard time keeping quiet and still, even if a national told you it was the right way? =) How does our desire to get things accomplished get in the way sometimes?

5. Do you think some things Americans see as good qualities are actually faults? Can you think of any Bible verses that refute the American ideals of climbing the ladder, the end justifies the means, follow your heart, or do what makes you happy?

6. Does your idea of or appreciation of God change when you hear about the gods others worship? How or why?

7. What do you think about the idea that getting medical care is only if you can afford it? If you had to choose between food or medicine, would there be any choice?

8. Do you feel Rashid was in the wrong, or a victim, or both? In his society, could he have done anything?

9. When you were young, did you ever feel pressured or trapped into doing wrong by someone older, or a peer group? What can we teach teens about their options in such circumstances?

10. Do you think if we took the time to hear people's stories, we would tend to judge less by our initial impressions?

READER CLUB/DISCUSSION QUESTIONS
PART THREE: Chapter 24-35

1. The verse on page 139—who or what group does this make you think of most?

2. What do you think of Mark's dad? Are people more than they may seem?

3. If you had a friend who grew up with the idea that girls are worth less or deserve to be mistreated, what would you tell her about her worth to God?

4. When you read that Asha's mother knew all along about how Asha was taken, how did you feel? Did she have any other options? Does it make you see her differently?

5. Were you surprised the author didn't get Mark there in time to rescue Asha? Should the guy always rescue the girl? =)

6. Have you ever been stuck and not able to fix something (like Mark not being able to get to Asha)? Were you tempted to keep pushing your own way rather than trusting in the Lord? In Genesis, Sarah, Abraham's wife tried to push God's promise along—how did that work out?

7. How did you feel when Mark had to stay and help the pastor rather than going to find Asha?

8. How would it feel to finally find each other and not be able to hug or even really talk? Were you frustrated that all these other things kept them busy before they had time together?

9. In chapter 34, Shazari says her anger has hurt her more than anyone else. Do you believe that is true?

READER CLUB/DISCUSSION QUESTIONS
PART FOUR: Chapter 36-47

1. It's been said our actions speak louder than our words. How was that the case for the Christians and Shazari? Do you know someone who has either turned away or toward Christ because of a Christian's life?

2. Do you think the theme of forgiveness in Stolen Child is unrealistic? Is it possible to forgive even those who do not deserve it or ask for it? (If you're unsure, the author recommends reading The Hiding Place by Corrie Ten Boom.)

3. Forgiveness is more than a one-time choice. How do you forgive the next day and the next when your feelings attack? (Let's help each other with ideas!)

4. If you had been in Asha's situation, which would you long for most?
   a. A soft bed?
   b. Air-conditioning?
   c. Comfort food?
   d. Clean clothes?
   e. A shower?
   f. A real toothbrush? =)

5. How would it feel to have to rebuild your village knowing you'll have to do it again when another cyclone hits or enemies come? (Does it change the idea of not getting too attached to things, not making this world our home?)

6. It is a current trend for Americans to feel threatened about our economy, society, and freedoms. However, what if something terrible really did happen? According to the Bible, do we have rights? How should we view what we "deserve"?

7. Why do you think Shazari was the first to forgive the father rather than Asha? Do we have things we could learn from new believers?

8. Were you happy the parents came back into the story?

9. What would you like to see happen in the final book?

FACT OR FICTION? A Verbal Visit with Author Kimberly Rae

Why did you choose an international setting for the Stolen Series?
I lived in Bangladesh for two years. Going to a third-world country changes you, and I wanted to share that with others. Now, because of my health condition, I can't even go back myself, so writing this series was like going back for a visit for me, and also through the series I get to take people on a trip (even if just through words!) to one of the places I love most in the world.

So some of the cultural scenes in the books are from your own experiences?
Yes. Like the scene where Asha and Mark watch the arranged marriage. That was entirely based on a real arranged marriage I watched—from the people calling it a love match, to them holding hands instead of kissing, even down to the flowergirl throwing her flowers right at the bride's face. =)

What are some of the cultural facts in Stolen Child that came from your memory—that are true rather than fiction?
Let's see…Driving on the left side of the road. Wedding roses really being put on cars with scotch tape. Guys letting their pinkie fingernail grow out to show they don't do manual labor. Using a special tree branch as a toothbrush. (I brought one home and gave it away—now I wish I'd kept it!) Roadside barbers cleaning out ears with a tiny ladle. (Yuck!)

Were you ever there when a cyclone hit?
Yes. And that part about sweeping water from the third floor and watching it waterfall down the stairs—that came from a memory, not my imagination.

Do you have any other true stories about your adventures in Bangladesh?
Oh, lots! It was such an amazing place. I wrote about the arranged marriage, about the year of the flooding, true stories about the real Milo, and even about the time I invited a snake charmer and his 8-foot-long king cobra to do his show in my driveway! You can read all of them on my blog at www.kimberlyraeauthor.blogspot.com under *True Stories from Bangladesh*.

ACKNOWLEDGMENTS

Thanks to everybody who voted to get this out before Christmas—I love a good challenge!

Thanks to my reader group, especially Bethany, Katie and Sandy for all your good suggestions, and to my Proverbs 31 critique group for the same.

Thank you, Jenny, for helping make my own proposal story so inspiringly unique!

Thanks to medical workers worldwide who give love and unceasing commitment to those who can never repay. God sees.

Thank you, Shawne, for your cultural insights and encouragement through both books. You can count on me sending you #3!

Jeannie, my first supporter and the one who told me I couldn't write it if I'd never lived it, thank you for your nudges in the right direction and for your faith in me, for writing *Bangladesh at a Glance* for culturally clueless people like I was, and for your fantastic edit of *Stolen Child*. You are officially my favorite editor!

Thank You, Heavenly Father, for giving me writing: a ministry I love, and one I can do even while being a mommy with a health condition.

As always, thanks Brian for listening to every word. I'm so glad you went through with your proposal to me despite the thunderstorm!

Lastly, thanks to my little boy, who loves to tell random people about "Mommy's book."

ABOUT THE AUTHOR

Kimberly Rae has visited the world's largest banyan tree in Kolkata, seen Mt. Everest, and eaten cow brains and cow bone marrow just to say she'd done it!

Rae has been published over 250 times and has work in 6 languages. She now lives in North Carolina, where she loves to take readers on "verbal tours" to international places and fascinating cultures. All three books in her Stolen Series—Stolen Woman, Stolen Child, Stolen Future—are Amazon bestsellers.

A wife and mother of two young children, Rae sees herself as a "writer on the side, but it's a good side!"

www.kimberlyrae.com
www.kimberlyraeauthor.blogspot.com,

Made in the USA
Charleston, SC
20 April 2013